11   Under the pear tree   215

12   Tearing along   221

13   Life's illusions   227

14   Not a particularly good impression   233

15   Black on white   238

16   Mönch, Eiger, Jungfrau   241

17   Too late   247

18   A little peace of mind   253

19   Pending proceedings   257

20   As if   263

21   Stuttering a little   269

22   Write an article!   273

23   R. I. P.   275

24   After Fall Comes Winter   281

25   That's strange   287

26   A pointed chin and broad hips   291

27   If we had put our money where our mouth is   295

28   Marked red   302

29   Another matter altogether   305

30   All's not lost   310

31   Rawitz laughed   316

32   Too late   322

33   Imprisoned   330

W9-CEI-802

Bernhard Schlink

SELF'S DECEPTION

Bernhard Schlink is the author of the internationally bestselling novel *The Reader* and of four crime novels: *The Gordian Knot, Self's Punishment* (with Walter Popp), *Self's Deception*, and *Self's Slaughter.* He is a professor at the Benjamin Cardozo School of Law, Yeshiva University, in New York.

SELF'S DECEPTION

SELF'S DECEPTION

Bernhard Schlink

TRANSLATED FROM THE GERMAN BY
Peter Constantine

VINTAGE CRIME/BLACK LIZARD
Vintage Books
A Division of Random House, Inc.
New York

A VINTAGE CRIME/BLACK LIZARD ORIGINAL, JUNE 2007

Cataloging-in-Publication Data:
Schlink, Bernhard.
[Selbs Betrug. English]
Self's deception / Bernhard Schlink ; translated from
the German by Peter Constantine.
p. cm.
ISBN 978-0-375-70908-1
I. Constantine, Peter.   II. Title.
PT2680.L54 S4313 2006
2006042169

www.vintagebooks.com

Printed in the United States of America
10 9 8 7 6 5 4 3 2 1

Contents

PART ONE

1   *A passport photo*   3

2   *Young Translators*   8

3   *Catastrophic thought*   13

4   *Her dear old uncle—how sweet!*   17

5   *Turbo on my lap*   23

6   *Well, what do you think?*   26

7   *Scratch a Swabian and you'll find a small Hegel*   31

8   *Davai, Davai*   36

9   *It was only later*   40

10   *Scott at the South Pole*   44

11   *Pictures from an exhibition*   47

12   *In vain*   51

13   *Yes and no*   54

14   *Twenty Smurfs*   58

15   *Smashed china*   61

16   *Wider, straighter, faster*   66

17   *In response to an official request*   70

18   *A demigod in gray*   75

19   *Why don't you go, too?*   79

20   *Stopping up holes* 84

21   *Very clear indeed* 90

22   *Pain, irony, or heartburn* 93

23   *The boy who lops the thistle's heads* 98

24   *Marble breaks and iron bends* 102

25   *Don't forget the kitty litter!* 107

26   *You're stubborn, just plain stubborn* 112

27   *My cards weren't all that bad* 114

28   *A trick that psychotherapists use* 119

29   *In this weather?* 124

30   *Spaghetti al pesto* 128

31   *Like in the days of Baader and Meinhof* 130

32   *Bananas in exhaust pipes* 136

33   *The Kaiser-Wilhelm-Stein* 144

34   *Angels don't shoot at cats* 151

35   *A nation of cobblers* 155

PART TWO

1   *A final favor* 165

2   *What insanity!* 169

3   *A bit flat* 174

4   *Peschkalek's nose* 179

5   *Gas needn't stink* 185

6   *A summer idyll* 190

7   *Tragedy or farce?* 194

8   *It makes sense, doesn't it?* 197

9   *Old hat* 202

10   *And both sound so harmonious together* 209

PART ONE

I

A *passport photo*

She reminded me of the daughter I've sometimes wished for. Lively eyes, a mouth prone to laughter, high cheekbones, and rich, brown curls hanging down to her shoulders. The photograph didn't indicate whether she was tall or short, fat or thin, slouching or poised. It was only a passport photo.

Her father, Under-Secretary Salger from Bonn, had called me. For months he and his family had not heard from Leonore. At first they had simply waited, then they put in calls to friends and acquaintances, and finally notified the police. No luck.

"Leo is an independent sort of girl who likes to go her own way. But she's always stayed in touch, visiting, calling us. We were still hoping she might turn up for the beginning of the semester. She's studying French and English at the Heidelberg Institute for Translation and Interpretation. Well, the semester started two weeks ago."

"Your daughter didn't sign up for her courses?"

His voice sounded irritated: "Herr Self, the reason I'm resorting to a private investigator is because I'm hoping he might be the one who will do the investigating—not I. I have no idea whether she signed up or not."

I patiently explained that every year thousands of people were reported missing in Germany, but that most of them disappeared and then reappeared of their own free will. They simply wanted to get away for a time from anxious parents, husbands, or loved ones. As long as you don't actually hear anything there's no reason to worry. When something bad does happen—an accident or a crime—that's when you hear.

Salger was aware of this. The police had already gone over it. "I respect Leo's independence. She's twenty-five and not a child anymore. I also understand that she might need some space. In the past few years there has been tension between us. But I have to know how she is, what she's up to, if she's OK. I don't suppose you have a daughter, do you?"

I didn't see that this was any of his business and didn't answer.

"It's not only me who's worrying, Herr Self. I can't tell you what my wife's been through these past few weeks . . . So I want quick results. I'm not asking you to confront Leo or embarrass her. I do not want her or any of her friends to know that there's a search on for her. I'm afraid she would take that very, very badly indeed."

This didn't sound good. You can tail a person in secret once the person has been located, and you can look for a person overtly if you don't know where that person is. But not to know where a person is and to look for that person without her or her friends catching on is difficult, to say the least.

Salger was growing impatient. "Are you still there?"

"Yes."

"I want you to start right away and report back as soon as possible. My number is . . ."

"Thank you, Herr Salger, but I must decline. Have a nice day." I hung up. I don't really care whether my clients' manners are good or bad. I've been a private investigator for almost forty years and have come across all types, those with proper upbringing and those without, timid types and audacious types, poseurs and cowards, poor devils and big shots. There were also the clients I had dealt with back in the days when I was a public prosecutor, clients who would have preferred not to be clients. But indifferent as I was, I had no wish to dance to the tune of the imperious under-secretary.

The following morning when I arrived at my office in the Augusta-Anlage, I found a yellow post-office notice hanging from the flap of the letterbox in my door: "Urgent. Express Mail. Please check your letterbox." They needn't have left the notice, as all the letters pushed through the slot fall onto the floor of the former tobacconist's store where I have my desk with my chair behind it and two chairs in front, a filing cabinet, and a potted palm. I hate potted palms.

The express letter was heavy. A bundle of hundred-mark bills lay inside a folded sheet of paper covered with writing.

Dear Herr Self,

I hope you will forgive my abruptness on the phone. My wife and I have been under great strain over the past few weeks. I do not, however, imagine that the tone of our conversation could have led to your refusal to help us, so allow me to offer the enclosed five thousand marks as a deposit. Please stay in touch with me by phone. Over the next few weeks you can reach me only on my answering machine; I must take my wife out of this hell of uncertainty. But I will be picking up my messages regularly and can call you back any time.

Sincerely,
Salger

I opened my desk drawer and took out a box of coffee beans, a bottle of sambuca, and a glass, and filled it. Then I sat down in my chair, cracked the beans between my teeth, and let the clear, oily sambuca roll over my tongue and down my throat. It burned, and the smoke of my first cigarette stung my chest. I looked out of the former storefront. It was raining in dense gray streams. In the murmuring traffic the hissing of the tires on the wet streets was louder than the droning of the engines.

After my second glass I counted the fifty hundred-mark bills. I looked at the envelope on both sides. Like the letter, it didn't have Salger's address. I called the telephone number in Bonn he'd given me.

"You have reached 41-17-88. Please leave a message at the sound of the tone. All messages will be answered within twenty-four hours."

I also called Information and wasn't surprised to hear that there was no number listed for a Salger in Bonn. Presumably his address wouldn't be in the phone book either. That was as it should be—the man was safeguarding his privacy. But why did he have to safeguard his privacy from his own private investigator? And why couldn't he have at least cooperated to the extent of letting me know his daughter's address in Heidelberg? Besides, five thousand marks was far too much.

Then I saw that there was something else in the envelope. Leo's picture. I took it out and leaned it against the small stone lion I had brought back years ago from Venice and which stands guard over the telephone, the answering machine, the fountain pen, the pencils and notepads, the cigarettes and lighter. An overexposed photo-booth picture on cheap paper. It must have been about four or five years old. Leo looked at me as if she'd just decided to grow up, to no longer be a girl but a woman. There was something more in her eyes: a question, an expectation, a reproach, a defiance. I couldn't put my finger on it, but it moved me.

2

Young Translators

When a person is reported missing and relatives want an investigation, the police go through a routine. They draw up a report in a number of copies, request photographs, staple them to the report and the copies, and send the whole dossier to the local criminal bureau, which files it and waits. Nowadays the information is often entered into a computer. But either way the file remains closed until something happens, something is found, or something is reported. Only in juvenile cases or when the police suspect foul play do they go public. An adult who hasn't committed a crime can pitch his tent when and where he likes without the police getting involved. That would be all we need!

When I'm hired in a missing person's case, the idea is for me to go farther out on a limb than the police ever would. I called the registrar's office at Heidelberg University and was told that Leonore Salger was no longer enrolled. She'd registered for the winter semester, but not for the spring semester. "Not that that means anything. Sometimes students simply forget to register, and only think of it when it comes to work or exams. I'm sorry, I can't give you her address. She's no longer in our system."

Work—that gave me the idea of calling the university chancellor's office. I could talk to the human resources department and see if Leonore Salger was on the books in some part-time position at the university.

"Who is making this request? According to our regulations, all personal information is confidential . . ." Her tone was as strict as her chirping little voice could manage.

But I didn't give confidentiality a chance. "Good Morning, this is Gerhard Self from the Federal Credit Union. I have Leonore Salger's file in front of me, and I see that the employee savings bonus has not been entered. You must take care of this right away! Frankly, I can't understand why . . ."

"What did you say her name was?" The chirping voice had become shrill with indignation. All confidentiality was swept aside, Leonore Salger's file was opened, and I was triumphantly informed that Frau Salger had not worked at the university since February.

"How so?"

"That's what it says here." Now she sounded snippy. "Professor Leider didn't send in a request for an extension, and in March the position was reassigned."

I got into my old Opel, drove up the autobahn to Heidelberg, and parked the car near the Plöck, where I found the Institute for Translation and Interpretation. Professor Leider's office was on the first floor.

"How may I help you?"

"Gerhard Self from the Ministry of Education and Science. I have an appointment with the professor."

The secretary looked at the appointment calendar, at me, and back at the calendar. "One moment, please." She disappeared next door.

"Herr Self?" Professors too are getting younger by the day. This one cut quite a stylish figure. He was sporting a dark moiré silk suit, a pastel linen shirt, and an ironic smile on his tanned face. He invited me into his office and offered me a chair. "Well, what brings you to us?"

"After our successful initiatives Young Scientists and Young Musicians, the minister of education and science has set up other youth programs over the past few years. Last year he initiated Young Translators. You might recall the information we sent you last year?"

He shook his head.

"Ah, you don't remember—I'm afraid Young Translators simply hasn't received the kind of publicity it needed over the last year in schools or universities. But this year I have taken the initiative, and I'm particularly interested in reaching out to universities. One of last year's participants recommended you to me, and also one of your assistants, a Frau Salger. What I have in mind is—"

The ironic smile had not left his face. "Young Translators. What's that all about?"

"It seemed a natural enough progression after Young Scientists, Young Musicians, Young Architects, and Young Doctors, to name just a few of our programs. In the meantime, I would say that for 1993 Young Translators will play a particularly important role. Our Young Pastors program has received the blessing of the divinity schools, and Young Lawyers has been approved by law schools. As for translation departments, or I should say institutes, unfortunately things haven't really taken off yet. But I envision an advisory committee—a few professors, one or two students, someone from the language department of the European community.

I was thinking of asking you to participate, Professor Leider, and perhaps also your assistant, Frau Salger."

"If you only knew . . . But I see you don't." He launched into a lecture about how he was a scholar and a linguist, and that he didn't think much of translation and interpreting. "One day we will figure out how language actually works, and then there'll be no need for translators and interpreters. As a scholar it's not my job to find a way of muddling through till then. My job is to figure out a way to end the muddle."

A professor of translation who doesn't believe in translation! How perfectly ironic. I thanked him for his openness, extolled critical, creative variety, and told him that I would like to stay in touch about the committee. "And what would you think of my asking Frau Salger to be the student representative on the committee?"

"I must tell you that she is no longer working for me. She has . . . you could say that she has in a sense left me in the lurch. After the winter break she simply didn't show up again—no explanation, no apology. I did ask colleagues and lecturers if they knew where she was. But she was no longer on campus. I even thought of calling the police." He looked concerned, and for the first time his ironic smile disappeared. Then it returned. "Perhaps she simply had had enough of studying, and enough of the university and the institute. I can't say that I'd be surprised. I guess I felt a bit hurt."

"Do you think she would make a good candidate for Young Translators?"

"She was my assistant, but she was never affected by my bleak view of translation. She's a hands-on girl, a good interpreter with the kind of quick tongue that is a must in this job, and was well liked as a tutor by first-year students. No, absolutely! If you find her, you should definitely bring her onboard. And please give her my regards."

We stood up and he walked me to the door. I asked the secretary for Frau Salger's address. She wrote it on a piece of paper: 5 Häusserstrasse, 6900 Heidelberg.

3

Catastrophic thought

I had come to Heidelberg in 1942 as a young public prosecutor and moved into an apartment on the Bahnhofstrasse with my wife, Klara. In those days it wasn't a good neighborhood, but I liked the view of the train station, the arriving and departing trains, the locomotives puffing steam, the whistle and rumble of the nocturnal shunting of freight cars. Today the station has been moved since the Bahnhofstrasse now runs past office blocks and court buildings with their smooth, gray functionality. If the law reflects the architecture in which it is proclaimed, then law in Heidelberg is in a bad state. If on the other hand the law is in any way reflected in the rolls, bread, and cakes that the court staff can buy around the corner, then one need have no fear. The Häusserstrasse branches off from the Bahnhofstrasse, and right past the first corner was the small bakery where over forty years ago Klara and I used to buy gray bread, a bakery that has now turned into an elegant and enticing bread and pastry shop.

Right next to it, at 5 Häusserstrasse, I put on my reading glasses to see the buzzers. And there was her name, next to the top one. I rang, the door clicked open, and I climbed the gloomy, musty stairwell. At sixty-nine, I am not as nimble as I used to be. On the third floor I had to stop and catch my breath.

"Yes?" came an impatient voice from above—either a high-pitched man's or a low-pitched woman's voice.

"I'll be right there."

The last flight of stairs led to the attic. A young man was standing in the doorway, through which I could see an apartment with dormer windows and slanted walls. He seemed to be in his late twenties, had black slicked-back hair, and was wearing black corduroys and a black sweater. He peered at me.

"I'm looking for a Frau Leonore Salger. Is she at home?"

"No."

"When will she be back?"

"Don't know."

"This is her place, isn't it?"

"Yep."

I simply can't keep up with the ways of the young. Is this modern tongue-tiedness? Modern introversion? Verbal anorexia?

I tried again. "I'm Gerhard Self. I run a small translation and interpreting agency in Mannheim, and Frau Salger has been recommended as someone who could work for me on short notice. I have a job that is quite urgent. Do you know how I can reach her? And can I come in and sit down for a few minutes? I'm out of breath, my knees are shaking, and my neck is getting stiff from having to stare up at you." There was no landing, and the young man was standing on the top step while I stood some five steps below him.

"OK." He moved out of the doorway and motioned me into a room with bookshelves, a tabletop resting on two wooden stools, and a chair. I sat down. He leaned against the windowsill. The tabletop was covered with books and papers. I saw French names, none of which rang a bell. I waited, but he showed no imminent signs of conversation.

"Are you French?"

"No."

"We used to play a game when I was a boy. One player had to think something up, while the others had to figure out what it was by asking all kinds of questions, to which he could only answer 'yes' or 'no.' The first one to guess what he was thinking was the winner. When there are a number of people playing, the game can be quite amusing. But when there are only two players it's no fun at all. So how about speaking in full sentences?"

The young man straightened up with a jolt, as if he'd been dreaming and had suddenly woken up. "Full sentences? I've been working on my dissertation for two years now, and for the past six months I've been writing nothing but full sentences, and I'm getting more and more lost. You seem to think that—"

"How long have you been living here?"

He was visibly disappointed by my prosaic question. But I found out that he'd been living in the apartment before Leo had moved in and had sublet it to her. The landlady lived on the floor below and had called him in February to say she was worried that there had been no sign of life from Leo—or her rent money—since the beginning of January. He was now staying in this apartment for the time being, as he couldn't get any work done at his new place because of his noisy roommates. "And then when Leo comes back she'll still have the apartment."

"Where is she?"

"I've no idea. I'm sure she knows what she's doing."

"Hasn't anyone come looking for her?"

The young man ran his hand over his smooth hair, pressing it down even flatter, and hesitated for a moment. "You mean for a job? You mean if someone like you . . . no, nobody's been here."

"What do you think—could she handle a job interpreting for a small technological conference, twelve participants, from German to English and English to German? Would she be up to it?"

But the student didn't let himself be drawn into a conversation about Leo. "You see?" he said. "Full sentences are of little if any use. Here I am, telling you in full sentences that she isn't here, and you ask me if she can handle a small conference. She's gone . . . disappeared . . . flown off . . ." He flapped his arms. "OK? If she happens to show up I'll let her know you came by."

I handed him my card—not the one from my office, but the one with my home address. I found out that he was working on a dissertation in philosophy on catastrophic thought, and that he'd met Leo at a university residence hall. Leo had given him French lessons. I had already started down the stairs when he again warned me against full sentences. "You mustn't think you're too old to grasp the idea."

4

Her dear old uncle—how sweet!

Back at the office, I gave Salger a call. His answering machine recorded my request that he call me back. I wanted to know the name of the residence hall in which Leo had lived so I could look into who her friends were and where she might be—not a hot trail, but I didn't have many options.

Salger called me back that evening just as I stopped by my office on my way home from the Kleiner Rosengarten restaurant. I had gone there too early. There was hardly anyone there, my usual waiter Giovanni was on vacation in Italy, and the spaghetti gorgonzola was too heavy. My girlfriend, Brigitte, could have made me a better meal. But the previous weekend she'd seemed a little too hopeful that I might learn to let her spoil me: "Will you be my cuddly old tomcat?" I don't want to become some old tomcat.

This time Salger was exquisitely polite. He expressed his deepest gratitude that I was taking on the case. His wife was grateful, too. Would it be all right if he gave me a further payment next week? Would I inform him the moment I found Leo? His wife begged that I . . .

"Could you tell me Leo's address before the Häusser-strasse, Herr Salger?"

"Excuse me?"

"Where did Leo live before she moved to the Häusser-strasse?"

"I'm afraid I can't tell you that offhand."

"Could you take a look, or ask your wife? I need her old address. It was a university residence hall."

"Oh yes, the residence hall." Salger fell silent. "Liebigstrasse? Eichendorffweg? Schnepfengewann? I can't think of it right now, Herr Self; the names of all kinds of streets are going through my head. I'll talk to my wife and take a look at my old address book—we might still have it somewhere. I'll let you know. Or I should say, if you don't find a message from me on your answering machine tomorrow morning, that means we couldn't find it. Would that be all? In that case, I wish you a good night."

I couldn't say I was warming up to Salger. Leo was leaning on the small stone lion, looking at me, pretty, alert, with a determination in her eyes that I felt I understood, and a question or a spark of defiance that I could not interpret. To have such a daughter and not know her address—shame on you, Herr Salger!

I don't know why Klara and I never had any children. She never told me she'd gone to see a gynecologist, nor had she ever asked me to take a fertility test. We were not very happy together; but no clear links have ever been drawn between marital unhappiness and childlessness, or marital happiness and an abundance of children. I'd have liked to have been a widower with a daughter, but that is a disrespectful wish, and I've only admitted it to myself in my old age, when I no longer keep any secrets from myself.

I spent a whole morning on the phone till I finally located Leo's residence hall. It was on Klausenpfad, not far from the public swimming pool and the zoo. She'd lived in room 408, and after crossing some grungy stairwells and hallways I found three students drinking tea in the communal kitchen on the fourth floor—two girls and a boy.

"Excuse me, I'm looking for Leonore Salger."

"There's no Leonore here." The young man was sitting with his back to me and spoke over his shoulder.

"I'm Leo's uncle. I'm passing through Heidelberg, and this is the address I've got for her. Could you—"

"A dear old uncle visiting his dear young niece—how sweet! Hey, what d'you say to that, Andrea?"

Andrea turned around, the young man turned around, and all three of them eyed me with interest.

Philipp, an old friend of mine who's a surgeon at the Mannheim Municipal Hospital, works a lot with young interns and tells me how well behaved the students of the nineties are. My ex-girlfriend Babs has a son who's studying to be a lawyer, and he's polite and serious, too. His girlfriend, a nice girl studying theology, whom I always addressed as "Frau," as the women's movement has taught me to do, corrected me gently, telling me that she is a "Fräulein."

These three students seemed to have missed this trend— were they sociologists? I sat down on the fourth chair.

"When did Leo move out?"

"Who says she ever—"

"It was before your time," Andrea cut in. "Leo moved out about a year ago, to somewhere on the west side, I think." She turned toward me. "I don't have her new address. But they must have it over at the registrar's office. I'm going there—want to come along?"

She led the way down the stairs, her black ponytail swinging, her skirt swaying. She was a robust girl, but quite pleasing to the eye. The office had already closed, as it was almost four. We stood irresolutely in front of the locked door.

"Do you happen to have a recent picture of her?" I went on to tell her that Leo's father, my brother-in-law, had a birthday coming up, and that we were going to have a party on the Drachenfels, and that all her aunts, uncles, and cousins would be coming from Dresden. "One of the reasons I want to see Leo is because I'm putting together a photo album of family and friends."

She took me up to her room. We sat down on the couch, and she pulled out of a shoebox a student's life of carnivals and end-of-term parties, vacations and field trips, a demonstration here and there, a weekend work study, and pictures of her boyfriend, who liked to pose on his motorbike.

"Here's one of her at a wedding." She handed me Leo on a chair, dark blue skirt and salmon-pink blouse, a cigarette in her right hand and her left hand resting pensively on her cheek, her face concentrating as if she were listening to or watching someone. There was nothing girlish about her anymore. This was a somewhat tense, assertive young woman. "In this one she's coming out of the city hall—she was one of the marriage witnesses—and in this one we're all on our way to the Neckar River. The wedding party was on a boat." I figured her to be about five foot six. She was slim without being thin, and had a nice, straight back.

"Where was this one taken?" Leo was coming out of a door in jeans and a dark sweater, her bag over her shoulder and her coat slung over her arm. She had dark rings under her eyes, her right eye squeezed shut, her left eyebrow raised. Her hair was tousled and her mouth a thin, angry line. I recognized the door and the building, but couldn't place them.

"That was after the demonstration we had back in June. The cops had arrested her and taken her in for fingerprinting."

I couldn't remember there being any demonstrations in June, but now I saw that Leo was coming out of the Heidelberg police headquarters.

"Can I have these two?"

"You want this one, too?" Andrea shook her head. "I thought you were planning a nice surprise for Leo's father, not trying to get her into trouble or something. You'd better leave this awful photo and take the nice one—the one where she's sitting, that's a good one." She gave me the picture of Leo on the chair and put the other pictures back in the box. "If you're not in a hurry, you could drop by the Drugstore Bar. She used to hang out there every evening, and I ran into her there this past winter."

I asked her the way there and thanked her. When I found the bar in the Kettengasse, it all came back to me. I had been shadowing someone once who had had a cup of coffee and played chess here. He's no longer alive.

I ordered an Aviateur, but the bar was out of grapefruit juice and champagne, and so I just had a Campari straight up. I struck up a conversation with the bored guy behind the bar and showed him Leo sitting in her chair. "When did you last see her?"

"Well, how about that, it's Leo! Nice picture. What do you want with her? Hey, Klaus, come here." He waved over a short stocky man with red hair, rimless glasses, and sharp, intelligent eyes. The spitting image of what I imagined an intellectual Irish whiskey drinker would look like. The two men talked in hushed tones, falling silent under my interested gaze. So I turned away and pricked up my ears. I could tell I wasn't the first one who'd come to the Drugstore Bar looking for Leo. Somebody had been here back in February. Klaus also asked me why I was looking for her.

I told him I was her uncle, that I'd been at the residence hall on Klausenpfad, and that Andrea had sent me over here. The two men were still suspicious. They told me they hadn't seen Leo since January. That was all I got out of them. They eyed me as I finished my second Campari, paid, left, and looked through the window one more time.

5

Turbo on my lap

My next move was to scour the hospitals, even though I knew in cases where they have patients who are unable to speak they contact relatives. They also notify the police when a patient's identity is unclear. But it's rare for a doctor to authorize that relatives be contacted against a patient's will. A person being sought by relatives could be lying in a hospital only a few streets away. Perhaps the patient doesn't care that his loved ones are crying their eyes out not knowing where he is. Perhaps that's just what he wants.

But neither of these possibilities fit the impression I had of Leo. Even if her relationship with her parents was more strained than her father had admitted, why would she want to keep her hospital stay a secret from Professor Leider or the catastrophe philosopher? But the devil works in mysterious ways, so I made my way through the Heidelberg university clinic, the Mannheim Municipal Hospital, the district hospitals, and the hospitals of the diocese. Here I didn't run the risk of ruffling any of her circle of friends. I didn't have to adopt any of my character roles but could be Private Investigator Self, hired by an anxious father seeking his missing daughter. I didn't rely on the phone, though it's a pretty dependable way of determining whether a person is in a certain hospital. But if you want to know whether someone was a patient somewhere a few weeks or months ago, then it is better to go there in person. I spent two whole days going from place to place. There was no sign of Leo.

The weekend came. The rain that until now had been accompanying April stopped, and the sun was shining as I went on my Sunday walk through the Luisenpark. I had taken along a little bag of stale bread and was feeding the ducks. I had also brought along a copy of the *Süddeutsche Zeitung*, intending to settle into one of the chairs there. But the April sun wasn't yet warm enough. Or my bones don't warm up as fast as they used to. I was quite glad, back home, when Turbo, my tomcat, curled up on my lap. He purred and blissfully stretched out his little paws.

I knew where Leo had lived, studied, and hung out, and that she wasn't in some hospital in or around Heidelberg, nor had she been. She'd been missing since January, and in February someone had been looking for her. In July of last year she'd been arrested and fingerprinted. Her professor had good things to say about her, as did her roommates. Her contact with her parents left a little to be desired. She smoked. I also knew where to find Leo's friends and acquaintances, colleagues, and teachers. I could make inquiries at the translation institute, at the Drugstore Bar, and in neighborhood stores. But I wouldn't be able to manage that without disturbing any of her friends. So I had to give Salger the option of either giving up the case or allowing the possibility that Leo might get wise to the search. This was the second point that I made a note of for Monday.

The first point ought to have been on my to-do list of the previous week: the State Psychiatric Hospital outside Heidelberg. It had not been an oversight on my part—I'd just kept putting it off. Eberhard had spent a year and a half there; I had visited him quite often, and those visits always took it out of me. Eberhard is a friend of mine, a quiet person who lives off his modest fortune. He is a chess grand master, and in 1965 came back completely bewildered from a tournament in Dubrovnik. Philipp and I set him up with a string of housekeepers, none of whom could deal with him. So he ended up in the psychiatric hospital. The patients were crammed into large rooms, slept in double-decker beds, and didn't even have their own closets or lockers—not that they needed any, as all their personal belongings, even wristwatches and wedding rings, had to be handed in. For me the worst was the sweetish smell of food, cleansing agents, disinfectants, urine, sweat, and fear. How Eberhard managed to get well again in these circumstances is a mystery to me. But he made it, and is even playing chess again, against the advice of his doctor, who had read Stefan Zweig's *Royal Game*. From time to time Eberhard and I play a game or two. He always wins. Out of friendship he sometimes leads me to believe that I play a tough game.

6

Well, *what do you think?*

The State Psychiatric Hospital lies out where the mountains begin. I was in no hurry and took the long way through the villages. The nice weather was holding, the morning was bright, and there was an explosion of fresh green and bright blossoms. I opened the sunroof and put on my cassette of *The Magic Flute*. It was great to be alive.

The old building is the core of the hospital complex. It had originally been constructed in the shape of a large U toward the end of the nineteenth century and used as barracks for a Baden bicycle regiment. In World War I it served as a military hospital, then later as a homeless shelter, and finally in the late 1920s as a sanatorium. World War II turned the large U into a large L. The walls that had closed off the old building into an elongated rectangle disappeared, and the courtyard now extends into the hilly terrain where many new clinic buildings have sprung up. I parked my car, closed the sunroof, and turned off the music. The columns around the entrance of the old building, as well as the whole edifice, were covered in scaffolding, and unpainted brickwork glowed around the

26

windows. Apparently thermoglass windows had just been installed, and painters were busy applying a new coat of delicate yellow. One of them had picked up on the Queen of the Night aria and kept whistling it as I walked over the gravel toward the entrance.

The doorman told me the offices were on the second floor, to the right. I climbed the wide, worn, sandstone steps. By the door to room 107 was a sign, ADMINISTRATION/RECEPTION. I knocked and was told to enter.

The receptionist drew a blank at the name Leonore Salger, and returned to her medical records. Passport photos were stapled to some of them, which gave me the idea of showing her Leo's picture. She took it, studied it carefully, asked me to wait for a moment, locked her filing cabinet, and left the room. I looked out the window at the park. The magnolia trees and forsythia bushes were in full bloom, and the lawn was being mowed. Some patients in everyday clothes were sauntering along the paths; others were sitting on benches that had been painted white. How everything had changed! Back in the days when I used to visit Eberhard, there were no lawns beneath the trees, just trodden earth. In those days patients had also been let out for fresh air, but in gray institutional overalls, walking one after another in a circle at a certain hour every day for twenty minutes, like the yard exercise of prison inmates.

The receptionist didn't come back alone.

"I am Dr. Wendt. Who are you, and what is she to you?" He held Leo's picture in his hand and looked at me coldly.

I handed him my card and told him of my search.

"I am sorry, Herr Self, but we can only provide patient information to authorized individuals."

"So she is—"

"That is all I am prepared to say. Who was it who commissioned you to undertake this search?"

I had brought along Salger's letter and handed it to him. Wendt read it with a frown. He didn't look up, although he most certainly had finished reading it. Finally he got a grip on himself. "Please follow me."

A few doors down he showed me into a conference room with a round table. This room also faced the park. The workers had not finished renovating here. The old frames and glass had been removed from the windows, which were now sealed with a temporary transparent plastic sheet. A fine layer of white dust covered the table, shelves, and filing cabinets.

"Yes, Frau Salger was a patient here. She came about three months ago. Somebody brought her here; he had picked her up . . . hitchhiking. We have no idea what happened before or during that car ride. The man just told us he'd picked her up and taken her along." The doctor fell silent and looked pensive. He was still young, wore corduroys and a checked shirt beneath his open white gown, and looked athletic. He had a healthy complexion and his hair was artfully tousled. His eyes were too close-set.

I waited. "You were saying, Dr. Wendt?"

"As they were driving, she had begun to cry and simply wouldn't stop. That went on for over an hour. The man didn't know what to do, and finally decided to bring her to us. Here she continued crying till we gave her a Valium injection and she fell asleep." Again he stared pensively.

"And what then?"

"Well, what do you think? I initiated her therapy."

"No, I mean where is Leonore Salger now? How come you didn't contact anyone?"

Again he took his time. "We didn't have . . . well, it's only now that I find out from you what her real name is. If our receptionist"—he waved his hand in the direction of room 107—"hadn't happened to deal with her a couple of times . . . she doesn't usually get to see our patients at all. And then you come with a passport photo . . ." He shook his head.

"Did you notify the police?"

"The police?" He fished a crumpled pack of Roth-Händle cigarettes out of the pocket of his pants and offered me one. I preferred to smoke my own, and took out my pack of Sweet Aftons. Wendt shook his head again. "No, I don't like the idea of having the police here at our hospital, and in this case having her questioned by the police would have been utterly inappropriate from a therapeutic standpoint. And then she got better soon enough. She was here voluntarily and was free to leave any time she wanted. It's not like she was a minor."

"Where is she now?"

He cleared his throat a couple of times. "I should inform you . . . I have to . . . um . . . Frau Salger is dead. She . . ." He avoided my eyes. "I am not exactly sure what happened. A tragic accident. Please extend my sincerest condolences to her father."

"But Dr. Wendt, I can't just call her father and tell him that his daughter died in some tragic accident."

"True . . . true. Well, as you see"—he pointed at the window—"we're installing new windows. Last Tuesday, she . . . On the fourth floor we have these large windows along the hallway from the floor to the ceiling, and she fell though the plastic cover down into the courtyard. She died instantly."

"So if I hadn't happened to come to see you now you'd have authorized her burial without informing her parents? What kind of a crazy story is this, Dr. Wendt?"

"Of course her parents have been informed. I'm not certain of the exact procedure our office followed, but her parents were most definitely informed."

"How could your office have informed them if you only found out her name from me?"

He shrugged his shoulders.

"And what about the burial?"

He stared at his hands as if they could tell him where Leo was to be buried. "I suppose that is waiting on the parents' response." He got up. "I've got to go back to my station. You can't imagine the commotion this has created: Her fall, the ambulance sirens, our patients have been very shaken up. May I show you out?"

I tried to take leave outside room 107 but he pulled me away. "No, our offices are now closed. Let me say how pleased I am that you came. I would be grateful if you would speak to her father at your earliest convenience. That was a point you had there—perhaps our office didn't manage to reach her parents." We stood by the main entrance. "Good-bye, Herr Self."

7

Scratch a Swabian and you'll find a small Hegel

I didn't drive far. I stopped at the pond by Sankt Ilgen, got out of the car, and walked over to the water. I threw a couple of stones, trying to make them skip over the water. Even as a boy on Lake Wannsee I'd never got the knack. It's too late to learn now.

All the same, I wasn't about to let some young kid in a white gown pull the wool over my eyes. Wendt's story stunk. Why hadn't the police been called in? A woman who's been in a psychiatric hospital for three months falls out of an unsecured fourth-floor window, and it doesn't cross anybody's mind that negligent homicide or worse might be at play and that the police should be called? OK, Wendt hadn't exactly said that the police hadn't come and investigated. But he'd only mentioned ambulances, no police cars. And if the police had been brought in on Tuesday, Salger would have been informed by Thursday at the latest, regardless of what name Leo might have registered under. The police wouldn't have taken long to figure out that Frau so-and-so didn't exist but that Leonore Salger was missing, and that consequently Frau so-and-so was none other than Leonore Salger. And if Herr Salger had been contacted on Thursday, he'd surely have called me by now.

I had lunch in Sandhausen. It's no culinary Mecca. After lunch I got into my old Opel, which I'd parked on the market square in the sun, and the heat inside was stifling. Summer was just around the corner.

At half past two I was back at the hospital. It was cat-and-mouse. The receptionist in room 107—a different receptionist from the one in the morning—had Dr. Wendt paged but couldn't find him. Finally she showed me the way to his station through long, high-ceilinged corridors in which footsteps echoed. The nurse was sorry, but Dr. Wendt was definitely not to be disturbed. And I'd have to wait in the reception area; waiting at the station was against regulations.

Back in reception, I managed to barge all the way through to the office of Professor Eberlein, the director of the hospital, and explained to the secretary that Eberlein would doubtless rather see me than the police. By now I was fuming. The secretary looked at me uncomprehendingly. Could I please go to room 107?

When I got back out into the corridor, a nearby door opened. "Herr Self? I am Professor Eberlein. I hear you are kicking up quite a fuss."

He was in his late fifties, small and fat, dragging his left foot and leaning on a cane with a silver knob. He studied me with deep-set eyes that peered out from beneath thinning black hair and bushy black eyebrows. His lachrymal glands and cheeks hung limply. In nasal Swabian he asked me to accompany him in his leisurely limping gait. As we walked, his cane tapped out a syncopated beat.

"Every institution is an organism. It has its circulation, breathes, ingests and eliminates, has infections and infarctions, develops defense and healing mechanisms." He laughed. "What kind of an infection are you?"

We descended the stairs and went out into the park. The heat of the day had turned muggy. I didn't say anything. He, too, had only puffed and wheezed as he slowly negotiated the stairs.

"Say something, Herr Self, say something! You'd rather listen? *Audiatur et altera pars*—You're on the side of justice. You are something like justice, aren't you?" He laughed again, a smug laugh.

The flagstones came to an end and gravel crackled beneath our feet. The wind rustled through the trees of the park. There were benches along the paths and chairs on the lawn, and there were many patients outside, alone or in small groups, with or without white-gowned hospital staff. An idyll, except for the twitching, hopping gait of some of the patients, and the empty gazes and open mouths of others. It was noisy. Shouts and laughter echoed against the wall of the old building like the impenetrable confusion of voices in an indoor swimming pool. Eberlein periodically nodded to or greeted this or that person.

I tried this approach: "Are there two sides to this matter, Dr. Eberlein? Either an accident or something else? And what might that something else be? Involuntary manslaughter? Or did somebody murder your patient? Or was it suicide? Are we dealing with a cover-up? I'd like some answers, but all my questions fall on deaf ears. And you come along and start talking about infections and infarctions. What are you trying to tell me?"

"I see what you mean. Murder most foul, or at least suicide. You like dramatic effect? You like imagining things? We
have a lot of people here who like imagining things." He drew
a wide arc with his cane.

That was impudent. I didn't quite manage to swallow my
anger. "Only patients, or doctors, too? But you're quite right:
When the tales I'm being told have holes in them, I start imagining what might fit into these holes. The story your young
colleague fed me had neither rhyme nor reason. What do you,
as director of this institution, have to say about a young
patient falling out a window?"

"I'm no longer a young man, and wouldn't be one even if
I still had my left leg. And you"—he looked me up and
down with an affable expression—"aren't either. Were you
ever married? Marriage is also a kind of organism where bac-
teria and viruses work, and sick cells grow and proliferate.
'Lay a brick, lay a brick, and your house will be built,' as we
Swabians say, and let me tell you, bacteria and viruses are real
Swabians." Again the smug laugh.

I thought about my marriage. Klärchen had died thirteen
years ago, and my grief about our marriage long before that.
Eberlein's image left me cold.

"So what's festering inside the organism of this psychiatric
hospital?" I asked.

Eberlein stopped in his tracks. "It was a pleasure to
meet you. Look me up whenever you have any questions.
I've got into the habit of philosophizing a little. Scratch a
Swabian and you'll find a small Hegel. You're a man of
action, with clear sight and sober reasoning, but at your
age you should be careful about your circulation in this
weather."

He left without saying good-bye. I followed him with my eyes. His walk, his tense shoulders, the short jolting of his whole body as he swung his left leg forward around its axis, the hard thumping of the cane with the silver knob—there was nothing soft or limp about this man. He was a bundle of strength. If he was out to confuse me, he had done so.

8

Davai, Davai

The first drops fell, and the park emptied. The patients ran to
the buildings. The loud chirping of agitated birds hung in the
air. I took refuge under an old, half-open bike shelter, between
slanting rusty racks that had not seen a bicycle for a long
time. There were lightning and thunder, and the pelting rain
hammered on the corrugated iron roof. I heard a blackbird
sing, leaned forward to catch a glimpse of the bird, and pulled
my head back completely wet. The bird was sitting under the
regimental coat of arms up in the corner of the old building.
The first blackbird of summer. Then I saw two figures coming
slowly toward me through the pouring rain. An attendant in
a white gown was calmly talking to a patient in an oversized
gray suit and gently pushing him along. The attendant was
holding the patient's hand behind his back in a police grip
that wasn't painful, but could quickly force one into submis-
sion. As they approached, I could understand the attendant's
words, appeasing nonsense, along with an occasional sharp,
"Davai, Davai!" Both men's clothes were sticking to their
bodies.

Even as they were standing next to me under the corrugated roof the attendant didn't let go of his patient. He nodded to me. "New here? Administration?" He didn't wait for my reply. "You guys up there have it easy while we here have to do all the dirty work. Nothing personal, I don't even know you." He was broad and heavy and towered over me. He had a massive, rough nose. The patient was shivering and looking out into the rain. His mouth formed words I didn't understand.

"Is your patient dangerous?"

"You mean because I've got a tight grip on him? Don't worry. What do you do up there?"

There was a flash of lightning. The rain was still streaming down, drumming on the corrugated roof and splashing up from the gravel onto our legs. Rivulets poured over the shelter's concrete floor, and a smell of wet dust hung in the air.

"I'm from outside. I'm looking into the accident of that female patient last Tuesday."

"You're from the police?"

The thunder came roaring over us. I flinched, which the attendant might well have taken for a nod, and me for a policeman.

"What accident?"

"Over in the old building—a fatal fall from the fourth floor."

The attendant looked at me blankly. "What are you talking about? That's the first I've heard about a fall last Tuesday. And when I don't know a thing, it never happened. Who's supposed to have fallen?"

I handed him Leo's picture.

"That girl? Who told you such bullshit?"

"Dr. Wendt."

He gave me back the picture. "In that case, I didn't say anything. If Dr. Wendt . . . if the director's golden boy said so"—he shrugged his shoulders—"then I guess we had an accident. A fatal fall from the fourth floor of the old building."

I put off acknowledging what the attendant had retracted. "And your patient here?"

"He's one of our Russians. He gets into a crazy mood now and then. But he needs his fresh air, too, and I've got a good grip on him. Right, Ivan?"

The patient became agitated. "Anatol, Anatol, Anatol . . ." He was shouting the name. The attendant tightened his grip and the shouting stopped. "There, there, calm down, Ivan, nothing will happen to you, it's just thunder and lightning, there, there, what will this nice policeman think?" He spoke in the kind of crooning voice with which one reassures children.

I took my pack of Sweet Aftons out of my pocket and the attendant took one. I offered the patient one, too. "Anatol?" He cringed, looked at me, clicked his heels together, bowed, and, turning his head away, fished a cigarette out of the pack.

"Is his name Anatol?"

"How am I supposed to know? You can't get anything out of these guys."

"And who are 'these guys'?"

"We've got all kinds here. They're left over from the war. They were workers in the Third Reich, or foreign volunteer helpers, or fought for some Russian general. Then we've got those from the concentration camps, both inmates and guards. When they're crazy, they're all the same."

The rain grew weaker. A young attendant, his coat billowing, ran past us, jumping over puddles. "Hey, hurry up," he called. "It's almost time to clock out."

"I guess we ought to go." The attendant next to me let his cigarette fall, and it went out on the wet ground. "Come on, Ivan. Time to grab some grub."

The patient had also let his cigarette fall, trod it out, and with his foot carefully buried it in the gravel. Again he clicked his heels together and bowed. I watched the two men slowly make their way to the new building at the other end of the park. The thunder rumbled in the distance, and the rain rustled with gentle monotony. Figures appeared in the doors, and from time to time a doctor or attendant with an umbrella crossed the park with quick steps. The blackbird was still singing.

I remembered the senior public prosecutor's note that had crossed my desk in 1943 or 1944 at the Heidelberg Public Prosecutor's Office, which had decreed that any Russian or Polish workers not meeting their quotas were to be sent to forced labor in a concentration camp. How many had I sent? I stared into the rain. I shuddered. The air after the storm was clear and fresh. After a while I only heard the drops falling from the leaves of the trees. The rain had passed. The sky split open in the west, and pearls of water sparkled in the sun.

I returned to the main building, crossed the stairwell, passed the main entrance, and went out through the columns of the portal. It was five o'clock, change of shift, and employees were streaming out. I waited, keeping a lookout for Wendt, but he didn't appear. The attendant from before was one of the last to come out, and I asked him if he wanted me to drop him off somewhere. In the car on our way to Kirchheim he reiterated that he hadn't said anything.

9

It was only later

It was only later that the shock of Leo's death kicked in, and then, even later, relief that the information could not be right. If the attendant didn't know something, it never happened. I believed him. Also Eberlein would have reacted differently had the fatal fall from the window really taken place. Was he merely trying to provoke me in order to probe me? Be that as it may, in our exchange he'd found out more about me than I had found out about him. I was angry that I hadn't realized this, too, until later.

When I got back home I called Philipp. Sometimes it's a small world—perhaps Philipp, as a surgeon at the Mannheim Municipal Hospital, might know something about the State Psychiatric Hospital and its doctors. He was on his way to a house call and promised to get back to me. But an hour later the doorbell rang and there he was. "I thought I'd better drop by. We don't see enough of each other."

We sat on the leather couches in my living room, which also served as my study, the door to the balcony open. I uncorked a bottle of wine and told Philipp about my investigation at the psychiatric hospital. "I can't make heads or tails of it. Wendt with his silly lies, sinister old Eberlein, and the attendant's hints about Wendt being the director's golden boy—do you see rhyme or reason in any of this?"

Philipp downed the glass of good Alsatian riesling in one gulp and held it out to me. "We're having our spring festival at the yacht club on Friday. I'll take you along and you can have a nice chat with Eberlein."

"Eberlein's got a yacht?"

"The *Psyche*. A Halberg-Rassy 352, sails like a three-quarter-ton vessel, top of the line." Philipp's glass was empty again. "You call Eberlein sinister," he said. "All I know is that people see him as an energetic, unconventional boss. The psychiatric hospital had taken a nosedive, and he put it back on track again. He is seen as a traditionalist in the field, but I don't think that a reformer could have gone a different route and done a better job. Wendt being his protégé doesn't fit the picture, though. Then again, one wouldn't expect him to esteem all doctors the same way—perhaps he likes Wendt particularly. But if Wendt, whom I've never heard of, is behind the mess you're describing, I wouldn't want to be in his shoes."

"And what about your shoes?" I asked. Philipp had knocked back the third glass, too, and rolled the stem between his fingers and looked unhappy.

"Füruzan has moved in with me."

"Just like that?"

He smiled sourly. "It's just like in that building and loan commercial. The bell rings, and there she is at my front door with all her earthly belongings, along with some furniture mover, to move her things into my apartment."

I was impressed. Ever since I'd known him he hit on women, took them out a few times, got them into bed, and that was that. Nurses and hospitals are exactly the same, was his motto: Either you get out quickly, or you're a hopeless case. So he was always particularly careful with nurses. Also because of the working atmosphere. And Füruzan, the proud, voluptuous Turkish nurse, brought everything tumbling down with the flick of a wrist.

"When did this happen?"

"Two weeks ago. I had to slam the door in her face. And then turn the key. It wasn't fair of her. I just couldn't handle it."

Turbo crossed the roof and came into the room from the balcony.

Philipp said, "Here kitty, kitty," and held out his hand. The cat marched straight past him. "See how things are with me? He can sense that I'm a castrated man and turns his back on me."

I sensed something else. Philipp hadn't just dropped by because we don't see enough of each other. As I brought out another bottle from the kitchen, he spilled the beans. "Thanks, just one more sip, I'll have to get going. And if Füruzan should call here and ask for me . . . I don't know if she'd do that, but if she does . . . could you . . . I mean, as a private investigator, you know how to handle these things. Could you tell her, for instance, that I had trouble with my car and that I had to take it to some mechanic you recommended who could only take a look at it this evening . . . I'm hanging around there, and he doesn't have a phone. How's that?"

"Who's the other one?"

He shrugged his shoulders and raised his hands. "You don't know her. She's a student nurse from Frankenthal, but she's got a figure . . . breasts, I swear, she's got breasts like ripe mangoes and a bottom like . . . like . . ."

I suggested pumpkins.

"That's it, pumpkins. Or perhaps melons, not the yellow ones, the green ones with the red flesh. Or perhaps . . ." It was on the tip of his tongue.

"Do me a favor and tell Füruzan that you and I went out," I said to him, "and I won't pick up the phone tonight if it rings."

He left, and I sat there looking into the twilight thinking about my case and my friend Philipp. Füruzan didn't call. At ten o'clock Brigitte came over. My curiosity had been piqued: Before she slipped into her nightgown I took a quick, meticulous look. A pumpkin? No, and not a melon either, nor a muskmelon or a watermelon. A Belgian tomato.

10

Scott at the South Pole

Chief Inspector Nägelsbach is always restrained and polite. He was that way when we met during the war at the Heidelberg Public Prosecutor's Office, and this was how he remained toward me when we became friends. We're both well past the age when friendships thrive on emotional outpourings.

When I visited him the following morning at the Heidelberg police headquarters, I could tell right away that something wasn't quite right. He remained sitting at his desk and only shook my outstretched hand when I was about to withdraw it.

"Please be seated." He waved me to a chair by the filing cabinets, quite a distance from his desk. He frowned when I picked up the chair and brought it closer to his desk, as if I were invading his space.

I came straight to the point. "A case has taken me to the State Psychiatric Hospital. There's something fishy going on there. Can you tell me if the police have been there recently?"

"I am not in a position to provide you with such information. That would be against regulations."

We have never kept to the regulations, but made each other's work and life easier. He knows I can be trusted with the confidential information he gives me, just as I know I can trust him with the information I provide him. I couldn't figure out what was going on. "What are you talking about?"

"Nothing." He peered at me hostilely through the small round lenses of his glasses. I was about to say something curt, then I realized that his expression was not one of hostility, but unhappiness. He had lowered his eyes and was looking at the newspaper. I got up and came to his side.

"Cork Monuments of Italy." It was a newspaper article about an exhibition in Kassel of cork models of ancient buildings, from the Pantheon to the Colosseum, that had been made in Rome by Antonio Chichi between 1777 and 1782. "Read the last bit!"

I quickly ran an eye down the column. The article ended with a quote from a Leipzig art dealer who, in 1786, had proclaimed that these masterful cork models were the best possible medium for conveying a precise and sublime impression of the original monuments. In fact I would have mistaken the picture of the model in the paper for the real thing if it had had the right background.

"I feel like Scott when he reached the South Pole, only to find the tent Amundsen had pitched. Reni wants us to drive over to Kassel this weekend. She says I could see for myself that it's comparing apples and oranges. But I don't know."

I didn't know either. When he was fifteen, Nägelsbach had begun building models of major monuments out of matchsticks. From time to time he would attempt to build something else, like Dürer's *Praying Hands* or the golden helmet of Rembrandt's *Man in a Golden Helmet*, but his mission in life,

45

to which he was going to devote his retirement, was to build a model of the Vatican. I know and value Nägelsbach's works, but to be honest they did not achieve the kind of illusion of reality that those cork models did. What could I tell him? That art was more a matter of creation than an attempt to portray reality? That in life the goal wasn't as important as the journey? That today the world remembered Scott, not Amundsen?

"What are you working on right now?" I asked him.

"On the Pantheon, of all things. For four weeks now. Why didn't I go for the Brooklyn Bridge?" His shoulders drooped.

I waited for a bit. "Can I drop by again tomorrow?"

"It's the State Psychiatric Hospital, right? I'll call you when I have the information."

I drove back to Mannheim with a deep feeling of futility. My old Opel purred over the asphalt. Sometimes the tires thumped over the yellow bumps marking the shifting of lanes where road work was being done. Failure late in life is no easier to bear than failure when one is young. It might not be the first time one is knocked down, but it might well be the last.

Back at my office, Salger's strained voice sounded from the answering machine. He was most anxious for news and wanted me to leave a message on his machine with an update on my investigation. He was sending another payment. His wife was also anxious for news. He didn't want to keep pestering me, but he did until my answering machine cut him off after two minutes.

Pictures from an exhibition

Nägelsbach didn't keep me waiting. He told me he had put his ear to the ground but hadn't found out much. "I can tell you the long and the short of it on the phone." But I wanted to meet with him instead. "This evening? No, I can't. But I'll be back in the office tomorrow morning."

It was to be a drive I shall never forget. It was almost the end of everything. At some construction near Friedrichsfeld, where neither a center planting nor barriers separate the lanes of the autobahn, a large furniture truck skidded, crossed my lane toward the embankment, and rolled over. I froze. The truck slid across my lane; my car was headed toward it as if to ram it, and the truck grew bigger, came nearer, and towered above me. I didn't brake or swerve my car to the left. I simply froze.

Within a fraction of a second everything was over. The truck had rolled over with a loud crash: Brakes screeched, horns blared, and a car that had careened out of its lane sideswiped another car that had come to a standstill. I stopped on the shoulder of the autobahn and got out but couldn't walk a step. I began shivering; I had to tense my muscles and grit my teeth. I stood there and saw the line of cars grow longer, the driver of the truck climb out of his cabin, a crowd of onlookers cluster around the rear door that had burst open, and the arrival of a police car and also an ambulance that immediately drove off again. My teeth kept chattering.

A man got out of the car that had come to a stop behind my car and walked up to me. "Do you need a doctor?" I shook my head. He took hold of my arms, shook me, made me sit down on the embankment, and lit a cigarette. "Would you like one, too?"

All I could think of was that you're not supposed to sit on the bare ground in any months that have an "r" in them, and it was April. I wanted to get up, worried about my bladder and prostate, but the man held me down.

After the cigarette, I pretty much came around again. The man was talking up a storm—after a few sentences I had already lost the thread. When he left, I didn't even remember what he looked like. But now I was capable of making a statement to the police without trembling.

Car by car, the traffic was waved past the capsized truck, its back door wide open. Its contents had fallen onto the autobahn, pictures from an exhibition in Mannheim. They were to be recovered and placed under the charge of the curator of the Mannheim Kunsthalle. I drove to Heidelberg along an almost empty autobahn.

The information Nägelsbach had found came from the file of a colleague of his who was on sick leave. "His reports are in quite a bad state. It seems he's not been well for some time. But one thing's clear, there's been trouble off and on at the psychiatric hospital over the last few years."

"Trouble? What do you mean? Trouble, as in a patient falling out a window and breaking his neck?"

"Good God, no. I'm talking about small slipups and glitches. I guess 'trouble' isn't even the right word. It's things like a failure in the hot-water supply, food that's gone bad, workers finding windows they had stacked in the courtyard smashed, a patient being released a few days too late, an attendant falling from a ladder—I don't know if any of this is even significant. And the reports were never made by the management, but always by patients, their families, or anonymously. If only one didn't have to be so goddamn careful nowadays in wards and institutions . . ."

"Do the problems go beyond what happens in any large institution?"

Nägelsbach got up. "Follow me." We went out into the corridor, turned around the corner, and looked out the window into the courtyard of the police headquarters. "What do you see, Herr Self?"

On the left, three police cars were parked, and on the right the ground was dug up and pipes were being laid. Some of the windows looking out on the yard were open, some closed. Nägelsbach looked up at the blue sky, across which a fresh wind was blowing little white clouds. "Wait a few more minutes," he said. And then, as a cloud covered the sun, the blinds suddenly closed in all the windows. The cloud moved on, but the blinds remained closed.

"Of the three cars down there, two are almost always here because they need repairs, the sewer pipes have already been dug up once this year and then covered up again, and every summer the blinds come up with some new prank. Would you say that all this is within the bounds of what can happen in any large institution? Or is this the work of terrorists, libera-tionists, anarchists, or skinheads?" Nägelsbach looked at me blankly.

We went back to his office. "Do you have anything on a Dr. Wendt?" I asked.

"One moment. The computer terminal is in another office." He came back with a blank expression on his face. "There's nothing in the computer. But the name rings a bell. I don't know if that's for any specific reason. I'll have to look through the paper files that we'll be shredding for security reasons, which can't be pulled up on the computer. I'll try to do it as fast as I can, but it might take a while. When do you need this?"

I said "yesterday" and meant it. But what I had to do was clear even without a file on Wendt. Wendt was my lead, regardless of whether the lead was hot, warm, or cold. I had to dig up what sort of man he was, who his friends were, if he'd had dealings with Leo. Leo and her friends were not sup-posed to get wind of my investigation. But with Wendt I didn't have to mind my p's and q's.

12

In vain

I followed Wendt when he came out of the psychiatric hospital at about seven. He got into his car and drove off in the direction of Heidelberg. I'd been waiting for two hours and thrown my butts out the window because the ashtray was full. Sweet Aftons have no filter and are environmentally friendly cigarettes that burn out completely.

Route 3 is a smooth ride, and Wendt hit a good speed in his little Renault. From time to time I lost him, but caught up with him again at traffic lights, followed him down the Rohrbacher Strasse and through the Gaisberg tunnel, around Karlstor and up Hauptstraße. My Opel rattled over the cobblestones. We both parked in a garage beneath the Karlsplatz. Wendt pulled into a handicapped parking space, I into a well-lit parking space for women. Wendt got out of his car quickly, rushed up the stairs, and ran across the square, up Hauptstraße, past the Kornmarkt and the Heilig-Geist church. I couldn't keep up with him. His silhouette in the billowing beige raincoat grew smaller. I stopped at the corner of the city hall, pressing my hand to my side and trying to ease the pounding and stinging.

After the Florin-Gasse he hurried into a doorway over which hung a sign with a golden sun. I waited for the pounding in my side to grow weaker. The marketplace and the main street were quiet. It was too late for people to be shopping, and too early for strolling. On the houses around the marketplace a tax-advantaged historic renovation spree had left its mark. I noticed that in the niche at the corner of the city hall the stone statue of a prisoner of war was missing. He had stood there waiting for decades in a long coat, with hollow cheeks and emaciated hands. I wondered who might have taken him back home.

Beneath the sign of the golden sun was the Ristorante Sole d'Oro. I peeked inside. Wendt and a young woman were being given menus. Across the street, in the Café Bistro Villa, I found a table by the window where I could keep my eye on the restaurant's entrance. Long after the cassata, while I was on my second espresso and second sambuca, Wendt and his companion came out onto the street. They sauntered past a few houses to the Gloria movie theater. I watched the movie from three rows behind them. What I remember of the movie is the desperation of a woman who is becoming schizophrenic, and images of grand old facades, of a table festively decked on a terrace overlooking the sea, and of the sun hanging large and red in a hazy evening sky. As I came out of the theater I was dazed by the images and let my attention slip. Wendt and his companion were gone. A thick stream of students was moving down the main street, some with bright caps and headbands, along with American, Dutch, and Japanese tourists and loud young people from the provinces.

In the garage I waited for Wendt a long time. When he finally turned up, he was alone. He drove slowly: Friedrich-

Ebert-Anlage, Kurfürstenanlage, along the Neckar River as far as Wieblingen. There he parked at the end of the Schustergasse. I couldn't make out the house number but saw him opening the garden gate and then closing it, walking around the house, and then disappearing down some stairs. Then the windows of the basement apartment lit up.

I drove home through the villages. The full moon cast its white light on fields and roofs. That night the moon kept me awake for a long time, and then I dreamed about it. It shone onto a terrace with a festively decked table, and I waited in vain for guests I had not invited.

13

Yes and no

One of the advantages of advancing years is that people believe everything you tell them. A man my age is simply too weary to try his hand as a con artist or a marriage swindler— what would he need the money for, anyway?

When I introduced myself as Wendt's father, his landlady didn't doubt my word for a minute.

"Ah, so you are Dr. Wendt's father!"

Frau Kleinschmidt eyed me inquisitively. Her flowery smock enclosed a good three hundred pounds, which protruded in small bulges between the buttons. The lower buttons had got in the way of her bending down and so were open, and her blue and pink petticoat peeked out. Frau Kleinschmidt had been busy with her strawberry beds when I had gone down the stairs to Wendt's basement apartment, rung the bell, and knocked on the door in vain. When I came back up the stairs, she had called me over.

I looked at my watch, and shook my head: "My son said he'd be home by five today. It's already a quarter past, and he's still not here."

"He's usually never back before a quarter to seven."

I sincerely hoped that today would be no exception. Twenty minutes earlier his car had still been parked outside the psychiatric hospital. I had taken up my post at four thirty, got fed up with waiting, and remembered the trustworthiness of the elderly. "I know he usually works till six or even later, but he told me he'd get away earlier today. I'm in Heidelberg on business and have to leave this evening. May I sit down on the bench for a moment?"

"I'll be happy to let you into your son's apartment. One moment; I'll go get the keys."

She came back with the keys and a plate of marble cake. "I was intending to leave this on his doorstep." She pressed the plate into my hands and unlocked the door. "Perhaps you'd like to try a piece. What did you say you were doing in Heidelberg?"

"I'm with the Union Bank of Baden." As a matter of fact I do have an account there, and the old gray suit I was wearing fitted the image of a Baden official who had erred into banking. Frau Kleinschmidt found me sufficiently reputable and kept nodding her head respectfully. Her chin doubled, tripled, and quadrupled.

It was cool in Wendt's apartment. There were four doors in the hallway. The bathroom was to the left, the living room and the bedroom, which also served as his study, to the right, and the broom closet straight ahead. The kitchen lay beyond the living room. I hurried, as I wanted to be out of there by six. I looked for the telephone, to no avail. Wendt didn't have one. So there wasn't going to be one of those little books with names, addresses, and phone numbers lying next to a phone. In the chest of drawers I found only shirts and linen, in the closet only pants, jackets, and sweaters. In the wooden cabinets that Wendt used as supports for his writing desk there were ring binders, technical books, and a dictionary that was still in its shrink-wrap. Also loose letters, and letters in bundles, bills, reminders, traffic tickets, and thick reams of writing paper, as if he were planning to write a big book and had wanted to make sure that he wouldn't run out of supplies. Pinned on the cork board above the desk were a movie schedule from the Gloria Theater, a brochure for a water pick, a postcard from Istanbul and another from Amorbach, a key, a shopping list, and a cartoon showing two men. "Do you find it hard to make a decision?" one man was asking the other. "Yes and no."

I took down the postcards. A thankful former patient and his wife had sent greetings from Istanbul, while Gabi, Klaus, Katrin, Henner, and Lea sent greetings from Amorbach, with the message that Amorbach was beautiful in the spring, that the children and Lea were getting on well together, that the renovation of the mill was almost finished, and that Wendt should come visit them soon. Gabi had been the one who wrote the postcard, Klaus had signed with a flourish, Katrin and Henner had scrawled something in childish letters, and from Lea came: "Hi, Lea." I looked carefully, but Lea remained Lea, not Leo.

In the ring binders I found the notes and drafts of Wendt's doctoral dissertation. The letters that were bundled together were ten or more years old; in the loose letters his sister described her life in Lübeck, his mother her vacation, and a friend wrote on professional matters. I rummaged through the pile of books, newspapers, patient files, and papers and found a bank savings book, a checkbook, a passport, travel brochures of Canada, a draft for a job application to a hospital in Toronto, a Wieblingen parish newsletter, a note with three phone numbers on it, and the beginning of a poem.

> *Who can tell*
> *if parallel lines*
> *meet*
> *at infinity?*
> *Who can tell*
> *if you and I . . .*

I would have liked an optimistic continuation for that "you and I." My father, an official with the German railways, with tracks in mind, had answered the question of whether parallel lines meet in infinity with a "no."

I jotted down the three phone numbers. On the bookshelf I found a photo album documenting Wendt's childhood and youth. In the bathroom there was a picture of a naked girl stuck to the mirror. Under the mirror was a packet of condoms.

I gave up. Whatever Wendt might be hiding, his apartment didn't reveal it. I stood a few more minutes with Frau Kleinschmidt by her strawberry patch. I showed her Leo's picture and told her how happy my wife and I were that our son had met this nice young woman. She had never seen Leo before.

14

Twenty Smurfs

Back at my office I found an envelope with Salger's next payment. Again, fifty hundred-mark bills. I called Salger's answering machine, confirmed that I had received his payment, and informed him that Leo had been a patient at the State Psychiatric Hospital, had checked out again, and that for the time being that was all I knew.

Then I called the numbers that Wendt had jotted down: a number in Munich, one in Mannheim, and one that Information identified as an Amorbach number. Nobody answered in Munich, in Mannheim the Institute for Mental Health replied, and in Amorbach a woman with a heavy American accent.

"Hello, Dr. Hopfen's residence." Children were making a racket in the background.

I tried a simple ruse: "Could I speak to Dr. Hopfen? We worked on the insulation at the mill, and this is a follow-up call to see if everything is fine."

"I can barely hear you." The children had come closer and were making even more noise. "Who is this?"

"My name is Self, insulation services. The cellar in the mill was damp, and we . . ."

"One moment, please." She held her hand over the receiver, but I could hear every word of the children's shouting match, and her reply: Henner had given Katrin twenty-three Smurfs— No, Katrin had only gotten twenty-one, and he'd only gotten eighteen back—No, she'd given him back nineteen. "Eighteen!" "Nineteen!" "Seventeen!" Lea established the facts. "One, two, three . . . twenty. You have twenty Smurfs, which is more than you counted. That's more than enough!" Twenty— that threw the kids for a loop and shut them up for a while. "You want to speak to Dr. Hopfen, because you're wanting to go in the mill?" She asked in a thick German accent, slipping up on nouns and verbs. "The painters are there, you can go inside the cellar with no problems. Now they're off work, but tomorrow morning the painters will be working again."

"Thank you very much. Are you English?"

"I'm from America, the Hopfens' au pair."

For a moment we both waited, in case she or I might say something more. Then she hung up without a word. I watered my potted palm. Something had caught my attention, but I couldn't pin it down.

Philipp called. "Gerhard, don't forget the spring festival tomorrow evening at the yacht club. It'll start at around seven, but most people will turn up between eight and nine. Eight would be a good time, otherwise you might lose Eberlein in the crowd. And bring Brigitte."

I spent the following day at the municipal library, reading up on psychiatry. I thought that if I picked up a few pointers I might get more information out of Eberlein about the State Psychiatric Hospital, and about what Wendt had done there for or against Leo and what he might be hiding. I learned that the psychiatric hospital in Trieste had been closed down and that the State Psychiatric Hospital in Wunstorf was being restructured, which made me realize that the changes I had noticed at Eberlein's hospital were part of a major development in psychiatry from incarceration to healing. I found mental health defined as the ability to play the social game well. Someone is mentally ill when we no longer take him seriously because he does not play along or does not play along well. A chill ran down my spine.

15

Smashed china

Yacht clubs, rowing clubs, riding clubs, and tennis clubs may all be lavish to a greater or lesser degree, but they look like they've sprung from one and the same unimaginative clan of architects. On the ground floor are the equipment rooms, shower rooms, and changing rooms; on the first floor the lounge with the bar for social events, one or two adjoining rooms, and a terrace, which looked out over the Rhine and Friesenheimer Island.

On my way through the lounge I lost Brigitte. We'd had another of our spats in the car, because she wants us to get married and I don't. Or at least not yet. Then she tells me that at sixty-nine I'm not getting any younger—I tell her that one never gets any younger—and she tells me I'm talking non-sense. When she's right, there are no two ways about it. So I shut my mouth and dug in my heels. We parked among the many Mercedeses, BMWs, and even two Jaguars and a Rolls-Royce, but by the time I had walked to the other side of the car to open the door for her she had gotten out, cool and haughty.

Philipp, Füruzan, and Eberlein, who had a young woman on his arm, were standing by the railing of the terrace.

"Gerhard!" Füruzan gave me a kiss on each cheek, and Philipp squeezed my arm.

Eberlein introduced me to his wife and then grabbed the bull by the horns. "Why don't you young people leave us alone for a while? We elderly gentlemen have a thing or two we need to confer about."

He steered me to a table. "You're obviously here to talk to me, so why keep you on tenterhooks? You came to our hospital inquiring about a young lady, but all you managed to find out was that she was a patient. Wendt fobbed you off with some story, and I started philosophizing. Now you've come to sound me out on neutral territory. Fair enough, fair enough." He laughed his smug laugh and exuded harmlessness. He accepted a cigarette, refused a light, and twirled the cigarette between the tips of his thumb and middle finger while I smoked. His fat fingers executed the movement tenderly.

"I've come to sound you out? As far as I'm concerned, we can call it that. A young doctor in your institution tells me that a patient, whose father commissioned me to find her, fell out a window and died. Nobody else knows anything about this. An employee at your institution tells me that someone's pulling my leg, but when I inform him where I got my information from, he suddenly retracts what he said. Then I hear about small slipups and glitches at your hospital, while you spin a yarn about infections and infarctions, viruses and bacteria. Yes, I would be grateful for an explanation."

"What do you know about psychiatry?"

"I've read this and that. Years ago a friend of mine was a patient at your hospital, and I've seen firsthand how things were done back then and how much things have changed."

"And what do you know about the responsibility and burden of psychiatric work? Of the worries a psychiatrist can't leave behind in his locker along with his white gown, worries that follow him home, pursue him in his sleep, and are waiting for him the next morning when he wakes up? What do you know about that? You with your jokes about viruses, bacteria, infections, and infarctions . . ."

"But it was you who . . ." I couldn't figure out where he was coming from. Or is it with psychiatrists as it is with the kind of firemen who are covert arsonists and policemen who are covert criminals? I looked at him, bewildered.

He laughed and cheerfully tapped the floor several times with his cane. "Can a man with a face that is so easily readable be a private investigator? But don't worry, I'm just confusing you a little so that you can better understand the confusion about which you are asking me." He leaned back and took his time. "Don't be too hard on young Wendt. He isn't having an easy time of it. All things considered, he might well be a good doctor some day."

What I needed now was time before I could continue. "You're saying I shouldn't be too hard on him. Well, before I do anything, I want to give him one last chance." I didn't have a clear concept of what I was talking about. Needless to say, it had gone through my mind to tell Nägelsbach about Wendt's behavior, or someone from the medical association or the appropriate board of physicians. But I couldn't see what I would gain by doing that. That would get Wendt into trouble, so I could perhaps try to put pressure on him by threatening such an action. But there was also the problem that Leo wasn't supposed to realize that I was looking for her, and were I to carry out my threat, I didn't know if that could be avoided.

"Of course it was foolish of Wendt to invent a fatal accident," Eberlein said. "But imagine that you are a dedicated therapist, conscious that the relationship between your client and her father is the core issue, are working on it, have successes, setbacks, and finally a breakthrough that will bring your client back on the right track. And then suddenly a private investigator appears, and through that private investigator the father raises his fist—Wendt simply reached for the first lie he could think of to shake you off and shield his client."

"So where is she?"

"I have no idea, Herr Self. I also do not know if things happened as I told you. The reason for my telling you this is so you can understand what might drive a doctor like Wendt to invent a foolish story like that."

"So it could have been altogether different?"

He ignored my question. "I liked that girl—a cheerful spirit beneath a depressive veneer, not to mention her good pedigree. I hope she'll make it." He thought a while. "Be that as it may, I have neglected my wife long enough. Let's go back."

He got up and I followed him. The band had begun to play, and couples were whirling over the floor. We didn't have to force or edge our way through the crowd—standing and dancing couples spontaneously parted before Eberlein. We found the others. I danced with Frau Eberlein after he tapped his cane against his wooden leg and gave me a prompting glance, and then with Füruzan, and with a woman who approached me during ladies' choice and towered a head above me. By eleven thirty the crowd became too much for me, the room too small, the music too loud.

I found Brigitte on the terrace. She was flirting with a nobody in a turquoise suit and with an oily slick of hair.

"I'm leaving. Are you coming along?" I asked her.

She stayed. I drove home. At six thirty in the morning the doorbell rang, and there was Brigitte with a packet of fresh rolls. I didn't ask her where she'd just come from. Over breakfast I was going to propose to her, but as she got up to get the eggs from the stove she stepped on Turbo's tail.

16

Wider, straighter, faster

After lunch things suddenly fell into place. I'd swum a few laps at the Herschelbad on account of my back, and then, returning from the market, saw Giovanni standing outside the door of the Kleiner Rosengarten restaurant.

I greeted him. "You back? No more *Mama-mia* and *Solemio*?" But he wasn't in a mood to play our German-converses-with-immigrant-worker game today. He had a lot to tell me about things back home in Radda, and found it easier to do so in his fluent German than in our bumbling pidgin. Then he brought out my food, which finally was again the way I liked it. He himself had gone shopping in the morning to the market and the slaughterhouse. The veal cutlet was juicy and the sauce had been pureed from fresh tomatoes and seasoned with sage. He brought me espresso and sambuca without my having to ask.

"Do you count in Italian?" I asked him. Giovanni was standing next to my table with his pad, adding up my order.

"You mean, even though I speak good German? I think when people count, they fall back into their mother tongue. Even though numbers aren't really that difficult."

I thought of the Hopfen family's au pair. One, two, three . . . she had counted twenty Smurfs. In German, despite her thick accent and her slipping up on nouns and verbs. Brigitte's son, Manu, who had lived for a long time in Brazil with his father but by now speaks good Mannheim German, still counts in Portuguese, even when I'm helping him with his homework and math problems. On the other hand, Lea might have been counting in German just to settle the children's argument.

I wanted to see her. Only I couldn't remember where I'd parked my car. At the Herschelbad? The market square? At home? It's sad when you have to use your detective's nose to make up for the shortcomings of age. The price tag on the shampoo bottle gave me a clue. It came from a drugstore in Neckarstadt. I remembered that I had driven Brigitte to her place in the Max-Joseph-Strasse after breakfast, had bought the shampoo there, and then had crossed the Kurpfalz Bridge and walked over to the swimming pool.

I found my car, took the autobahn to Heidelberg, and drove along the Neckar to Eberbach. I hadn't known that all of Route 37 was under construction, that it was being made wider, straighter, and faster, and that it even tunneled under the mountain at Hirschhorn. Will it one day turn into an autobahn? Will one day a monorail line run through forest and meadow, mountain and valley, replacing the dignified sandstone viaducts over which the Grand Duke sent the first trains across the gorges of the Odenwald? Will a Club Med one day take over the enchanted complex of old guesthouse, hunting lodge, and disused factory in Ernsttal? There, on the road from Kailbach to Ottorfszell, the trees are at their green-est and the sandstone at its reddest, and on the shaded terrace beer tastes like ambrosia. Why does it always have to be coffee and cake in the afternoon? I had a schnitzel with my beer, and a salad with a dressing that didn't come out of a bottle, and blinked in the sunlight that breached the leafy canopy.

In Amorbach I found Dr. Hopfen's office on the market square, and one of his patients told me the way to his home. "Head past the train station, over the tracks, and up toward the Hotel Frankenberg. Keep following the signs for Sommerberg. The doctor's house is the last one on the left before you get to the driveway of the hotel."

After I negotiated the steep and narrow lane and made a U-turn in the hotel's driveway, a little girl opened the gate in front of the Hopfen residence, and a Land Rover pulled out. The girl closed the gate again and got into the car. Two other children were romping around in the backseat. A woman was at the wheel. The engine died a few times, and I looked around: I gazed at the fruit trees on the slope, the building supplies warehouse in the valley, and the church of Amorbach with its two onion domes beyond the railway tracks. I followed the Rover back into town. The throng of tourist cars in front of the abbey left only two parking spaces—one for the Rover and one for my old Opel.

I followed the woman and the three children on foot to the market square. I still wasn't certain. But then they went into Hopfen's office, and when they came out again I had the young woman in full view, and there was no doubt. She was Leo. Leo in pink sunglasses, a peroxide blond mop of curls, and a man's checked shirt over her jeans. She had done her best to look like an au-pair girl from the American Midwest.

I followed Leo and the children. They shopped at the butcher's and at the cheese store, and while the children were having their hair cut at the salon, Leo browsed the shelves of the bookstore across the street. Before they got back in the car and drove home, they stopped at the church with the onion domes. I followed them inside and drank in the bright, spacious interior and the sounds of the organ, on which an organist happened to be practicing. In the nave, Saint Sebastian was being shot with arrows and nursed by Saint Irene. Leo and the children were kneeling in the back row. The little girl was looking around the church and the two boys were popping their bubble gum. Leo leaned her elbows on the back of the pew in front of her, rested her head on her hands, and stared into the emptiness.

17

In response to an official request

I was back in Mannheim at four thirty. On my way there I
had still not figured out what to make of all this. I wanted to
talk to Salger, but not on the phone and definitely not by way
of his answering machine. It was clear that he knew more
than he had led me to believe.

I drove straight over to the Max-Joseph-Strasse. Brigitte
greeted me as if our spat had never taken place. We embraced.
She felt good, warm, and soft, and I only let go of her when
Manu tugged at us jealously.

"Why don't the two of you take Nonni out?" she suggested. "And come back around seven thirty. I'll finish my tax
returns and cook something—the sauerbraten should be
ready by seven thirty."

Nonni is Manu's dog, a tiny creature, a fluffy toy. Manu
put him on a leash and we made a grand tour of the town: the
Neckar embankment, the Luisenpark, the Oststadt, and the
Water Tower. We made slow progress. In general I have my
doubts when it comes to evolution and progress, but the fact
that erotic attraction between humans doesn't involve sniffing

tree trunks and corners is without doubt a clear sign of evolutionary progress.

I called Salger from Brigitte's place. The answering machine wasn't on. Was Salger back in Bonn? The phone rang futilely. I tried again at nine and at ten, but still nobody picked up.

On Sunday, too, and even Monday morning at eight my attempts were futile. At nine I took Manu to school and Brigitte to her massage practice at the Collini Center, and then drove on to the main post office to look through the regional phone books. If Salger was back in Bonn, he had to be back at work, too. I found Bonn in phone book number 53, and under Federal Government found the number of the chancellor and seventeen federal ministries. I started with the Federal Chancellery and the Press and Public Relations Office. They didn't have an Under-Secretary Salger. There was no Salger at the Federal Ministry for Work and Social Services, nor at any of the other ministries listed. At the Federal Ministry for Justice nobody picked up until ten fifteen, at which point the lady on the phone, though sounding rested and exceptionally friendly, had never heard of an Under-Secretary Salger. I turned to phone book number 39 and called the various departments at the state government in Düsseldorf. It didn't seem too farfetched that Salger might be living in Bonn but working in Düsseldorf. But no regional minister of Nordrhein-Westfalen had an under-secretary by the name of Salger.

I drove over to the Municipal Hospital. It was time to find out a few things. I wanted to pin down my client: the mysterious under-secretary without a department, the owner of a phone number that was listed nowhere, the sender of letters containing five thousand marks without a return address.

I had his telephone number, but Information will only disclose a subscriber's name and address in response to an official request or in a case of an emergency. A doctor who finds nothing but a telephone number in the pockets of an unconscious patient and needs to know his name and address can call Information and put in his request, and he will be called back. Philipp had to help me make this request official.

Philipp was still in the operating theater, and the head nurse showed me into his office. I had intended to ask him to put the call through to Information, but then I decided to save him the trouble and do my own lying.

"Hello, this is Dr. Self, Mannheim Municipal Hospital. We have an accident patient without ID. All we have is a number in Bonn: 41-17-88. Can you please provide me with the name and address for this number?"

I was put on hold twice. Then they promised to check and call me back. I gave them Philipp's number. Five minutes later the phone rang.

"Hello."

"Dr. Self?"

"Speaking."

"41-17-88 belongs to a Helmut Lehmann . . ."

"Lehmann?"

"Ludwig, Emil, Heinrich, Marta, Anton, Nordpol, Nordpol. The address is Niebuhrstrasse 46a in Bonn, District 1."

I made a cross-check, calling Information in Bonn and asking for the number of Helmut Lehmann, Niebuhrstrasse 46a, and was given 41-17-88.

It was twenty past twelve. I checked the train schedule: There was an intercity train from Mannheim to Bonn at 12:45. I didn't wait for Philipp.

By 12:40 I was standing in the long line in front of the only open ticket window. By 12:44 the bored clerk and his boring computer had served four passengers, and I could see that I wasn't going to get to my ticket before 12:48. I rushed out onto the platform. No train came at 12:45, 12:46, 12:47, 12:48, or 12:49. At 12:50 there was an announcement that intercity train 714 was running five minutes late, and it pulled into the station at 12:54. I get worked up, even though I know that this is how things are nowadays with the train system, and that getting worked up isn't good for me. I remember the railways in the old days, punctual and treating passengers with sober, firm, Prussian respect.

I won't waste any words on the lunch in the restaurant car. The ride along the Rhine is always beautiful. I like seeing the railway bridge from Mainz to Wiesbaden, the Niederwald Memorial, the Kaub Castle on the island, the Loreley, and Castle Ehrenbreitstein. At 2:55 I was in Bonn.

I won't waste any words on Bonn either. A taxi took me to Niebuhrstrasse 46a. The narrow house was, like most houses on that street, a product of the mid-nineteenth century Gröünderzeit period with columns, capitals, and friezes. On the ground floor, next to the entrance, was a tiny shop in which nothing was on display or being sold anymore. The pale black lettering on the gray frosted glass above the door announced HABERDASHERY. I ran my eye over the names on the buzzers: There was no Lehmann.

I didn't find a Lehmann on the buzzers of Niebuhrstrasse 46 or 48 either. I read the buzzers of number 46a once more but found no further information. I was on the point of giving up, but then I hesitated, perhaps because I had glimpsed something from the corner of my eye that had been picked up by my subconscious. The tiny plaque by the door of the shop read HELMUT LEHMANN. Helmut Lehmann—nothing more. The door was locked. Inside the shop there were a counter, two chairs, and an empty display stand for pantyhose.

On the counter stood a telephone and an answering machine.

18

A demigod in gray

I knocked, but nobody emerged from a hidden trapdoor or stepped out of a secret panel. The shop remained empty.

Then I rang the second-floor apartment and found the landlord. He told me that the old widow who had run the haberdashery had died a year or so ago and that her grandson had been paying the rent ever since. "When might I be likely to find young Herr Lehmann?" The landlord eyed me with his piggish little eyes and spoke in a whiny Rhineland tremolo. "I have no idea. He told me that he and his friends want to turn the shop into a gallery. Sometimes one of them is here, sometimes another, and then for days on end I don't see or hear anyone." When I delicately tried to ascertain if he was certain about the identity of the grandson, Lehmann, the landlord's whininess turned to outrage. "Who are you? What is it you want?" His tone smacked of bad conscience, as if he had let his doubts be bought off by a high rent.

I went back to the station. There wasn't a train until 5:11 in the afternoon, so I sat down in a café across the street. I sipped some hot chocolate and went over what I knew and didn't know.

I knew that Lea was Leo. I could also imagine why Leo had altered her name to Lea. I, too, always chose aliases close to my real name. In one of my past assignments I had used the alias Hendrik Willamowitz to infiltrate a gang that traded in American cigarettes and stolen German antiquities. There was something I liked about the name. But on two occasions I didn't react fast enough when someone called me Willamowitz, and that was that as far as the gang boss was concerned. Ever since, I have been Gerhard Sell, or Selk, or Selt, or Selln whenever I needed an alias, and these are the names I also have on my fake business cards.

But what did Leo need a fake name for? She'd turned up at the psychiatric hospital under a fake name and was registered under that name—the receptionist there had no information on a Leonore Salger, and Dr. Wendt, too, had said that he'd only learned her real name from me. A patient at the State Psychiatric Hospital and an American au-pair girl in a remoter part of the Odenwald—a good move if one wanted or needed to go underground. But why would Leo want or need to hide? It was crystal clear that she was not hiding within the guise of therapy from a threatening father, but from the phony Herr Salger, the phony or real Herr Lehmann, or myself—his informant or client. Did Wendt know more about this? Everything undeniably pointed to Wendt's having arranged the au-pair position for Leo in Amorbach. Even Eberlein seemed to assume that Wendt had something to do with Leo's disappearance. Maybe he had even helped her hide out in the psychiatric hospital in the first place.

I ordered another cup of hot chocolate and a chocolate meringue. Who was the mysterious Herr Salger? He had played the role of under-secretary from Bonn quite convincingly on the phone. He knew that Leo had studied French and English at the Heidelberg Institute for Translation and Interpretation. He had a photograph of Leo that came from her. Had she given it to him?

As I nibbled at my meringue I sketched out a love story. Leo, wearing a crumpled yellow blouse, is cutting class. She is sitting on the bank of the Rhine. A young attaché from the Foreign Ministry comes sauntering by. "Hello young lady, may I . . ." They go for a walk. More walks follow. The banks of the Rhine are not the only place where they kiss. Then the attaché is posted to Abu Dhabi and she stays behind, and while he only sees veiled women who remind him of Leo, she meets a handsome young man or two. The attaché returns from Abu Dhabi—there is jealousy, arguments, stalking—she moves from Bonn to Heidelberg—he follows her, threatens her. A foolish story. But what made it compelling was the locality. Salger/Lehmann had to have a reason why he would choose to play the role of the father from Bonn, and the most obvious reason was that Leo was from Bonn.

I finished my chocolate, asked the waitress the way to the main post office, paid, and left. It was only a few steps. I already knew that I would not find the name Salger in phone book number 53 under Bonn. But perhaps the widow of an under-secretary, whom I could picture as Leo's mother, might be living out in the suburbs. I could see the private home bought with a state subvention, small and white, in a pretty, colorful garden with a lodger's apartment and a rustic fence. I didn't find the name Salger in Bad Honnef, Bornheim, Eitorf, Hennef, Königswinter, or Lohmar. I did find a landscape designer by the name of Günter Salgert in Meckenheim, and a management consultant called Philipp Salsger. Encouraged, I worked my way through Much, Neunkirchen-Seelscheid,

Niederkassel, Rheinbach, and Ruppichteroth to St. Augustin. There I found an E. Salger, and that was that. Siegburg, Swisttal, Troisdorf, and Windeck only offered up an M. Sallert who specialized in renovating frame houses, and a nurse by the name of Anna Salga. I wrote down the address and phone number of E. Salger and went into a phone booth.

"Yes, hello?" It was the shaky voice of a woman who had been struck by congestive heart failure, had had a stroke, or was an alcoholic.

"Good afternoon, Frau Salger. My name is Self. Your daughter Leonore will have told you about my son. My wife and I are so pleased about the two of them and think it is high time that we met you. You see, I happen to be in Bonn today and I thought—"

"My daughter isn't here. Who is this please?"

"My name is Self. I am the father of her friend . . ."

"Ah, you are the TV repairman. I was expecting you yesterday."

I could rule out congestive heart failure. It had to be a stroke or alcoholism. "Will you be home around six?" I asked her.

"I couldn't see my TV movie yesterday. And now I can't even see the movies I have on video." The voice shook once more and broke. "When will you come?"

"I'll be over in half an hour." I bought a small black-and-white TV set at Hertie for 129 marks, and a screwdriver for 9.99, and gray overalls for 29.90 at a sale. Then I was ready to make my appearance as a demigod in gray at Frau Salger's sickbed.

19

Why don't you go, too?

The taxi driver in front of the train station was pleased. The trip to the Drachenfelsstrasse in Hangelar is one of the good longer fares. But when I struggled into my gray overalls on the backseat, he peered at me, frowning, through the rearview mirror, and when I walked through the garden gate carrying the TV set, his wary eyes followed me. He waited with the engine running; I have no idea why. I rang twice. There was no answer, but I didn't go back to the taxi. He finally drove off. Once I could no longer hear him, there was total silence. Sometimes a bird chirped. I rang a third time, the doorbell echoing and dying away like a weary sigh.

The house was big, and there were tall old trees in the garden. Only the fence was as I had imagined it. I made a wide detour over the lawn and reached the terrace at the back. She was sitting on a wicker lounger under an awning with green and white stripes. She was asleep. I sat down across from her on a cane chair and waited. From a distance, she could have been Leo's sister. Close up, her face was deeply furrowed, her shoulder-length ash blond hair had gray strands, and her freckles had lost their mirth. I tried to immerse my own face in those furrows and gauge the inner state that would correspond to them. I felt the harsh wrinkles over my own nose and the sharp lines in the corners of my eyes as I defensively strained to narrow them.

She woke up, and her gaze, blinking carefully, flitted over me, to the bottle on the table, and back to me again. "What time is it?" She burped, and a haze of alcohol wafted over to me. I ruled out a stroke, too.

"A quarter past six. You have—"

"Don't think you can hoodwink me like that. You haven't been here since six!" She burped again. "So I won't let you charge me from six. You can go fix my TV now. It's over there on the left." Her hand pointed to the terrace, seized the bottle on the way back, and poured a glass.

I remained seated.

"What're you waiting for?" She downed the glass.

"Your TV can't be repaired. Here, I've brought you a new one."

"But mine is . . ." Her voice became whiny.

"OK then, I'll take your set back to the shop with me. I'll leave you this one here anyway."

"I don't want that thing." She pointed at the 129-mark television as if it had a disease.

"Then give it to your daughter."

Surprise livened her glance for an instant. She asked me in a normal voice to bring her a bottle from the refrigerator. Then she sighed and closed her eyes. "My daughter . . ."

I went to the kitchen to get the gin. When I came back onto the terrace, she was asleep again. I took a tour of the house and found a room on the second floor that I guessed had once been

Leo's. On the corkboard above the desk were several photos of her. But the closet, the bureau, the desk drawers, and the bookshelves revealed as good as nothing about the room's former occupant. She had played with stuffed animals, had worn Betty-Barclay clothes, and read Hermann Hesse. If the drawings on the wall that were signed L. S. were hers, she definitely had a knack for sketching. She had been a fan of an Italian pop star who was smiling from a poster on the wall and whose records stood on the shelf. I was at a loss. I sat down at her desk and studied the photos more carefully. With the opening at knee height, the desk had been built as if each minute a young girl spent sitting there was a minute wasted. As if the idea was to keep girls from learning the basics of reading, writing, and arithmetic. I have my doubts: Is this really the way to solve the issue of women's emancipation?

I took along Leo's photo album, a thick volume with a linen cover that documented her life from the cradle to her first day at school, the school dances, class excursions, her matriculation party, all the way to university. Why are girls so eager to keep photo albums? They also like showing them, and therein lies a hidden mystery, a matriarchal magic. When I was a young man I always viewed the invitation "Would you like to see my pictures?" as a signal to flee. With my wife, Klara, I either didn't pick up this signal or felt that I couldn't keep fleeing forever and had to stand my ground.

I descended the winding staircase without aim or plan, sauntered through the large living room, and stopped in front of a shelf unit filled with videos. Frau Salger was snoring outside on the terrace. For a moment I was tempted to steal *The Wild Bunch*, a Peckinpah movie I love that can't be found anywhere on video. It was six thirty and it began to rain.

I went out onto the terrace, rolled up the awning, and sat down across from Frau Salger again. The rain was light. It gathered in the hollows of her eyes and ran down her cheeks like tears. Waving her right hand erratically, she tried to shoo away the drops. It didn't work, and she opened her eyes. "What's going on?" Her look was vacant, reeled, and then fled back behind her closed lids. "Why am I wet? It's not supposed to rain over here."

"Frau Salger, when did you last see your daughter?"

"My daughter?" Her voice became whiny again. "I don't have a daughter anymore."

"Since when don't you have a daughter?"

"Go ask her father that."

"Where can I find your husband?"

She looked at me slyly through narrowed eyes. "You're trying to con me, aren't you? I don't have a husband anymore either."

I made a new attempt. "Would you like to have your daughter back?" When she didn't answer I became more generous. "Would you like to have your daughter and your husband back?"

She looked at me and for an instant her eyes were awake and clear before they became rigid and stared through me. "My husband's dead."

"But your daughter is alive, Frau Salger, and needs help. Doesn't that interest you?"

"It's been ages since my daughter needed any help. What she needed was a good spanking. But my prick of a husband . . . my limp prick of a husband . . . my . . ."

"How long has it been since you've heard from Leo?"

"Leave me alone. Everyone's left me all alone. First he went, then she did. Why don't you go, too?"

The rain had become heavy, and our hair stuck to our heads. I tried again.

"When did she go?"

"Right after he went. And that's just what the other guy had been waiting for. I guess she wanted to . . ."

"What?"

She didn't answer. She'd fallen asleep in midsentence. I gave up, rolled the awning back down, and listened for a while to her snoring and the rain rustling on the sailcloth. I left her the TV set.

20

Stopping up holes

"If you want some insider information about the comings and goings of the Bonn political scene, then go talk to Breuer. He's your age, has been living in Bonn since 1948, writes for various small newspapers, and used to do *Interfactional*, a TV show with politicians about the first to cross party lines. He brought together backbenchers from all the parties and talked politics with them as if they were interested in politics or knew anything about it. We all had a good laugh, but the party leaders saw to it that the show was canceled. Breuer's a clever and funny guy." I got this lead from Tietzke, an old Mannheim friend who used to write for the *Heidelberger Tageblatt* and was now at the *Rhein-Neckar-Zeitung*. I gave Breuer a call. He agreed to meet me early in the morning the following day.

So I stayed over in Bonn. I found a quiet hotel behind the trees and the pond around Poppelsdorf Castle. From there it wasn't too far to Breuer's office. Before going to bed I called Brigitte. The strange sounds of a strange city, the strange room, the strange bed—I did feel homesick.

The following morning Breuer greeted me with bubbling loquacity. "The name's Self, right? You're from Mannheim? An old friend of Tietzke's? Who'd have thought the *Heidelberger Tageblatt* would have folded, just like that! With every passing day I find myself thinking more and more . . . Ah, well, it's the same old story. Come in, come in!"

The walls of his office were lined with books, the view through the large window was of backyards with old trees and beyond them two tall smokestacks. His desk by the window was covered in papers, a small green triangle was blinking insistently on the screen of a word processor, and water was hissing in the coffeemaker. Breuer offered me an armchair, sat on the swivel chair at his desk, reached under the seat and pulled a lever, and he and the seat went down with a clang. Now we sat facing each other at the same height.

"Shoot! Tietzke says I've got to help you any way I can. I'm ready and willing. The ball's in your court. Are you a detective?"

"Yes, and I'm working on a case that involves a young woman by the name of Salger, whose deceased father must have been a big shot here in Bonn. That's if being the undersecretary in one of the ministries means being a big shot. Does the name Salger mean anything to you?"

He'd been watching me attentively, but now was looking out the window, lost in thought. He massaged his left earlobe with his left hand.

"When I look out the window . . . Do you know why I like those two smokestacks over there? They're harbingers from another world. Perhaps not a better one, but a world that's more complete, where, unlike here in Bonn, you don't just have officials, politicians, journalists, lobbyists, professors, and students, but people who work, who build something—machines, cars, ships, whatever—who establish, run, and ruin banks and companies, who paint pictures and make movies, who're poor, panhandle, commit crimes. Can you imagine a crime of passion being committed here in Bonn? Passion for a woman, for money, even for becoming the next chancellor? No, you can't imagine that, and believe you me, neither can I."

I waited. Does it speak for a journalist if he asks questions and then answers them himself? Does it speak against him? Breuer massaged his earlobe again. A high forehead, sharp eyes, a weak chin—he looked intelligent. And I liked listening to him; there was a pleasant twang in his voice, and what he said about Bonn sounded appealing. Yet at the same time I felt that I was privy to a routine performance. He had probably expounded on the smokestacks and Bonn a thousand times.

"Salger . . . yes, I remember him. I'd have thought you'd have remembered him, too. What newspapers do you read?"

"Nowadays the *Süddeutsche*, but I used to read all kinds, the *Frankfurter*—"

"Maybe the *Süddeutsche* didn't write much about Salger. Less than the other ones. He made headlines in some of them."

I looked at him, puzzled. He enjoyed toying with my curiosity. But I was glad to humor him. If people give me what I want, I don't care what detours and diversions there are.

"Some coffee?"

"Please."

He poured me a cup. "Salger was, as you yourself said, an under-secretary. He was in acquisitions at the Ministry of

Defense, the way anyone who was anybody was back then. Remember the fifties and sixties? Life, politics—everything was about acquisitions." He took a slurping sip from his cup. "Remember the König scandal?"

I had no idea what he was talking about. "In the late sixties?"

"That's right. König was an under-secretary and the president of a fund that could be used to bypass the federal budget to finance large public construction projects of the armed forces. It was a peculiar setup, what with the under-secretary also being president of the fund. But that's how it was, and Salger was an under-secretary and also a board member of the fund. Is it all coming back to you?"

Nothing was coming back to me, but I had got one guess right and tried my luck again. "Embezzlement?" How else could the president of a fund and a board member cause a scandal?

"Biafra." Breuer reached for his earlobe again, as if he wanted to milk from it the continuation of the story, and looked at me meaningfully. "König had speculated with loans to Biafra. If Biafra had managed to secede from Nigeria, he would have made millions. But as we know, Ojukwu lost, and so did König. I don't know if he embezzled the money from the fund in the legal sense of the term, or misappropriated the money, or what. He hanged himself before the verdict was announced."

"And Salger?"

Breuer shook his head. "That was one crazy guy. I guess you don't remember. Suspicion first fell on him. He was interrogated and arrested, but kept his mouth shut. The way he saw it, there was nothing that he could be reproached for. He got in a huff and saw the whole thing as a personal insult. When it finally came out that König . . ."

"How?"

"König was drowning in debt, and when the Biafra money he was counting on didn't materialize, he tried to stop up the holes in other ways, with more and more building grants and credits from the fund, and the whole thing blew up on him."

"How long was Salger in prison?"

"About six months." He stretched out his arms. "That's a long time. And all his colleagues, superiors, and political buddies turned their backs on him. They were sure he was the culprit. When it became clear that he wasn't, they tried to pin dereliction of duty as a board member on him. But that didn't stick either. A report surfaced showing that he had drawn attention to all the irregularities. So he was rehabilitated. There was even a promotion in the works. But he couldn't deal with the fact that the same people who had suspected and already convicted him were now patting him on the back and acting as if nothing had happened. He dropped everything and broke off contact with everyone: with his colleagues, superiors, and political buddies. He was barely fifty and had ended up retired and totally isolated. It's a crazy world." He shook his head.

"Does the story go on?"

Breuer poured us another cup of coffee and reached for a pack of Marlboros on his desk. "My first one today. Would you like one, too?" I fished my yellow pack of cigarettes out of my pocket and offered him one, and he took it with great aplomb. A smoker of filter cigarettes who at the sight of a Sweet Afton doesn't say "Oh, but those don't have a filter!" and takes one with interest. I like that.

"There's more. Salger joined the Free Democratic Party, put himself up as a candidate for parliament, and mounted a futile campaign with a fervor that he would have done well to invest in a better cause. He wrote a book into which he poured all his experiences, a book that nobody wanted to publish and nobody wanted to read. He got sick, cancer, was in and out of hospitals, you know. He died a few years ago."

"What did he live on?"

Breuer milked his earlobe. "He had a private fortune, quite a large one. That just goes to show—money doesn't guarantee happiness."

21

Very clear indeed

On my trip back home the train was diverted through Darm-stadt and along the Bergstrasse route. It was the first time I noticed the many quarries at the edge of the Odenwald Range. They made the mountains look like red Jell-O covered in green mint sauce, of which God had taken a few bites with a spoon.

In Bonn I had again dialed 41-17-88 and let it ring a long time in vain. The answering machine remained silent. But I'd barely set foot in my office when the phone rang.

"Hello."

"Hello, Herr Self, Salger here. Have you tried reaching me over the past few days?"

So he, too, had noticed that his answering machine wasn't reacting. Had one of his friends turned the machine off by mistake?

"I'm glad you called, Herr Salger. I have a lot of informa-tion for you and would like to give it to you in person. I'd be happy to come see you in Bonn, but perhaps you will be passing through Mannheim one of these days? I take it you're back in Bonn, you see, your answering machine . . ."

"It must be broken, or the maid turned it off by mistake. But no, we're not back in Bonn, and as I can't arrange a meeting in the foreseeable future, I must ask you to give me the information over the phone. Have you found Leonore?"

"I'd rather not discuss the whereabouts of Leonore on the phone, since—"

"Herr Self, you took on this case and are obliged to report your findings. You accepted the case from me over the phone, and you must also make your report over the phone. Have I made myself clear?"

"Very clear, Herr Salger, very clear indeed. But I will not make my report over the phone, only in person. Furthermore, you did not commission me over the phone, but by letter. I am quite happy to make a report, but it will have to be in person."

We continued haggling back and forth. He had no reason to refuse to meet me, and I had no reason to insist on it. He argued that his wife was close to a nervous breakdown, that she needed him constantly at her side, him and him alone. "She cannot bear the presence of strangers."

I wedged the receiver between my chin and shoulder, got out my bottle of sambuca and poured myself a glass, lit a Sweet Afton, and explained to Salger in no uncertain terms that first, I always made my reports in writing or in person, and second, I always made a point of meeting my clients. "That is how I have always worked."

He changed his tactics. "In that case, how about providing me with a written report? In the next few days I shall be taking my wife to see a doctor in Zurich, and we could pick up your report at the Baur au Lac when we get there."

It had been a long day. I was tired and had had enough of this absurd conversation. I'd had enough of the Salger case. On my way home on the train I had admitted to myself that right from the start the case had stunk to heaven. Why had I even taken it on? Because of the hefty fee? Because of Leo? And, as if I felt that I wanted to close this case just as unprofessionally as I had undertaken it, I heard myself say: "I could also send my report to Niebuhrstrasse 46a in Bonn, care of Helmut Lehmann."

For a moment there was silence on the line. Then Salger slammed down the receiver. Resounding in my ear was the hoarse *tak-tak-tak* with which sound waves mark time when they have nothing to transmit.

22

Pain, irony, or heartburn

For two days nothing happened. Salger didn't call me, and I didn't call him. I didn't give the case much thought. I opened a special account at the Badische Beamtenbank in order to deposit Salger's ten thousand marks, which I had initially locked up in my desk drawer. To these ten thousand marks I added the interest that would have gathered had I deposited it right away.

One afternoon, as I was repotting my palm, I had a visitor.

"Don't you remember me? Well, I guess you were quite shaken up at the time. My name's Peschkalek. We met on the autobahn."

This was the man, in a green loden coat—midforties, bald, with a thick mustache and a pleasant, wry smile—who had walked me over to the embankment and given me a cigarette after the furniture truck had crashed. I thanked him.

"You're welcome, you're welcome. We should thank our lucky stars that the accident wasn't serious. The paintings also seem to have come out of it unscathed—do you want to come along to the Mannheimer Kunsthalle to see the exhibition that nearly cost us our lives?"

He turned out to be a photographer, a photojournalist, and had quite a few clever things to say about the composition of the photo-realistic pictures on show. I noticed details on the pictures that had eluded him. "Aha, quite a detective!" he said. It was a pleasant afternoon, and we said good-bye and hoped we would soon meet again.

There have been times when I've had the feeling of calm before the storm. But I've never known how to make provision for the storm. Furthermore, feelings can be misleading, just as thoughts can be.

On the third day, I was in the mood to go out for breakfast. Since the Café Gmeiner has been replaced by a restaurant serving foie gras in Jurançon gelée and monkfish slices in mustard seed and similar fripperies, I go instead to the Café Fieberg in the Seckenheimer Strasse. The waitress there is a boisterous but kind soul who has taken me under her wing and has made sure the kitchen knows how I like my eggs—fried eggs flipped over just before being served.

She brought pepper and nutmeg. "Another pot of coffee?"

"I'd like one, too, please." He pulled up a chair and sat down opposite me. I recognized his voice even before he introduced himself as Salger. I only nodded and looked at him. A full face, high forehead, heavy frame, an aura of bourgeois ponderousness. I could imagine him in the gray flannel of a teacher, the dark blue pinstripes of a banker, or even the robes of a judge or pastor. Now he was wearing a leather jacket, flannel pants, and a sweater. He must have been in his midforties. If I had been able to see his eyes, I could have decided if the expression around his mouth indicated pain, irony, or heartburn. But his eyes remained hidden behind mirrored sunglasses.

"I owe you an explanation, Herr Self. I knew you were a good detective, and I should have known that you'd be able to see through my little game of hide-and-seek. I hope you won't hold it against me. It would be terrible if you took all this as a lack of confidence in your competence and integrity. It was more a matter of . . ." He shook his head. "No, let me put it differently . . ." The waitress brought two pots of coffee, and he asked her to bring him some honey. He silently added cream and honey to the coffee, stirred it, and sipped it with delight.

"You see, I've known Leonore Salger for many, many years. I can't really say that we grew up together, because of the difference in our ages. It was a kind of big-brother and baby-sister thing, far apart in age but inwardly close—you know the connection I mean? A bitter father, a drunken mother," he shook his head again. "That made Leo look for the kind of stability in an older brother that one would usually look for in one's parents. Do you know what I mean?"

I didn't say anything. I could take a look in Leo's album later on. If his story was true, I would find pictures of him.

"You could say that I didn't lie to you about my paternal concern for her. I felt, and still feel, the way you experienced me on the phone. Leo disappeared at the beginning of the year, and I'm worried that she has ended up in bad company and a bad situation. I think she needs help, even though she perhaps doesn't know it. I'm really, really worried that—"

"Is it your help she needs?"

Salger demonstrated a penchant for dramatic effect. He leaned back in his chair, slowly raised his right hand, took off his sunglasses, and looked at me calmly. Pain, irony, or heartburn? The look beneath his heavy eyelids didn't tell me more than the expression about his mouth.

"*My* help, Herr Self, *my* help. I know Leo, and I also know"—he hesitated—"the situation she might have gotten herself into."

"What situation?"

"Some of it you know, some of it you might suspect—that is enough. I haven't come here to give information but to get information. Where is Leo?"

"I still don't understand what you want from her. You have also not clarified why you lied to me. You haven't even introduced yourself. Herr Salger? No, that you are not Herr Salger we already know. Herr Lehmann? The grandson who wants to open a gallery where his grandmother barely had enough space to lay out her buttons and threads? And what am I supposed to know or suspect about Leo's dangerous situation? I've had enough of your tactics and lies. I am not demanding when it comes to the extent of the trust between my clients and myself. I don't expect all-out openness. But you will either lay the facts on the table or we will go to the Badische Beamtenbank where you can take back your ten thousand marks and we can say good-bye."

First he closed his eyes tightly. Then he raised his eyebrows, sighed, smiled, and said: "But Herr Self." His hand slipped into the pocket of his jacket and reappeared with a business card that he placed before me on the table. Helmut Lehmann, investment consultant, Beethovenstrasse 42, 6000 Frankfurt am Main 1. "I want to speak to Leo. I want to ask her if I can help her, and how I can help her. Is that so difficult to understand? And why the high horse?" His eyes had narrowed again, and his voice was low and sharp. "You accepted my assignment and my money without too many questions. A lot of money. I'm willing to offer you a bonus for the successful completion of the assignment, let's say another five thousand. That's all I can offer. Where is Leo?"

I knew exactly how much fried eggs and two pots of coffee cost at Café Fieberg. I didn't wait for the waitress, laid the money on the table, got up, and left.

23

The boy who lops the thistle's heads

That evening I went to see Nägelsbach in his workshop, a converted shed in an old building in the Pfaffengrunder settlement from the 1920s. He had given me a call. "I've got some information on Wendt."

It was still light outside, but a fluorescent fixture was already on over his workbench. "What you're doing isn't going to be the Pantheon, right?" I said. From what I could see, the gnarled structure on his workbench could evolve into a clenched fist, a tree stump, or a rock, but not a domed structure.

"You said it, Herr Self. I've been doing some thinking. I see now that I shouldn't have just launched into my models, but done some thinking first. Doing buildings was the wrong way to go: the Cologne Cathedral, the Empire State Building, Lomonosov University, all built to scale with matchsticks. That was just childish nonsense. I was like the boy in that Goethe poem 'who lops the thistle's heads.'" He shook his head despondently. "What I worry about is that I'm all burned out."

"What should you have done instead?"

He took off his glasses and put them back on again. "Do you remember my efforts with the praying hands and the golden helmet? In principle, that was the right path for me, but what I'd done wrong was that I'd taken the paintings as my models. A matchstick sculptor needs to find his models in sculptures of wood, stone, or bronze. Are you familiar with Rodin's *Kiss*?"

On the wall were some twenty photographs of two kissing figures taken from every perspective. They were seated next to each other, she with her arm around his neck, he with his hand on her hip. "I've also ordered a cast that has a patina of bronze, of course an altogether different model than these photos." He looked at me as if waiting for approbation. I dodged into a question about his wife. Whenever I came to his workshop, she had always been sitting in a chair with a book. For years she had read to him as he worked. Instead of answering my question, he rang a bell. After a short, uncomfortable wait, Frau Nägelsbach appeared. She greeted me warmly, but self-consciously. It was evident that Nägelsbach's creative crisis had spilled over into a marriage crisis. Frau Nägelsbach's plumpness had lost its cheerful ruddiness.

"Why don't we all go outside?"

He picked up three folding chairs, and we sat down beneath a pear tree. I asked him about Wendt.

"What I know lies a long time back. Ages ago, Wendt had been a member of the leftist terrorist group SPK, the Socialist Patient Collective. We don't know whether he belonged to the small circle surrounding the notorious Dr. Huber or to those who were members more out of curiosity than anything else. He was driving a stolen vehicle without a driver's license and had an accident, and the woman who was in the car with him—she was also in the SPK—soon afterward went underground and joined the Red Army Faction. He was only seventeen. His parents and teachers stood behind him all the way, so his past didn't really cause him any trouble until two years ago, when he was hired by the State Psychiatric Hospital. Word got around that he'd been a terrorist, and the old story was dug up again."

I remembered. In 1970 and 1971, the papers were full of reports on Dr. Huber, who had been fired from the Heidelberg University Neuropsychiatry Clinic and had then gone on to round up his patients and create the SPK. He had commandeered rooms at the university and prepared for revolution. Revolution as therapy. By 1971 all was over, Dr. Huber and his wife had been arrested, and the patients were scattered in all directions—except for a few who went over to the Red Army Faction. "Nothing has come up about Wendt since then?" I asked.

"Nothing. How come he interests you?"

I told him about my search for Leo in Heidelberg, in Mannheim, and finally at the State Psychiatric Hospital; of Wendt's foolish lies; and of my mysterious client.

"What is the young woman's last name?"

"Salger."

"Leonore Salger from Bonn?"

I hadn't even mentioned Bonn. "How come—"

"And you know where Frau Salger is right now?" His tone became official and inquisitorial.

"What's going on? Why are you asking?"

"We're looking for Frau Salger. I cannot disclose the reason, but you can believe me, it's no trifle. Where is she?"

In the many years of our friendship we had always been aware that he was a policeman and I a private investigator. In a sense, our friendship lived off the fact that we were acting out different roles in the same play. He never treated me like a witness, and I never used the kind of tricks on him with which I find out from people things they don't want to disclose. Was that only because the cases had never been all that important, while this one was? There was a sharp retort on the tip of my tongue, but I swallowed my words. "No, I don't know where Frau Salger is right now."

He wasn't satisfied. He continued digging, and I continued dodging. The tone became increasingly tense, and Frau Nägelsbach looked at the two of us with mounting alarm. She repeatedly tried to pacify us. Then she got up, went into the house, and came back with a bottle of wine and some glasses. "I don't want to hear another word about this case or this woman," she cut in. "Not another word. If you won't stop," she turned to her husband, "then I'll tell Herr Self what's what. And if you won't stop"—now she turned to me—"I will tell my husband, perhaps not everything—because I don't have all the facts—but everything that you have said without intending to, and what my husband hasn't heard because he's become too furious to listen."

We both fell silent. Then we slowly started chatting again, about Brigitte and Manu, vacations, old age, retirement. But our hearts were not in it any longer.

24

Marble breaks and iron bends

Driving back home, I brooded over why I'd been so intent on keeping Leo's whereabouts to myself. Was she worth it? Did it help her in any way? By all accounts she'd been unlucky in her father, and I doubted that the counterfeit Salger had brought her much luck either, though he often appeared in her photo album, with her as a little brat on his knee, him pushing her swing, or with his arm around the growing girl. How was I to reconcile Salger the paternal friend with Salger the wannabe father? I didn't know who she was, what she'd done, why she was hiding. It was high time I had a word with her.

It was only ten thirty when I arrived in Mannheim, and the mild night beckoned me out for a walk. I went to the Kleiner Rosengarten restaurant and had a bottle of Soave with my vermicelli alla puttanesca, a dish that is not on the menu but which the chef makes for me if I ask him nicely and he happens to be in the mood. After my meal I was slightly tipsy.

In the old days, when I climbed the stairs up to my attic apartment, I only needed to stop once for a breather. Then it became twice, and now, on a bad day, I have to stop on every landing. Today was a bad day. I stopped, steadied myself on the banister, and could hear my heart pounding and my breath whistling. I looked up and saw that the landing in front of my apartment was dark. Was the lightbulb out?

Then I attacked the last flight of stairs. We Prussians have fought the battles of Düppeler Schanzen, Gravelotte, and Langemarck and stormed greater heights. When I got to the last few stairs I took the key out of my pocket. There are three doors on my landing. One is to my apartment, the second to that of the Weilands, and the third up to the attic—I have my back to that one when I unlock my door.

He had been standing in the doorway to the attic waiting for me. When I unlocked my door he came up behind me, laid his left hand on my shoulder, and with his right poked a gun into my side. "Don't try anything foolish!"

I was too taken aback, and also too exhausted and drunk, to be able to dodge him or throw a punch. Maybe I'm also too old. I'd never been threatened with a weapon before. During the war I was in the tank division, but in a tank you're not threatened, you're simply hit. Our tank had been hit one beautiful day, the sky blue, the sun warm, little white clouds—bang.

He remained behind me as I reached for the light switch in my front hall. It was gloomy out on the landing, and my windowless hall would be completely dark if the door closed before I turned on the light. An opportunity? I hesitated and waited for the door to fall shut. But he kicked me in the hollow of the knees and as I went down he closed the door and turned on the light. I staggered back to my feet, and he shoved the gun into my side again. "Keep walking!" In the living room he not only kicked me, but I also banged my shin against the coffee table. That really hurt. I sat down on one of my two leather couches and massaged my leg. "Get up!" he shouted, but I refused. So he fired. The thick leather of my couch comes from the broad nape of Argentinean buffalo and has stood its ground against my shoes, the embers of my cigarettes, and Turbo's claws. Faced with the projectile, it surrendered. I didn't. I remained seated, continued to massage my leg, and looked at my guest.

The shot had only made a popping sound, but the gun with its silencer looked vicious. He was wearing his mirrored sunglasses again and had turned up the collar of his coat. He looked at the gun, then at me, and then at the gun again. Suddenly he burst out laughing and let himself fall on the couch opposite me.

"We had trouble communicating earlier today, Herr Self, so I brought along an assistant, a therapist, so to speak." He looked at his gun again. Turbo came into the living room, jumped up on the couch next to me, arched his back, stretched his paws, and began grooming himself. "I've also brought a lot of time with me. Perhaps our morning conversation simply suffered from a lack of time. You were in such a terrible hurry. Did you have an important appointment, or are you just obstinate as a mule? Do we have a pleasant or a difficult evening ahead of us? Whatever is obstinate and will not bend, ultimately breaks. How does Drafi Deutscher's song go? 'Marble breaks and iron bends . . .' I can assure you that there is a general rule behind that." He raised his gun. I couldn't see where he was aiming—at me, over me, next to me—I could only see myself in the reflection of his sunglasses. He fired. Behind me, on the old pharmacy shelf where I keep my books and records, a bust of Dante's Beatrice, the work of an early-twentieth-century Munich artist, shattered. "See? That's how it is with marble," he said. "And it isn't any different with everything that lives and breathes. Only there are no shards." He raised the gun again.

I didn't try to figure out if he was aiming at Turbo or if it only looked that way. I staggered to my feet and slapped his arm out of the way. He immediately struck me back, hit me across the face with the gun, and pushed me back onto the couch. Turbo caterwauled and ran off.

"Just try something like that again!" he hissed angrily. Then he laughed once more and shook his head. "What an old fool you are!"

I tasted blood on my lip.

"Well, let's have it! Where's Leo?"

"I don't know. I've got a couple of leads, but that's all, just a couple of leads. I don't know where Leo is."

"It's been three days since we spoke on the phone. Have her whereabouts slipped your mind since then?" He sounded surprised and ironic.

"It was a fishing expedition. It's not that I've forgotten her whereabouts, I just never knew them. Just a fishing expedition, know what I mean? I didn't like it that I could never get to see you."

"Do you think I'm stupid or something?" he shouted, his voice breaking. But he immediately calmed down again, smiled, and shook his head. He got up, stepped in front of me, and waited for me to look up at him. Then he hit me again with the butt of his gun, just like that. Pain tore across my cheek and chin.

He didn't lose control when he shouted. He shouted with a cool head. I was frightened. I had no idea what . . .

The doorbell rang. We both held our breath. The doorbell rang a second and then a third time. There was a knock. "Gerhard, open up! Open up! What's going on in there?" Brigitte could see a glimmer of light under the door.

My guest shrugged his shoulders. "I guess we'll catch up some other time." He left the room. I heard him open the front door, say "Good evening," and descend the stairs with quick steps.

"Gerhard!" Brigitte kneeled next to me on the couch and took me in her arms. When she let go of me her blouse was stained with blood. I tried to wipe the blood away, but couldn't. The more desperately I ran my hands over her blouse, the worse the bloody scrawl became. I gave up.

25

Don't forget the kitty litter!

After Brigitte washed my face and cleaned up the cuts, she put me to bed. My face was on fire, but otherwise I felt cold. My teeth kept chattering. Drinking was difficult: My swollen lip couldn't hold the liquid in. During the night I was feverish.

I dreamt of Leo and Dr. Eberlein. The two were going for a walk, and I handed them an official document forbidding them to go on walks together as father and daughter. Eberlein laughed his smug laugh and put his arm around Leo. She snuggled up to him and threw me a shameless, disdainful glance. I was about to specify that not only were they to refrain from acting as father and daughter, but also as . . . when Eberlein suddenly whistled, and Anatol or Ivan hurled himself at me. He had been cowering at Eberlein's feet, waiting for his whistle.

When I fell asleep again, Chief Inspector Nägelsbach was walking me through a town. The buildings were of wood, as were the streets and sidewalks. There wasn't a soul about, and whenever I managed to peek into a house it turned out to be an empty shell without rooms or stories. Nägelsbach was walking so fast that I couldn't keep up with him. He turned around, waved, and called to me, but I couldn't hear him anymore. Then he was gone, and it dawned on me that I would never be able to find my way out of this maze of empty streets and houses. I realized I was in a Nägelsbachian matchstick town. I was tiny, no bigger than a watch hand or a jelly bean. No wonder I feel so cold, I thought, tiny as I am.

Brigitte brought me a hot water bottle and heaped blankets on the bed. In the morning I was bathed in sweat, but the fever had gone down.

Shaving was out of the question. And yet the scabby welts on my cheeks, lips, and chin did not split open when I brushed my teeth. I looked quite rakish, and decided against wearing a tie. Out on the balcony the sun was shining, and I unfolded my lounger and lay down on it.

What was next? Salger was a clever man. He had a repertoire of faces, vocal registers, patterns of expression, and behavior. There was something playful about how he made use of them, and our encounters brought to mind face-offs on a chessboard. Not the kind of chess evenings I had with Eberhard, whom I could never hope to beat or even think of beating, where I just enjoyed the beauty of his moves and our being together, but chess games of the kind I used to play in the past, determined to beat my opponent. Chess games that were like sword fights, where the aim was to destroy your opponent—that is, not him, but his self-confidence.

I remembered how I had once battled a whole evening with my future father-in-law, who initially had treated me dismissively. His son and I had been schoolmates and later fellow students. "Well, well, I see you're trying your hand at chess," he said to me ironically when he found us over a chessboard.

Klara was standing right there, and I could barely hide my shivering agitation. To be insulted like this in front of her. "Do you play, too?" I asked with as much coolness as I could muster. Old Herr Korten was assured by his son that I played a passable game, and challenged me to a round the following Saturday. He offered a bottle of champagne as a prize, and I had to promise that I would clean and oil his gun collection if I lost. All that week I lived and breathed chess, worked my way through openings, went over the moves of games, found out when and where Berlin chess clubs got together. In the first and second games old Herr Korten still had a chance. But he lost, even though I allowed him to retract the moves he called his "foolish little slipups." By then I knew how he played, and I toyed with him. That was the last time he challenged me to a game. And the last time he treated me dismissively.

So Salger wanted to play with me? Let him try.

Turbo looked at me obliquely. He was sitting in the flower box, steadying himself with his front paws, his head tilted to the side.

"I know, I know, Turbo, no need to look at me like that. That was just hot air." He listened attentively. When I didn't continue, he turned away and began grooming himself. I suddenly remembered how Turbo had sat on the couch next to me last night, while Salger was facing us with his gun. What if Salger were to take aim and fire faster the next time he showed up? I got up and walked over to the phone. Eberhard? No, he's allergic to cats. Brigitte? Nonni and Turbo fight like cats and dogs. Philipp? I didn't manage to reach him or Füruzan, and was told at the clinic that he was at a conference in Siena. Babs? She was home. She was having a late-afternoon cup of coffee with her two grown-up children, and invited me over right away. "You want to put Turbo up here? No problem, bring him along, and don't forget the kitty litter."

Turbo always has a fit in the car. I've tried baskets, I've tried collars, I've tried nothing at all. The sound and vibration of the engine, the quickly changing images, and the speed are all too much for my cat. His world is the rooftops between the Richard-Wagner-Strasse, the Augusta-Anlage, the Moll-strasse, and the Werderstrasse, the few balconies and windows he can reach over the rooftops, the few neighbors and cats living behind those balconies and windows, the pigeons and the mice. Whenever I need to take him to the vet, I carry him under my coat, and he peeks out between the buttons the way I would out of a space shuttle. That was how we made the long trip to the Dürerstrasse.

Babs lives in a large apartment with Röschen and Georg, who, if you ask me, are old enough to stand on their own two feet. And yet they prefer to keep their feet firmly planted on mummy's hearth rug. Georg is studying law in Heidelberg, and Röschen can't ever decide whether she wants to study, get some kind of vocational training or a job, or which of her admirers to choose between. She had kept them dangling so long that they finally gave up, and now she was absolutely miserable.

"Were they so great?"

She had either been crying or had a cold. "No," she sniffled, "but . . ."

"No buts. If they weren't that great, then you should be glad you got rid of them."

She sniffled. "Do you know anyone I can date?"

"I'll get back to you on that one. Do you think you can look after Turbo in the meantime? Think of it as practice. Men and tomcats are one and the same thing."

She smiled. She is a punk rocker with violet and yellow hair, alligator clips in her earlobes, and a computer chip in the side of her nose. But she smiled in a nice, old-fashioned way. "Jonas has—"

"Is that one of the two beaus?"

She nodded. "Jonas has a rat called Rudi. He never goes anywhere without him. I could invite him over for dinner— he did say we should remain friends—and while he eats his spaghetti, Turbo can eat Rudi." Her eyes misted over. "What do you say to that, Uncle Gerhard?"

26

You're stubborn, just plain stubborn

Back home I lay down again. Brigitte came over, sat on the edge of my bed, and asked me what actually had happened yesterday. I told her.

"Why didn't you want to let Inspector Nägelsbach know where that girl is? And why not tell the man who hired you? You don't owe her anything."

"I don't know why the police and Salger are looking for her. I need to know that first. She didn't do anything to me, and I don't want to hand her over just to get them off my back and pocket ten thousand marks."

Brigitte got up and poured herself an amaretto and a sambuca for me. She sat down again and said, "May I ask you something?"

"Sure." I smiled encouragingly, though I knew it wasn't going to be a question but a reproach.

"I don't want to tell you how to do your job. When you didn't have a case over the past few months, I thought to myself: Fine, that's his business, not mine. Sometimes I would ask myself if it could work out, us getting married I mean, and having kids, if it would work out financially. But that's not the issue. It's the way you're handling this case. And not just this case. I get the feeling that you'll only be satisfied when you've quarreled with everyone and are at loggerheads with all the different parties. Not that it seems to be giving you any satisfaction. Does it have to be this way? Is it . . ."

"Old age? Are you asking if I'm becoming stubborn and bad tempered in my old age?"

"You're becoming more and more of an outsider. That's what I mean."

She fixed me with her sad gaze, and I could not escape into anger. I tried to explain to her that the only way one can see clearly is from the outside. "So of course I'm an outsider; it's part of my job description. Maybe I stumble around a bit more as I get older, but do I have any choice? And you mustn't forget that it's natural for an outsider sometimes to be at loggerheads with the different parties. You wouldn't want to side with every party either, would you?"

Brigitte looked at me skeptically. "You're stubborn, just plain stubborn."

27

My cards weren't all that bad

The men from the Federal Criminal Investigation Agency turned up the following morning just after eight. Bleckmeier, gaunt and sour in his gray suit and beige coat, and Rawitz in a suede jacket over a polo shirt and linen pants, playing the nice little fat guy. His affability was as put on as a clown's nose. "Dr. Self?"

This form of address was bad news. As a public prosecutor I had been proud of my title, but as a private investigator I found it absurd. There's no "Dr." on the door to my office or my apartment, and no "Dr." in the phone book or on my letterhead. Whoever approaches me with "Dr." knows things about me that are none of his business. I showed the two men into my living room.

"What brings you here?" I asked.

Bleckmeier spoke up. "We hear that while working on a case you have, so to speak, stumbled over a certain Leonore Salger. We are looking for her. If you—"

"Why are you looking for Frau Salger?"

"That is, so to speak, a delicate matter. I would—"

"Why is it delicate?" Rawitz interrupted Bleckmeier, looking at him reprovingly and then at me apologetically. "The Federal Criminal Investigation Agency targets criminals who work internationally, or at least beyond a specific region. We are the coordinating body for all the regional agencies and for Interpol. We also take on police duties in matters of law enforcement, particularly in cases when the chief federal prosecutor issues an order. Needless to say, we then immediately inform the appropriate regional agency."

"Needless to say," I replied.

Bleckmeier took over again. "We're looking for Frau Salger, so to speak, in an official capacity. We know that she was in the State Psychiatric Hospital, that she was in Dr. Rolf Wendt's care, and that she disappeared a few weeks ago. Do you know where she is?"

"Have you spoken to Dr. Wendt?"

"He invoked doctor-patient confidentiality and is refusing to cooperate in any way," Bleckmeier said. "Not that we're surprised. Dr. Wendt is not entirely unknown to us, so to speak."

"Did you inform him why you are investigating Frau Salger?"

"Dr. Self." Rawitz again took over. "I am sure we all want to keep things nice and simple. As a former public prosecutor you're an old pro. You can't expect us to go around disclosing that kind of information. We can only tell you what we can tell you, and if you're prepared to tell us what you know, then things will stay nice and easy." He was sitting across from me, and as he said "nice and easy" he actually leaned forward and patted me on the knee.

"Are we right in our surmise that you have been commissioned to locate Frau Salger by an individual who is, so to speak, passing himself off as her father? Are you still in contact with this individual?"

"You are confusing Dr. Self by asking him all those questions at once," Rawitz said to Bleckmeier in a mildly admonishing tone. I didn't know if this was their own version of the good-cop-bad-cop act, or whether Rawitz was the one with the higher rank and say. Bleckmeier was clearly the older of the two, but in the world of government bureaucracies, politics sends the strangest characters floating to the top. "If you ask a question and then immediately go on to the next question without insisting on an answer to the first question," Rawitz said to Bleckmeier, "then the person you are questioning gets the impression that you're not serious about the question you asked. Not serious, *so to speak*, as you yourself would put it. And yet we are quite serious about finding Frau Salger." Bleckmeier, his face bright red, nodded quickly. Then both men looked at me expectantly.

I shook my head. "First I want to know what this is all about."

"Dr. Self," Rawitz said, enunciating my name with painstaking clarity, "whether we're dealing with narcotics, counterfeit money, terrorism, or an attempt on the life of the German president, you have no right to hamper our inquiries. You have no right, neither as a private investigator nor as a former public prosecutor, and if you, of all people, a former Nazi, are intent on supporting the work of terrorists, then you can hardly expect much sympathy from us."

"I don't think your sympathy is particularly important to me. If we're talking terrorism, then why not go ahead and name names?"

"He doesn't think our sympathy is particularly important to him," Rawitz said scornfully, and slapped his startled colleague on the thigh. "I've already told you more than I have to, Dr. Self. But if you don't want to listen"—he peered at me over the tip of his index finger—"you'll have to bear the consequences. You have no choice but to give us a statement."

"You know as well as I do that I don't have to give you a statement."

"I'll have you dragged before the public prosecutor. Then you'll have to talk."

"But only if he tells me what it is he is investigating."

"What?"

"If I do not know who or what he is investigating and the reason for this investigation, I cannot assess if I am incriminating myself through my statement."

Rawitz turned to Bleckmeier. "Did you hear that? He doesn't want to incriminate himself. There are incriminating circumstances, but he doesn't want to incriminate himself. Is anything he's saying of interest to us? No. Incriminating things do not interest us in the least, do they? There's only one thing we want to know, and that is the current address of Frau Leonore Salger, which is exactly what the public prosecutor will tell you, too, Dr. Self. All I want to know, the public prosecutor will say, is the current address of Frau Salger. There can be no question of incrimination. 'Spit it out!' is what the public prosecutor will say." Rawitz looked me in the eye and raised his voice. "Spit it out! Or are you in any way involved with Frau Salger? Is she your fiancée? Your cousin twice removed? Your mother-in-law's niece? What game are you playing here?"

I took a deep breath. "I'm not playing any game. You are right, my case did put me on the trail of Frau Salger. But you're going to have to leave to me what I feel I can disclose concerning an ongoing case of mine."

"You're talking like you're her pastor or her doctor—or her lawyer. All you are is a nasty little private snoop with a shady scar on his face. Where'd you get that?"

I wanted to ask him where he had picked up his ridiculous interrogation techniques. The police academy? But Bleckmeier jumped in before I could open my mouth.

"All we have to do is snap our fingers, Dr. Self, and you'll be before the public prosecutor, even the judge. Your cards aren't all that good."

But the way I saw it, my cards weren't all that bad either. Perhaps my claim that I had to know what they were investigating in order not to incriminate myself had hit the mark with them. If not, they could slap me with a fine or arrest me for contempt, but even if they wanted to, they couldn't be that fast on the trigger. I also got the impression that the Criminal Investigation Agency and the chief federal prosecutor were not that eager to create a ruckus, and where a trigger is pulled there's noise.

"We'll be seeing you again." Rawitz stood up and Bleckmeier followed suit. I showed them out and wished them a nice day. So to speak.

28

A trick that psychotherapists use

I put in a call to the psychiatric hospital. I couldn't get Wendt on the phone, but I did find out that he was on duty. So I headed over. The April wind chased gray clouds across the blue sky. From time to time some gathered into sudden downpours. Then the wet asphalt shone in the sun again.

Wendt was in a hurry. "Oh, you again? I've got to go over to the other unit."

"Have they been here?"

"Who?" He found my presence irritating, but at the same time he was curious. He stood strangely twisted, his legs ready to walk away, his head turned toward me, his hand on the doorknob.

"The men from the Federal Criminal Investigation Agency and Leo's big brother."

"Leo's father, Leo's big brother? What other relatives are you going to pull out of the hat?" His tone was superior, but did not sound convincing.

"He isn't Leo's big brother. He just feels he is. He's looking for her."

He opened the door. "I really have to head over to the other unit."

"The guys from the Agency have bad manners. But Leo's brotherly friend has a gun with a silencer. And a strong fist. If he'd had more time with me, he would perhaps have beaten Leo's whereabouts out of me."

Wendt let go of the doorknob and turned to me. His eyes studied my face, as if they could read what he wanted to know from my forehead, nose, or chin. He seemed at a loss. "Have you . . . Do you know . . ."

"No, I didn't tell him Leo's whereabouts. And I didn't tell the guys from the Agency either. But you and I have to talk. What has Leo done? Why are they looking for her?"

He cleared his throat a few times, opening his mouth then closing it again. Then he got a grip on himself. "I'm on duty till noon. Let's meet at one o'clock at the restaurant on the main street." He walked off down the corridor with quick steps.

Shortly before one I was sitting at a table with an oilcloth cover in the restaurant garden. I kept my eye on the door that led into the restaurant and the door that led out into the street, but the waiter didn't come out of the former door, nor Wendt out of the latter. I was the only customer. I studied the oilcloth, counting the squares and watching the drops from the last downpour drying.

At one thirty a dozen or so young women appeared. They parked their bicycles, sat down at the long table next to mine, and boisterously placed their order with the shuffling waiter, who also sullenly took my order. They grew even more lively once their beers and sodas arrived. "Are we going bowling today?" "Sure, but without the guys." Of course they all were different, but they all looked the same. A little fashionable, a little athletic, a little professional, a little bit of hausfrau, a little bit of mother. I imagined them in their marriages. They stay faithful to their husbands the way one stays faithful to one's car. They're resourceful and cheerful with their children. Occasionally there's a touch of alarm in their shrill laughter. The way we Germans conduct our marriages, it's no wonder we've never had a revolution.

By two I had finished the cold cuts and drunk my apple spritzer. There was no sign of Wendt. I drove back to the hospital and was told he had left around one. I knocked on Eberlein's door.

"Come in!" He was standing by the window in his white gown. He had been looking out into the park and turned to me.

"First your patients disappear, then your doctors," I said, and told him about the appointment Wendt had missed. "Did two men from the Federal Criminal Investigation Agency visit you recently? And did someone else come, too: Tall, broad, midforties, could be anything from a banker to a pastor, perhaps wearing mirrored sunglasses? Asking about your former patient Leonore Salger, about Dr. Wendt, or about both?"

Again Eberlein took his time. I believe this is a trick that psychotherapists use, which is designed to make one nervous. But this time there was something else, too. He seemed worried. There was a sharp crease between his eyebrows that I hadn't seen before, and he kept tapping the floor impatiently and indignantly with his cane. "Who are you working for, Herr Self? Still for Leonore Salger's father?"

"She doesn't have a father. I imagine that's why Dr. Wendt told me that cock-and-bull story about her falling out a window. I guess he was sure that the man posing as her father wouldn't dare step forward and would have to accept that story. But the story was too flimsy, and as it turns out the fake father has no qualms about coming out of hiding, with or without his mirrored sunglasses. Who am I working for? I'm no longer working for him, and not for anyone else either. I don't have a client, just a problem child."

"Is that usual for a private investigator?"

"No. It's always best if the problem child is also a client. Just like in your world, Dr. Eberlein. Private investigators and psychotherapists should not work without remuneration. In my field, too, if the clients don't feel their pain, there's no hope for a cure."

He laughed. "I didn't know detectives were healers—I thought their job is to investigate."

"It's just like in your field. If we don't find out what really happened, people can't rid themselves of old issues."

"I see."

That sounded so reflective that I wondered if the stuff I was rattling on about was worth taking seriously. But Eberlein's thoughts were elsewhere. "I wonder what's going on with Wendt?" he said. "Yesterday the two men from the Agency were here, and today I told him to come see me. But he didn't show up. He can't think he . . ." Eberlein didn't finish what Wendt couldn't think. "The man you described to me was also here. Lehmann from Frankfurt. He wanted to see Wendt, but Wendt wasn't here, so he came to see me. He introduced himself as an old friend of the Salgers, particularly of their daughter Leonore. He spoke of his paternal interest in her and his feelings of responsibility, and of the difficulties she's in. He wanted to know her current whereabouts. Not that I have any idea. Nor would I have told him if I knew. I just hope he won't find her."

"So do I. But why would you hope such a thing?"

He opened the window and let some cool, damp air into the room. The rain was falling in vertical streams. "Perhaps you were wondering the other day why I have a yacht. Well, the fact is, I am interested in fish. There's a shark in the Indian Ocean that bears some resemblance to a dolphin. Sharks are loners, while dolphins are herd animals. But this particular shark can also display quite a bit of similarity to dolphins. He joins a herd of dolphins, swims with them, plays and hunts with them. That works well for a while. But then suddenly, we don't know why, he goes crazy and rips one of the dolphins to pieces. Sometimes the whole herd of dolphins will hurl itself at him, but usually they flee. Then he remains alone for weeks or months, until he goes and seeks out another herd."

"Lehmann reminds you of this shark?" I had no reason to prize Lehmann particularly, but the parallel Eberlein was drawing seemed a bit strong.

He raised his hand appeasingly. "What is fascinating about this shark is that it seems to be playing a part among the dolphins. But animals don't play parts. They don't have the necessary self-awareness. So there have to be two programs in our shark's brain: a shark program and a dolphin program. At times the animal is entirely a dolphin, and at other times entirely a shark. That is why Lehmann reminded me of this shark. I was certain he was serving me a pack of lies, but I was just as certain that he felt that what he was saying was utterly true. Do you know what I mean?"

I nodded.

"Then you also know why I find the man dangerous. Perhaps he has never harmed a hair on anyone's head and never will. But if he feels he needs to, he will do it without hesitation and with the clearest conscience."

29

In this weather?

I drove over to Wieblingen, to the Schusterstrasse. I rang
Wendt's bell and knocked on his door in vain. As I returned to
my car I saw Frau Kleinschmidt standing at her front door.
She must have been watching me from behind her curtains.

"Herr Wendt!" she called over to me.

I hopped over two puddles, got drenched by a gush of
water from the porch gutter, and joined Frau Kleinschmidt in
her front hall. I wiped my glasses dry.

"Are you looking for your son again? He was here—see,
there's his car—but a man drove up and then the two of them
went for a walk."

"In this weather?"

"Strange, isn't it? I think it's strange. And three-quarters of
an hour later the other man came back alone, got in his car,
and drove off. That's strange, too, isn't it?"

"You have sharp eyes. What did the man look like?"

"My husband's always saying that, too. 'Renate,' he tells
me, 'Renate, you've got a good pair of eyes in that head of
yours.' But I didn't get a good look at the other man. He'd

parked back over there. See? There, where the Ford is standing. It was hard to get a good look at him in the rain. In the rain, all cats are wet. But I did see that he was driving a VW Golf," she said brightly, like a child eager for praise.

"Which way did the two of them walk?"

"Down the street. It's the way to the river, you know, but you can't see that far from here, no matter how good your eyes are."

I refused a cup of freshly brewed coffee and got back in my car. I slowly drove down the street that ran along the Neckar River. Houses, trees, and cars were shrouded in a veil of rain. It was just after four, but it looked like early twilight.

After a while the rain grew lighter, and finally my wiper blades scratched over the dry windshield. I got out. I followed the path that crosses the Neckar Meadows from Wieblingen to Edingen and then goes past the sewage plant and the composting plant and under the autobahn bridge. At one point I thought I saw a piece of clothing that might belong to Wendt, trudged through the wet grass to take a look, and came back with wet feet. I generally like being outside when the earth is aromatic after a rain and the air tingles on my face. But this time I only felt clammy.

I found him, his arms outstretched and his eyes fixed. Above us the traffic rumbled. The way he was lying there, he could have fallen from the autobahn bridge onto the slabs that had been put down when the bridge was built. But there was a small hole in his light raincoat where the bullet had pierced his chest. It was dark red, almost black. On his raincoat, around the hole, the red gleamed brightly. There wasn't much blood.

Next to him lay his briefcase, as if it had slipped out of his hand. I took some tissues out of my pocket and used them to pick up the briefcase and take it under the bridge, where it was dry. With the tissues wrapped around my fingers, I pulled out a newspaper, a large notebook, and a copy of a map. The notebook was Wendt's hospital appointment calendar, and had no entry for this afternoon. The map had no place names on it, and I didn't recognize the terrain it showed. There was no town, river, or colors that might indicate a forest or houses. Most of it was divided into small numbered squares. A double line vertically cut the map in half, and several double lines veered from it to the left and extended into another double line that led straight to the edge of the map. I committed a few of the numbers to memory. At the bottom there was 203. At the top, 537, 538, and 539. On the left side, 425, and on the right side, 113. Then I put the briefcase back exactly as I had found it.

Wendt's head was slightly raised, propped up by a stone jutting out from a slab, and it was as if his fractured gaze was reaching longingly into the distance. I would have liked to close his eyes. It would've been the proper thing to do. But the police would not like it. In Wieblingen I called from the nearest phone booth and asked to be put through to Chief Inspector Nägelsbach's office.

"I can't believe you sent me your colleagues from the Agency." I had to get that off my chest first.

"I sent you who?" Nägelsbach asked.

"This morning I had a visit from Bleckmeier and Rawitz, from the Federal Criminal Investigation Agency. They wanted to know the whereabouts of Leonore Salger."

"I had nothing to do with that. What you and I spoke about that evening . . . How can you think I would abuse your trust like that?" Nägelsbach's voice was shaking with indignation. I believed him. Should I be ashamed? Had he been more straightforward with me than I had been with him? "I apologize. I simply couldn't imagine that the Agency would otherwise think of questioning me."

"Hmm."

I told him I had found Wendt. Nägelsbach asked me to wait for him by the phone booth. Exactly five minutes later a patrol car and an ambulance appeared, along with Tietzke from the local paper, and three minutes after that Nägelsbach himself pulled up with a colleague. I got into their car and showed them the way to Wendt's corpse, and they set to work. I was free to go. "Let's talk tomorrow," Nägelsbach said. "Can you come by my office in the morning?"

30

Spaghetti al pesto

The lightbulb on my landing was still out. I saw it as I stopped to catch my breath on the floor below and went back down again.

Brigitte wasn't home yet. Young Manu and I made my spaghetti carbonara—it's never too early for a child to be taught that cream is the body of a light pasta sauce, and vermouth the soul.

When Brigitte and I took the dog out for a walk late that evening, she wanted to know what was going on. "It's so great you're here and that the two of you cooked supper—and you even washed up—but I know you didn't come over just to please me."

"How about to please *me*—wouldn't that be enough?"

She sensed that I wasn't telling her the whole truth, but she didn't want to push the matter. Back at her place we watched a movie and the late news. Before the weather report there was a bulletin in which the Federal Criminal Investigation Agency made a special public appeal for information. There hadn't been a bulletin earlier that evening when I'd watched the news with

Manu. I didn't recognize the pictures they showed of the two nameless men. But the woman they showed was Leo, and they gave her name. The bulletin disclosed that there had been a terrorist attack on an American military installation and that there had been two casualties. Then a press officer from the Criminal Investigation Agency appeared on the screen and spoke of a new generation of part-time terrorists who lead normal lives during the day, and at night launch attacks with murder and fire. He asked the public to cooperate and to expect roadblocks and checkpoints over the next few days. He promised that any information that was provided would be handled in the strictest confidence and mentioned a substantial reward.

"Isn't that the girl whose picture is leaning on the small stone lion in your office?"

I nodded.

"I hope you don't think I'm thinking of the reward. What I'm thinking of is how I found you the other day. You told me you'd tell the police where she is when you know why they're looking for her. Now you know."

"Do I really? There was a terrorist attack on an American base and there were two casualties; that's all I know. But how come I don't know when and where the attack took place? Leo went into hiding in January, now it's May. The way they're talking, you'd think the attack took place yesterday, and that she'd gone into hiding yesterday. No, Brigitte, I know next to nothing."

As we lay in bed I made up my mind and set the alarm. I hoped that the people of Amorbach, and the Hopfen family in particular, hadn't seen the late-night news.

The following morning at six I was in my car, heading to Amorbach.

31

Like in the days of Baader and Meinhof

The streets were empty, and I was able to pick up speed. The sun rose as a pale red disk, but had soon steamed away the haze, blinding me in the many sharp curves between Eberbach and Amorbach. The rainy days were over.

The Badischer Hof Restaurant had opened already, and the breakfast buffet was laid out. At the table next to mine sat a married couple who were outfitted in knickerbockers and red socks. They looked out of place, almost like aliens, but they were ready for their hike through the Odenwald, and were reading the local *Bote vom Untermain* paper over coffee and rolls. I was itching to tell them how important it was in a marriage to talk to each other and to ask them to give me their paper. But I couldn't work up the courage. All the same, I could see that Leo's picture wasn't on the front page.

It was on page four. By the time I rang the doorbell in Sommerberg at a quarter to nine, I had bought the newspaper and was holding it under my arm. The children were making a great racket inside. Leo opened the door.

I had recently caught only a glimpse of her, and even then she had remained for me the girl in the first photograph, the girl with the mouth that liked to laugh, with the question and the reproach in her eyes, the girl who was leaning on the little stone lion on my desk. I had not really come to terms with the young woman whose picture I had been given at the Klausenpfad residence hall. Now she was standing in front of me, another year or two older. Her chin and cheekbones showed determination. I read in her eyes: "What does this old man want? Is he selling something? Some kind of door-to-door salesman? Or has he come to read the electric and gas meters?" She was again wearing jeans and a man's checked shirt.

"What can I do for you?" Her accent was as thick as the peanut butter on the sandwiches Manu makes for himself.

"Good morning, Frau Salger."

She took a step back. I was almost happy about the distrust in her eyes. Better a dangerous old man than a tiresome one.

"Excuse me?"

I handed her the newspaper, opened to page four. "I'd like to have a word with you."

She looked at her picture with a mixture of curiosity and resignation: That's supposed to be me? Who cares, it's all over anyway.

I imagined that the picture was from the police files, when she had been taken in for fingerprinting during the student protests. Sometimes there is talk about criminalization by the police, meaning that law enforcement creates breaches of law as much as it fights them. These are unacceptable generalizations. It is only police photographers who are capable of "criminalizing" a person. And they are masters of their trade.

Send them the most innocent and law-abiding individual you can find, and before you know it they will give him the mug of a criminal. Leo shrugged her shoulders and handed me back the newspaper. "Could you please wait a moment?" Her accent was gone.

I stood outside the door and heard snippets of Leo telling the children to put on their shoes, take along their jackets, and put their sandwiches in their schoolbags. Then she ran down the stairs and I heard her opening and shutting room and closet doors. When she came out of the house with the children, she was carrying a coat over her arm and a packed bag over her shoulder.

"Do you mind if I drive on ahead with the kids? I want to drop them off at the kindergarten and at the school and then leave the car outside Dr. Hopfen's office." She unlocked the Land Rover and helped the children get in.

I followed in my car, and saw the little girl go into the kindergarten and the boys into the school. Then Leo parked the Rover, dropped the keys into Dr. Hopfen's mailbox, and came over to my car with her bag and coat. "Let's go."

Did she think I was a policeman? Well, that could be cleared up later. When I turned into the road leading to Eberbach she looked at me with surprise but didn't say anything. We were silent all the way to Ernsttal. I parked the car under some trees. "Come along, let's have a cup of coffee."

She got out of the car. "And where are we going after that?"

"I don't know. Bonn? Heidelberg? Where would you like to go?"

We sat on the terrace and ordered coffee. "You're not a policeman—so who are you and what do you want?" She took tobacco and cigarette papers out of her bag, nimbly rolled herself a cigarette, and asked me for a light. She smoked and waited for my answer, looking at me not distrustfully but carefully.

"Wendt is dead, and everything points to this man being the murderer." I showed her one of the pictures from her album, in which the fake Herr Salger stood next to her with his arm around her shoulder. "You know him."

"What of it?" The caution in her eyes turned to defense. She had been sitting with her elbows propped on the table. Now she leaned back.

"What of it? Wendt helped you. First he hid you in the psychiatric hospital, then he got you the job as an au pair in Amorbach. I didn't know him well, but I admit that it troubles me that he might still be alive if I had told the police what they wanted to know, about you, about this guy"— I pointed at the picture—"and about Wendt. I am quite sure that he would still be alive if you had done one or two things differently."

The café owner brought us our coffees. Leo got up. "I'll be right back." Did she want to squeeze her way out the restroom window and head through the woods for Bavaria? I took the risk. The café owner began telling me that our forests have been dying since German boilers have been burning Russian natural gas. "They put something in it," he whispered. "Those Russians don't need war and weapons anymore."

Leo returned. Her eyes were swollen with tears. "Can you please tell me what you want from me?" She spoke in a natural voice, but not without effort.

I gave her a condensed version of the last couple of weeks.

"Who are you working for now?"

"For myself. I can do that from time to time, if it's not for too long."

"And you want to know what I know just out of interest and curiosity?"

"Not only. I also want to know what I might have to expect from him." I pointed again at the picture. "Incidentally, what's his name?"

"And when I've told you everything, what then?"

"You're asking me if I'll hand you over to the police?"

"That would be an option, wouldn't it? By the way, did you have a hard time recognizing me?"

"Not really. But recognizing people who don't want to be recognized is part of my job."

"Will you take me away from here?"

I didn't understand what she was getting at.

"I mean, can you take me somewhere where these pictures won't . . . They'll be up in every post office and police station, like in the days of Baader and Meinhof, won't they? And on TV—do you think they'll show them on TV, too?"

"They already have, yesterday."

"Do you have any ideas? If you do, I'll tell you what you want to know."

I needed some time to think. Supporting a terrorist organization, facilitation, obstruction of justice—all the things that could happen to me went through my head. Could I claim at my age a diminished capacity, or was that only permissible in Nazi trials? Would they impound my old Opel as an instrument of crime? I postponed the moral question of whether I would keep my promise to Leo if she had committed the most dreadful atrocities.

I got up. "Fine. I'll take you to France, and on the way to the border you can tell me what you know."

She remained seated. "And the official at the border will just wave us through with a smile?"

She was right. Even in a Europe of open borders, the police at border crossings take particular care during a hunt for terrorists. "I'll take you over a back road."

32

Bananas in exhaust pipes

The TV bulletin had warned the public to expect roadblocks and checkpoints. So I took country roads with their tractors, agricultural machinery, and hay carts, which the police avoid as much as everyone else does. We drove through Kleiner Odenwald and Kraichgau, crossed the Rhine at Leopolds-haven, and entered the Palatinate Forest at Klingenmünster. By two o'clock we were in Nothweiler.

"There's not all that much to tell," Leo had begun after Ernsttal, but then fell silent again. She sat brooding all the way to Neckarbischofsheim, rolling one cigarette after another and smoking it. "I don't get it. Rolf Wendt wasn't part of it at all. He didn't really participate. No one had any reason to kill him, no one. How was he murdered?"

"Why don't you tell me everything from the beginning?"

"OK, I'll start with Helmut Lemke. That's not what he calls himself anymore, but whatever. As it is, with that photo-graph you have of him, you would've had no trouble finding out his real name. You could say he was something like an older brother to me. I wasn't even at school yet when Dad

136

brought him home the first time. Helmut was already a young man, but was happy enough to play tag or hide-and-seek with me in the garden, and when I was older he taught me tennis. I guess he wanted a baby sister as much as I wanted a big brother."

"Where did your father know him from?"

"Helmut was a student, and during summer recess he worked as an intern at the ministry. Somehow he caught my father's eye. In 1967, Helmut moved from Bonn to Heidelberg, which kind of loosened the bond a little bit. But he always came back to Bonn and visited us, and he and I always had lots of fun. When my father ended up in prison and nobody wanted anything to do with us, Helmut still kept coming to see us like nothing had happened. But then, about six years ago, he disappeared as if the earth had swallowed him up."

"When did you see him again?"

"Last summer. *Comme ça.*" Leo snapped her fingers. He had appeared at her door one day and said "Hi," just as if they had been together the day before. In the next few weeks they met almost every day. "For us it was . . . Well, we'd known each other forever, and yet we were now experiencing each other in a completely new way." Did that mean that they had a relationship? At any rate, they did a lot together: tennis, hiking, theater, cooking. One day he told her of the six years he'd spent in prison. He had been sentenced for an attack on the army recruiting office in Heidelberg.

"He was sentenced to six years?" I asked. I didn't remember such an attack—and spectacular explosions in the Mannheim-Heidelberg area tend to stick in my mind.

"A night guard got the brunt of it. He was badly hurt. But Helmut had nothing to do with this attack. He was politically engaged and was involved with the Communist League of West Germany, and he kept provoking the police and the courts, so they finally framed him and put him away. That's how it was. He told me that a policeman actually said to him that he'd had his fun with the police long enough, now the police would have their fun with him."

"And all of that sounded plausible to you?"

"Sure, and I could see why Helmut wanted to pay them back. In the beginning he'd only considered blowing up the German army recruiting office, but now he was going to do something really big. He realized that what he had to do was target the people who were really behind everything: the Americans. Sometimes we walked down the Bunsenstrasse, and right around the corner from my apartment there's an old villa on the Häuserstrasse where the army recruiting office used to be and where the Americans now have some kind of office. 'You see,' he told me, 'the attack on the army recruiting office wasn't just a waste of time, because a recruiting office isn't just a recruiting office: The fact that the Americans came in and took it over shows more clearly than any bomb can that American imperialism is behind German militarism. It's an insult to my intelligence that they thought me capable of such an idiotic attack in the fight against capitalism and imperialism!'"

Even back in the sixties and seventies I'd had a hard time taking all this political jargon seriously. And the zeitgeist of the nineties doesn't make taking it seriously any easier. In spite of her self-rolled cigarettes I couldn't imagine Leo reading Marx and Engels. I carefully asked her about her own involvement in the fight against capitalism and imperialism.

"That was Helmut's soapbox. When someone has lived with it for such a long time and paid such a price for it, I guess he can't climb off it anymore. We sometimes made fun of him. He just couldn't see that good politics needs to be concrete, to hit the mark, to be fun. But I must say, he did teach us a lot."

"Us? You mean you and the other two in the police photos?"

"I mean just me. I don't want to drag anyone else into this. I don't even know the people in the newspaper shots."

I didn't push her any further. She continued talking, and I concluded from what she said that there were two others, a certain Giselher and a certain Bertram, that they had met at a demonstration, got together from time to time, and at first had only ranted and railed against the establishment.

"But there came a point when we had had it up to here! You talk and talk and don't change anything. All the mess goes on: forests dying, chemicals in the air and in the water, nuclear power plants, rockets, and the way they destroy the cities and arm the police. All you accomplish is that the papers and the media sometimes give these things a bit more coverage, but then the stories dry up, there's no more coverage on the forest, and people think that everything's A-OK, while things only keep getting worse."

So they decided to act instead of talk. They aimed fireworks at the nuclear plant in Biblis, set off stink bombs in Heidelberg and Mannheim sex shops, stuffed bananas in the exhaust pipes of police cars, tried but failed to stop a car race on the Hockenheim Circuit one night by blasting potholes in the track, and brought down a power pylon between Kirchheim and Sandhausen. Then Helmut Lemke joined them and convinced them that their tactics were just childish pranks.

"What role did Rolf Wendt play in all this? I know you don't want to drag anyone else into it, but after all . . ."

"I know, he's dead. As I've told you already, he wasn't part of any of this. We were just friends. He and Helmut somehow knew each other from before. We ran into Rolf at the Weinloch Bar, and Helmut introduced him to me. That's how I met him."

"The papers mentioned an attack on an American military installation."

"That was the result of our new tactics." Lemke had put them up to it. Their operations should not try to prevent the unpreventable, but simply expose all the terrible things that were going on. This made sense to Leo and her friends, so they planned to break into the Rhineland Chemical Works at Ludwigshafen and tamper with the plant's emissions so that the air and the water, which were already poisoned, would end up brightly colored, too. The poison would reveal itself in violet clouds and a yellow Rhine. They also planned an attack on the traffic network at Römerkreis, Bismarckplatz, and Adenauerplatz. They would disable the traffic lights during rush hour, bringing Heidelberg to a standstill that would underline the traffic overload. None of their plans panned out, so Helmut Lemke came up with Operation Bonfire.

"Why bonfire?"

"We wanted to set fire to an American installation so that the public would finally realize what it was the Americans were storing there. Normally they don't let anyone into such installations, but when there's a fire, all hell breaks loose and Germans appear on the scene: police, firemen, reporters. Of course it would have to be a big fire. But when a munitions depot goes up in flames . . ."

I was dumbfounded and looked at her dumbfounded. She defended herself against my accusations faster than I could come up with them. I realized that for weeks she had been her own prosecution, defense, and judge.

"Of course nobody was supposed to get hurt. We were unanimous about that and kept saying so to Helmut, who swore on a stack of Bibles that he agreed with us wholeheartedly. But even if people did get hurt—you mustn't get me wrong, we didn't take that into account—I just mean, even if people . . ." Her words trailed off.

I looked over at her.

She bit her lip defiantly, and one hand gripped the other so firmly in her lap that the skin beneath her nails gleamed white. "How can you expose something terrible without creating a terrible mess? If something happened, I mean if something *had* happened, then that would have still been better than if . . ."

I waited, but she didn't continue. "What did happen, Frau Salger?"

She turned and looked at me intently, as if it were I who was supposed to be offering her the key to a secret. "I'm not sure," she said. "I hadn't really been that involved in the preparations. The others did all of that, Helmut and Giselher. Bertram only came back from Tuscany the evening before. I knew I was going to be part of things, that I was going to participate. We always carried everything out together. Helmut was utterly opposed to me participating, but he didn't get his way. As it was, even with me there we were still missing one person. Helmut had initially tried to plan the operation with four people instead of five, but then he looked for a new, fifth person and found him. For his safety and for ours, Helmut didn't actually bring him into the group. We met only once the operation was under way. He was with Helmut in one car, while Giselher, Bertram, and I were in the other."

"And that was at the beginning of January?"

"Yes, January sixth. I don't even know where the meeting place was. I think somewhere outside Frankfurt. We headed up the autobahn for quite a while, north from the Heidelberg or Mannheim junction, and then drove onto the shoulder and down an embankment and onto a back road. We followed it till we came to the edge of some woods. There we met Helmut and the fifth man. Then we headed off."

"Did you know the fifth man?"

"We had all blackened our faces. I barely recognized Helmut. After a while we came to a fence, cut a hole in it, and climbed through. My job was to secure the way back. At midpoint I was supposed to keep an eye out in both directions in case a patrol turned up and either warn them or divert the patrol. But I guess you don't want to know all those details. It was quite foggy. I was supposed to wait for twenty minutes and then head back on my own." She shrugged her shoulders. "I waited twenty-five minutes. Then I heard shots. I ran back to the fence and got out of the compound. When I reached our cars, there was an explosion, followed immediately by another. So I went running to the road. At first nobody stopped. They must have thought I was some dangerous nut, my face all black the way it was. But then I realized that and quickly cleaned up. The third car stopped. The driver was a pharmacist from Schwetzingen who'd had a couple of drinks and hit on me. When I reacted hysterically and told him I wanted to go to the psychiatric hospital, he must have thought that that was where I belonged. He took me straight there and thanked his lucky stars that he wasn't arrested or questioned." She closed her eyes and leaned her head on the headrest. "Rolf was working the evening shift. He gave me a room and an injection, and I slept all the way through to the following evening."

33

The Kaiser-Wilhelm-Stein

As we drove through the bright, sunny countryside, Leo's account about dark and gloomy nights, blackened faces, holes cut into fences, bombs, and gunfire struck me as strangely unreal. In Nothweiler I parked the car in front of the church and we climbed up to the ruins of Castle Wegelnburg. The woods sparkled in fresh green, the birds were singing, and an aromatic tang hung in the air after the last few days' rain. Explosions at American installations? What Americans? What explosions? But Leo's thoughts did not leave that night so quickly.

"I felt that that fifth man was somehow fishy. He seemed jittery and all over the place: He'd be walking ahead, then he'd fall back, then he'd suddenly turn up on the side. He had all kinds of equipment with him. I don't know why, or what it was for. After all, we had brought along the explosives."

The path leading up to Castle Wegelnburg is steep. Leo hadn't let me carry her bag and coat, and I was glad. She was always a good bit ahead of me and would stop and wait. At first she walked as if she'd been wound up with a key. But gradually her steps grew lighter and freer. She took her bag off her shoulder and held it in her hand, swung her arms, threw her head back so that her hair flew, and when she waited for me she pranced backward in front of me. She returned to the subject of Operation Bonfire. An overgrown pile of rotting logs reminded her of the structures the Americans had put up at their installation. "Like garages, but a lot bigger, with slanted sides and covered with earth and grass. Then there were these really long objects, not quite as tall and wide as the garages, but also covered in grass. Who knows what they were." But the question did not really seem to preoccupy her. When I caught up with her and wanted to discuss the grass-covered garages, she laid her hand on my arm. "Shh." A rabbit was sitting on the path, watching us.

We stopped for a rest on the Kaiser-Wilhelm-Stein. At the gas station I had bought a kilo of Granny Smith apples and some chocolate with whole nuts. "What are you going to do on the other side?" I asked her. Just beyond the Kaiser-Wilhelm-Stein lies France.

"I'll take a vacation. As long as my money lasts. These past few weeks with the children were really exhausting. I think after that I'll find myself another au-pair job." She was sitting on the ground with her back to the Kaiser-Wilhelm-Stein. She bit loudly into her apple, her eyes blinking in the sun. The question of what would come after her au-pair job was on the tip of my tongue, of how she expected to live a normal life again. But why ask someone the kind of worrying questions they could easily ask themselves, but don't?

Then I had an idea. "We could make our way to the Tessin. I have friends there I've been wanting to visit for a long time.

If you can see yourself working as an au pair in the Tessin, my friend Tyberg has all kinds of connections."

She nibbled at the core of her apple and threw it away. She looked up at the sky and then at the trees, and wrinkled her nose. "*Comme ça?*" She snapped her fingers again.

"*Comme ça.*"

The path that went by the ruins of the Hohenburg and Löwenburg castles to Château Fleckenstein in France was relatively short, and Leo could take her time. I hurried back to Nothweiler and drove across the border by Wissembourg. A young border guard asked me where I was coming from and where I was heading, and an hour later I was at Château Fleckenstein. Leo was talking and laughing with a young Frenchman. She was engrossed in the conversation and didn't see or hear me approach. I was worried that she would give me the kind of look Manu gives Brigitte when he is playing with one of his friends and is ashamed that his mother is keeping an eye on him. But Leo greeted me quite unself-consciously.

That evening we didn't drive very far. At the Cheval Blanc restaurant in Niedersteinbach she ate oysters for the first time in her life and didn't like them. But she did like the champagne, and after the second bottle we felt like Bonnie and Clyde. If the pharmacy had still been open we'd have pulled up in front, wielded a gun, and gotten me a toothbrush and some razor blades. At ten I called Brigitte. She could hear I was tipsy and telling her only half the truth, and she was hurt. I didn't care, though I was still sober enough to register how unfair my indifference was. With Brigitte, who was generous, I was belatedly fighting for my independence—a fight I hadn't even started with my grouchy and whining wife, Klara, in all the years of our marriage. When I said good night to Leo at the door to her room, she gave me a kiss.

It took us two days to get to Locarno. We meandered through the Vosges and the Jura mountains, crossed from the French side to the Swiss, spent the night in Murten, and drove through passes the names of which I had never heard: Glaubenbüelenpass, Brünigpass, Nufenenpass. Even up in the mountains it was warm enough for us to spread out a blanket at noon and have a picnic.

As we drove, Leo talked about a thousand things: studying and interpreting, politics, even about the children she had looked after in Amorbach. She liked sitting with her legs on the dashboard or sticking her right foot out the window. She chose programs on the radio ranging from classical music to American pop, and in Switzerland included the farming broadcasts. From nine till ten, Jeremias Gotthelf's *Uli, the Farmhand* was broadcast in Swiss dialect. In *Uli, the Farmhand* all was still well with the world, while in the American pop songs the world was on its head: Men crooned and women had metal in their voices. Leo whistled along. She studied the countryside and the cities we drove through. On both days, after lunch she fell asleep in the car. Occasional periods of silence between the two of us made neither of us uncomfortable. I let my thoughts roam. Sometimes I would ask Leo a question.

"When you got to the psychiatric hospital, did you manage to find out what had gone wrong that night, and what happened to the others?" In our shared early-morning hangover we had began talking informally.

"I kept trying to find out. You can't imagine how happy I'd have been to hear that it was just a false alarm. But I could never reach Giselher or Bertram whenever I called, and it would have been too dangerous to try to get in touch with their friends."

I reminded her that two casualties had been announced. "And they're only searching for the three of you, even though five took part in the attack."

"Three of us? That's me in one of the pictures, but I don't know who the other two are." She immersed herself in the *Bote vom Untermain* newspaper. "Take a good look at that guy," she said, pointing at one of the two men whose pictures were next to hers. "Something about him reminds me of Helmut. It's not him, but he reminds me of him. Weird, isn't it?"

She was right. There was a vague similarity. Or does every picture start to resemble somebody if one looks at it long enough? Also, some of the features of the second of the two men suddenly seemed familiar.

Somewhere in the Jura Mountains, she asked me if Rolf Wendt's death could not have been an accident.

"Are you worried Helmut might have killed him?"

"I can't imagine anyone killing Rolf. I'd swear Rolf didn't have any what you would call enemies. He was far too cautious to lock horns with anyone. He was clever that way: He could always fend off a person and deflect tricky situations. I saw him do it a couple of times, both at the hospital and outside. Are you sure it couldn't have been been an accident?"

I shook my head. "He was shot. You don't know where Helmut and Rolf knew each other from?"

"It was only that once at the Weinloch Bar that I was with the two of them, and they only said a quick hi. I didn't ask Helmut or Rolf how they knew each other. At the hospital I told Rolf about Helmut—Rolf was my therapist and stuck to protocol as closely as possible. Of course he didn't always stick to protocol, but if he hadn't treated me as a regular patient, I'd have been exposed."

"Eberlein said something about . . . something about a depressive veneer, but that deep inside you were a cheerful girl."

"I *am* a cheerful girl, inside and out. When I feel fear coming on, I say 'Hello, fear!' and let it do its thing for a while, but I don't let it get the better of me."

"Fear of what?"

"Don't you ever have that feeling? It's not a fear that something bad will happen, but just like when you have a fever, or when you feel cold, or sick." She looked at me. "No, you don't ever have that feeling, do you? But I think Rolf did. He didn't get it just from his patients or from books. That's why he could help me a lot."

"Was he in love with you?"

She took her feet off the dashboard and sat up straight. "I'm not really sure."

I don't believe women when they say that they're not sure if they're attractive. Leo was sitting next to me in her jeans and a man's checked shirt, but I felt the woman in her voice, in her scent—even in the nervous movements with which she rolled her cigarettes. And she didn't know if Rolf Wendt was in love with her?

She could tell I didn't believe her. "OK, so he was in love with me. I didn't want to face up to it; I had a bad conscience. He'd done so much for me and got nothing in return, didn't even expect anything, but I'm sure he hoped I'd fall in love with him."

"What about Helmut?"

She looked at me puzzled.

"Is he in love with you? Why is he so eager to know where you are? Ten thousand marks is a lot of money."

"Oh." She blushed and turned her face to the window. "Does it surprise you that he wants to know where I am? He was my leader, was in charge of me, and then lost me."

34

Angels don't shoot at cats

That evening we sat in Murten, above the lake. From the terrace of the Hotel Krone we watched the late sailboats. In the evening lull they slowly made their way back into the harbor. The last steamer from Neuenburg forged past them with majesty, as if to prove the superiority of technology over nature. The sun set behind the mountains on the opposite shore.

"I'll go get my sweater." Leo got up and stayed away a long time. The waiter brought me a second aperitif. Silence rose from the lake and swallowed the buzz of voices behind me. I turned around just as Leo came out onto the terrace through the glass doors. She hadn't put on a sweater. She wore a tight, long-sleeved black dress that reached from her neck to just above her knees, and black high-heeled shoes. Her pantyhose, the stole, and the comb in her luxuriant pinned-up hair were red. She took her time crossing the terrace. She sashayed her way around tables, and when she squeezed between chairs that were too close together she pulled her shoulders up so high that her breasts were tight within the dress. Where there were no obstacles she walked with swaying hips, her head held high. I got up, pulled her chair out for her, and she sat down. The guests on the terrace had followed her with their eyes because of her swinging hips, and also because her dress was bare down the back.

"You're gorgeous."

We sat opposite each other. Her sparkling eyes—blue beneath a blue sky and sometimes gray or green beneath gray clouds—shone darkly. In her smile was delight at the game she was playing. A touch of seduction, a touch of complacency, a touch of self-mockery. She shook her head at my compliment, as if to say: "I know, but don't tell anybody else."

The waiter suggested fish from the lake and wine from the opposite shore. Leo ate hungrily. Over dinner I learned that she had spent a year in America as a high school student, that jersey sweaters don't get wrinkled, that the shirt and jacket I'd bought at her suggestion in Belfort suited me, and that her mother had been a voice-over actress and had previously been married to a washed-up movie director. It was clear that her relationship with her mother was not good. She asked me what life as a private investigator was like, how long I had been one, and what I had done before.

"You were a public prosecutor?" She stared at me in amazement. "How come you gave that up?"

During the course of my life I have given many different answers to this question. Perhaps all of them true. Perhaps none. In 1945, they turned their back on me for having been a Nazi public prosecutor, and when they wanted the old Nazis again, I turned my back on them. Because I was no longer an old Nazi? Because the let's-look-the-other-way attitude of my old and new colleagues at the bar rubbed me the wrong way? Because I had definitely had enough of others laying out for me what is just and unjust? Because as a private investigator I am my own boss? Because in life you should never pick up again what you've put down for good? Because I don't like the smell of government offices? "I can't quite say, Leo. Back in 1945, being a public prosecutor was simply over for me."

A cool wind rose and the terrace emptied. We sat down to finish our bottle on a bench that was shielded by a wall. Vully was an unpretentious local wine without frills that I had never tried before. The moon had risen and was mirrored in the lake. I felt a chill, and Leo snuggled up to me, warming and seeking warmth.

"My father stopped talking in the last years of his life. I don't know if he couldn't talk or just didn't want to. I guess a bit of both. I remember at first trying to have conversations with him—I'd talk to him about something or ask him a question. I hoped he'd tell me more about himself. There were also times when he'd try to speak, but only a croaking rattle would escape from his throat. Mostly he'd look at me with a kind of crooked smile that asked for forgiveness and understanding, but perhaps it was also the result of the minor stroke he'd had. Later I just sat by his bedside, held his hand, looked out the window into the garden, and let my thoughts wander. That's where I learned to be silent. And to love."

I put my arm around her shoulder.

"That was actually a nice time. For him and for me. Otherwise it was sheer hell." She took the pack of cigarettes out of my coat pocket, lit one, and smoked it, inhaling deeply. "He couldn't hold his piss or shit anymore in those last years. The doctor said his condition was psychological, not physical, which he also told my father. That was before things got really bad. The doctor wanted to help him, to give him a healing shock, but he accomplished the opposite. Perhaps my father wanted to prove that he really couldn't do anything else. It turned into a ritual between him and Mother, like a last dance that the two of them had before they were executed for a crime they had committed together. He would soil the bed, and his pride and dignity suffered. She would clean him up and change the sheets, her face turned away in disgust. He knew that he disgusted her, but that she would not shrink from tending him, even though she was slowly running herself into the ground. I shit on you, he wanted to tell her, but he could only tell her this by shitting on himself, and she could only show him that he was a pitiful shit by slaving over his shit."

Later Leo again returned to the subject. "When I was a little girl I wanted to marry my father. All girls do. Then when I realized that that wasn't possible, I wanted somebody like my father. You see, I've always liked older men. But those last years with Father . . . How ugly everything had become, how spiteful, nasty, dirty . . ." She looked past me, her eyes wide. "Sometimes Helmut seemed to me like an angel with a burning sword, destroying, judging, cleansing. You wanted to know whether I loved him. I loved the angel, and at times cherished the hope that he would take his sword and burn away my fear. But perhaps the heat was too much. I have . . . have I betrayed him?"

Angels do not shoot at couches and cats. I told her that, but she wasn't listening.

35

A nation of cobblers

I had put in a call from Niedersteinbach to Tyberg in Locarno. He told me he was looking forward to our visit. "You're bringing a young lady with you? My butler will prepare two rooms. I won't let you stay in a hotel, and that's that! You must stay at my place." We reached his Villa Sempreverde in Monti above Locarno at teatime.

Tea was served out in the arbor. The table and chairs were made of granite and were pleasantly cool in the heat of the summery afternoon. The Earl Grey gave off a strong aroma. The pastries were delicious, and Tyberg was attentive. And yet something wasn't quite right. His attentiveness was so formal that it struck me as forced and distant. I was taken aback: He had been so warm on the phone. Could it be because Judith Buchendorff, Tyberg's secretary and personal assistant, whom I had known slightly longer and better than I had known him, was away doing research for his memoirs? Or was the distance between us the kind of distance common between people who became important to each other under certain circumstances, but who in fact have nothing in common? Were we like vacationers, classmates, or war buddies who meet again?

After tea, Tyberg gave Leo and me a tour of the gardens, which extend far up the mountain behind the house. In his office he showed us the computer on which his memoirs were being written and told us how he had struggled to find the right title. "My whole life has been dedicated to the chemical industry—the only title I could think of was *He Who Touches Pitch and Sulfur*." But that reminded him too much of verse one of *Jesus Son of Sirach*, chapter thirteen. In the music room he opened a chest and took out a flute for me and then sat down at the grand piano. We played Telemann's Suite in A Minor, and after that, just as we had once before, the B Minor Suite by Bach. He played far better than I, and we started off shakily. But he knew where he had to slow down for me, and soon enough my fingers remembered the much-practiced runs. Above all, the two of us understood Bach the way one can only understand Bach when one is pushing seventy. That Tyberg and I came together so naturally and felicitously in his music convinced me that I had only imagined the atmospheric disturbances. But after dinner the storm broke loose.

With his full head of white hair, his gray beard, and bushy eyebrows, Tyberg looked like an elder statesman, a visionary Russian dissident, or Santa Claus after a Christmas party. His brown eyes stared at me sternly. "I have given the matter much thought, wondering whether I should talk to you privately. Perhaps it would make the matter easier. But then again it might make it harder, and I don't want to have to ask myself if I tried to skirt the issue." He got up and began pacing up and down behind the table. "Do you think we don't have German television here? Do you think you can simply come to the Tessin, an old man and a young woman, playing father and daughter, grandfather and granddaughter, or come visiting me in the guise of Uncle Gerhard and his young girlfriend?" Judith had first introduced me to him as her uncle Gerhard, and for him I had always remained Judith's "Uncle Gerhard," though he was well aware that it had only been a matter of incognito. "We have cable television here in Locarno, Uncle Gerhard, and I get twenty-three channels. And I'm not the only one who watches the *Tagesschau* around here—there are hundreds of Germans living here. You could argue that mug shots give a distorted picture, and blond hair can change one's looks to some extent"—he looked sternly at Leo—"but it didn't take me more than fifteen minutes to recognize you. And I'm not the only one here who has a good eye for people. There are many artists, painters, and actors in Monti, for whom a careful eye is part of what they do. All I can say is that it was a crazy idea to come here."

"It was my idea," I said.

"I am aware of that, Uncle Gerhard. I'm not reproaching her. Nor am I reproaching her—or you—for the crime they're after her for. For now, we are only talking about an indictment, not a conviction. I'm sorry I am being so brusque." Tyberg looked at Leo with a quick smile. "At my age, one aims to be as charming as possible to young ladies. But the matter is too important. It also has to do with an old story between Gerhard and me. Did he tell you how we met?"

Leo shook her head. I was filled with admiration for her. She sat there unperturbed, looking at Tyberg attentively and somewhat puzzled. She did not return his smile, nor did she rebuff it with a hard look. She was waiting. Every now and then her hands fiddled with a cigarette or brushed crumbs off her long white summer dress.

"But we can let that matter rest. I shall do things the way the Bedouins do. You can be my guests for three days. But I will ask you to leave my house on Saturday."

I stood up. "It wasn't my intention to put you in danger, Herr Tyberg. I am sorry if—"

"I'm surprised you don't understand. It's not a question of danger. It's just that I don't want to have anything to do with this flight from justice. The police are seeking Frau Salger, and she should be brought before a judge and found innocent or guilty. I would be glad to join you in hoping that she will be found innocent. But it is not my right, nor yours, Uncle Gerhard, to interfere in matters that are the job of the police and a court of law."

"What if they don't know their job? Something is wrong with their preliminary proceedings. First of all, they are looking for Leo without saying why. Then they make a public appeal for information, announcing an attack that is months old as if it happened yesterday. And they bring in people and faces that have nothing to do with the whole thing. No, Herr Tyberg, there's something fishy here." Tyberg's words had initially made me feel inconsiderate and reckless. I knew I wasn't putting him in any real danger, but the issue was not my view of things, but his. I had been ready to accept his reproaches, but the conversation was now taking another turn.

"You're not the one to judge that," he said. "You have to go through channels, there are public officials, there are investigative committees that deal with—"

"I can't just stick my head in the sand. There's something fishy about this, and the way the police are handling things definitely isn't aboveboard. If you want to know, the—"

"No, I don't want to know. Let's say everything that you're worried about is true—have you spoken to the commissioner in charge of the police officers who have acted wrongly? Have you spoken to your political representative? Have you contacted the press? I'm not saying you should stick your head in the sand, but how can you take it upon yourself to—"

"Take it upon myself?" I got angry. "I've been a man who minds his own business, a cobbler who has stuck to his last too often in life. As a soldier, as a public prosecutor, as a private investigator, I did what I was told, it was my job, and I didn't go messing about in matters that were in other people's domain. What we are is a nation of cobblers who mind their own business, and look where it's gotten us."

"You're talking about the Third Reich? If only everyone minded his own business But no: The physicians were not satisfied with curing patients, they had to advance the Volk and racial cleansing. The teachers were not satisfied with teaching reading and writing, they had to teach fighting for the fatherland. Judges did not ask what was just, but what they deemed to be good for the nation, what the Führer wanted; and as for the generals—their trade is to fight and win battles, not to transport and shoot Jews, Poles, and Russians. No, Uncle Gerhard, unfortunately we are not a nation that minds its own business!"

"What about the chemists?" Leo asked.

"What about them?"

"The chemists of the Third Reich—I wonder what, in your view, their business was and if they stuck to it?"

Tyberg looked at Leo with a frown. "I have been asking myself that question ever since I started working on my memoirs. I incline to the opinion that a laboratory is a chemist's business. But that would mean that others always bear the responsibility, and that we scientists are never responsible, and I can see the snag in that, especially when it comes from the mouth of a chemist."

For a while nobody spoke. The butler knocked, and then cleared away the plates. Leo asked him to compliment the cook for the corn biscuits with oxtail and green peppers that had been served as an appetizer. "Polenta medallions," he corrected her, flattered, as he himself was the cook, and the reintroduction of polenta as a culinary delicacy was a cherished objective of his. He proposed that we step into the drawing room for a liqueur.

Leo got up, came over to me, and looked at me questioningly. I nodded. "You don't have to come upstairs, Gerhard. I'll pack your things, too." She gave me a quick kiss and I listened to her steps as her bare feet pattered on the stone slabs of the stairs. The floorboards upstairs creaked.

Tyberg cleared his throat. He stood behind his chair, his shoulders drooping, his arms resting on the chair back. "At our age we don't get to know and treasure that many people that we can afford to lose them. Please don't leave now."

"I'm not leaving in anger, and I'd be happy to come back another time. But Leo and I—we really belong in a hotel."

"Let me have a word with her." He left the room and returned a little while later with Leo. She looked at me questioningly again and I smiled at her questioningly. She shrugged her shoulders.

We spent the evening on the terrace. Tyberg read to us from his memoirs, and Leo found out how his and my paths had crossed during the war. The candle, by the light of which Tyberg was reading, flickered. I could not interpret the expression in Leo's eyes. At times bats rustled over our heads.

They flew toward the house, and right before the wall their flight veered off abruptly into the emptiness of the night.

The following morning I was alone. Leo's things were no longer in the room. I looked in vain for a note. It was only later that I found one in my wallet in place of the four hundred francs I had changed in Murten. "I need the money. You'll get it back. Leo."

PART TWO

I

A *final favor*

I set out on my homeward journey with a hangover. The three days of sun, wind, and having Leo beside me had gone to my head.

I closed the book of my journey with Leo and put it away. It was at any rate only a thin little book. I had met her Tuesday morning in Amorbach, and by Friday evening I was back in Mannheim, though I felt I had been away for weeks. The traffic, the jostling pedestrians, the din of construction all around, the big, bleak palace in which there's supposed to be a university, the renovated Water Tower that looks as peculiar as Frau Weiland from next door when she comes back from the hairdresser, my apartment with its smell of stale smoke— what was I doing here? Wouldn't I have done better to head from Locarno down to Palermo, even without Leo, and swim from Sicily to Egypt? Should I get back in my car?

I quickly read through the newspapers that had piled up during my absence. They reported a terrorist attack on an American military installation, Leo's hiding in the State Psychiatric Hospital and the part Wendt had played in it, and an account of Wendt's life and death. There was nothing that I didn't already know. The Saturday edition reported that Eberlein had been temporarily suspended and that someone from the ministry had provisionally assumed his duties. I took note of that. I also took note of the fact that I had disappointed Brigitte.

A wanted poster with Leo's face on it had been put up at the post office, just as she had predicted. Ever since wanted posters, which I only knew from Westerns, had been reintroduced with the rise in terrorism, I have been expecting some roughneck with clanging spurs to come marching into the post office with a saddle bag slung over his shoulder and a Colt at his hip, stop in front of the poster, eye it, snatch it off the wall, roll it up, and put it in his bag. As the door falls shut behind him the dumbfounded customers hurry to the window to watch him swing himself up onto his horse and go galloping down the Seckenheimer Strasse. This time, too, I waited in vain. Instead, I came up with a few questions and answers. If the two dead men had belonged to the terrorist group, how did the police know that they had to search for Leo? For them to know about Leo, they had to have caught one of the terrorists and made him talk. And then, how come the police knew about Leo but not about the other members of the group? They must have caught one of them, and only one: the guy who Leo said had just come back from Tuscany, Bertram. He could have provided the police with only vague descriptions of Lemke and the fifth man, which was why the police had not managed to come up with particularly good composites. The other guy, Giselher, had to be dead.

But what really preoccupied me that weekend was my wanderlust and homesickness. Wanderlust is the longing for a new country that we don't yet know, and homesickness is a longing for an old country that we no longer know, even if we think we do. Why did I have this longing for the unknown? What did I want—to leave or to return? I puzzled over these thoughts until a toothache suddenly drove the nonsense away. It started Saturday evening with a slight twinge during the late movie, just as Doc Holliday rode out from Fort Griffin to Tombstone. By the end of the broadcast, as the camera passed above and beyond Helgoland, the pain, to the sound of the national anthem, was pulsating all the way up to my temples and my left ear. When the picture faded out at Helgoland's eastern tip with its crumbling tooth-shaped rock, I felt utterly demoralized. If only we could trade in Helgoland for Zanzibar again!

I haven't been to a dentist since my old one died ten years ago. I looked in the phone book and chose one two blocks away. The pain kept me awake all night. At seven thirty I started calling the dentist every five minutes. At eight on the dot a woman's cool voice answered. "Ah, Herr Self? Is your tooth bothering you again? Would you like to drop by now? We've just had a cancellation." I went over right away. The cool voice belonged to a cool blonde with flawless teeth. She sent me in right away, though I was not the same Herr Self who was already a patient there. I hadn't been aware that there was another Herr Self in the area. From what I know of our family tree, I'm the last twig to have sprouted.

The dentist was young, with a sure eye and a calm hand. The dreadful moment when the syringe approaches, fills your field of vision, and disappears because it has entered the oral cavity in search of a place to puncture, then the wait for the puncture, and finally the puncture itself—the doctor was so quick that I barely suffered. He managed to keep me calm, do his job, and flirt with his assistant. He explained to me that he wasn't sure if he could save tooth three-seven. It was deeply decayed. But he'd give it a try. He would remove most of the cavities, apply Calaxyl, seal it with Cavit, and put in a temporary bridge. A few weeks would show if tooth three-seven would hold. Was that all right?

"What are my options?"

"I could extract the tooth right away."

"And then?"

"Then we wouldn't opt for a permanent bridge, but we'd do something removable for three-five to three-seven."

"Do you mean I would be getting dentures?"

"Don't worry, not a full denture, just a removable prosthesis for the rear of the third quadrant."

But he could not deny that the prosthesis was meant to be put in and taken out, and was to remain overnight in a glass, where I would find it waiting for me in the morning. I quickly consented to any and all measures necessary to save tooth three-seven. Any and all measures.

I saw a movie once in which a man hanged himself because he was about to get dentures. Or had it been an accident? He had wanted to hang himself, but then as he was dangling there changed his mind but couldn't do anything because the dog had pushed over the chair on which he had been standing with the noose around his neck.

Would Turbo render me this final favor?

2

What insanity!

I went to Nägelsbach's office. He didn't ask me why I came only now, or where I'd been. He took down my statement. He already knew that I had passed myself off to Frau Klein-schmidt as Wendt's father. He also knew that she had let me into his apartment, thinking I was his father. But he didn't reproach me for that. I found out from him that the police were still completely in the dark about what Wendt's death meant.

"When is the funeral?"

"Friday, at the cemetery in Edingen. Wendt's parents live there. Remember the commercial back in the fifties? 'Want a house that's nice and new? Wendt will make your dreams come true!' Old Wendt used to have a small office in the arcade at the Bismarckplatz. Now it's grown into a big agency, with offices in Heidelberg, Schriesheim, Mannheim, and God knows where else."

I was already at the door when Nägelsbach touched on Leo. "Did you know that Frau Salger was hiding in Amorbach?"

"Have you arrested her there?"

He looked at me carefully. "No, she was already gone by the time one of the neighbors who'd seen her mug shot on TV called us. That's the way of the world—mug shots are also seen by the people you're looking for."

"Why weren't you able to tell me the other day why you had a search out for Frau Salger?"

"I'm sorry, I can't tell you that now either."

"The media says it's all about a terrorist attack on an American military installation—was that around here?"

"It had to have been in Käfertal or in Vogelstang. But we don't have anything to do with that."

"What about the Federal Criminal Investigation Agency?"

"What about it?"

"Has it been brought into the case?"

Nägelsbach shrugged his shoulders. "One way or another, the Agency's always involved in such cases."

What I was interested in was *how* the Agency was involved in all this, but I could see from his expression that there was no point in asking any more questions. "By the way, do you remember an attack on the army recruiting office in the Bunsenstrasse about six years ago?"

He thought for a while, and then shook his head. "No, there wasn't any attack in the Bunsenstrasse—not six years ago, nor at any other time. What's that all about?"

"Somebody mentioned it the other day, and I couldn't remember there having been such an attack either, though I wasn't as sure as you seem to be."

He was waiting for me to continue, but now it was my turn to stall. Our interaction had become extremely wary. I asked him about his work on Rodin's *Kiss*, but he didn't want to talk about that either. When I asked him to give my regards to his wife, he nodded. So the creative and marriage crises were continuing. When I was young, I thought that the worst was over once you made it through high school, then it became university finals, the first day at work, the wedding ceremony, and last of all, widowerhood. But things never get any easier.

Old Herr Wendt ruled his real-estate empire from an office in Heidelberg's Mengler-Bau. While I sat waiting in the reception area I watched the bulldozers digging up the Adenauer-platz yet again. On a big empty desk stood a small yellow bulldozer, a matching crane, and a small blue truck and trailer.

Wendt's executive secretary turned out to be more of an executive than a secretary. She was running the business until further notice. Herr Wendt had also entrusted her with the handling of his personal affairs, so could I please tell her how she might help me? Frau Büchler stood facing me, coolly toying with my business card. Gray hair, gray eyes, gray outfit—but she was no gray mouse. Her face was practically wrinkle free and her voice was young, as though a wily Brazilian cosmetic surgeon had lifted her vocal cords as well as her face. She moved as if today she owned the office, and tomorrow the world.

I informed her of my dealings with Dr. Rolf Wendt, of our last conversation, our scheduled meeting, and how I had gone looking for him and found him. I hinted at the connection between Wendt's death and the current investigation into Leonore Salger and told her how, in my view, these ought to be looked into. "Perhaps that is what the police are doing. But the way they're handling things seems suspicious. First they didn't want to say why they're looking for Frau Salger, and then they went on the air and publicly announced their hunt for terrorists, and as for Rolf Wendt's death: They either know more than they're saying, or less than they ought to know. Solving the Wendt case can't be left entirely up to the police. This is why I'm here. I want to take on the case. I stumbled into this case by chance, and now it won't leave me in peace. But I can't continue working on it at my own expense."

Frau Büchler showed me over to the lounge, and I sat down in a bulky construction of steel and leather. "If you work on this case, I assume you will want to talk to Herr and Frau Wendt, am I right? And you'll be asking them quite a few questions?"

I replied with a vague wave of the hand.

She shook her head. "It's not a question of money. In his own way, Herr Wendt has always been generous with his money, and now he has lost all interest in it. He intended it all for Rolf. Their relationship was not good, otherwise Rolf would not have lived in that hole—with a father with Herr Wendt's resources! But Herr Wendt had not given up hope. In the past, he had hoped that Rolf would join the family business and run it one day, but then later Herr Wendt hoped that Rolf might want to have his own psychiatric hospital. Herr Wendt would see to the construction of the hospital and its administration. This almost became an *idée fixe* with him. Time and again over the past few years we looked for old hospitals, schools, barracks, just for his son. Once we even bought some riding stables in the Palatinate because Herr Wendt felt they would be ideal for converting into an insane asylum. What insanity! Can you imagine? Throwing good money at some ramshackle stables, just like that? I'm only glad that we . . ." She smiled at me. "As you can see, Herr

Self, for me real estate is the be-all and end-all. But enough of that. If you are hired for this case, you must promise that, for a while at least, you will not disturb Herr or Frau Wendt. If you are hired, you would report to me. What do you say?"

I nodded. She sat with her legs neatly and symmetrically together, like a model in a fashion magazine. Her hands were clasped quietly, only to start up sometimes unexpectedly in a brisk gesture. This gave her an air of competence and authority. I decided to try that myself at the earliest opportunity.

She rose. "Thank you for dropping by. You will hear from us."

3

A *bit flat*

By that evening I had the case.

This time I didn't have to worry about ruffling anybody's circle of friends and could go at it no holds barred: Wendt's friends and girlfriends, his colleagues, his acquaintances, his landlady, his sports club, his local bar, his garage. I tracked down the young woman I'd seen him with at the Sole d'Oro, the friend from university with whom he'd traveled to Brazil, Argentina, and Chile, and his card-playing pals: an unemployed teacher, a tomato-fetishizing artist, and a violinist from the Heidelberg Symphony Orchestra. I also dropped in at the Eppelheim Squash Courts, where he was a regular. Everyone expressed their dismay at Wendt's death. But the dismay was not so much about Wendt's having died as the fact that somebody they knew had been murdered. Murder was something that only existed in papers and on TV! Rolf, of all people! He got on so well with everyone, he was so well-regarded!

The violinist was the third person who told me that.

"Well-regarded? Why 'well-regarded' and not 'liked'?"

She eyed her strong hands with their short nails. "We were together for a while, but somehow there wasn't much of a spark. You know what I mean?"

According to the young woman from the Sole d'Oro, there hadn't been much of a spark with her either. She worked at the Deutsche Bank where Wendt had an account. He'd approached her and asked her out. "He was utterly dependable, as dependable with his account as with our dates."

"That sounds a bit flat."

"What can I say? We never really hit it off. At first I thought he was a bit standoffish and didn't want me to get too close, because he went to university and had a doctorate, and me with my banking traineeship. But that wasn't it. He just couldn't break out of himself. I waited and waited, but nothing happened. Maybe there wasn't anything there. You'd think that there'd be more there when someone's a shrink, but I guess why should there be? I mean, I'm in banking and it's not like I've got any money."

I'd caught her on her lunch break, and she stood in front of me in her business outfit with her perfect hairdo and discreet makeup. Very appropriate for a young employee in a big German bank. But there was more to her than money and percentages. Rolf Wendt, who couldn't break out of himself, whom one is seriously interested in for a while, with whom one wonders at first if one did something wrong, and then if something's wrong with him—the others had not seen him or defined him as clearly as she did. And it wasn't a matter of his being reserved with women. His squash instructor said more or less the same thing: "He was a doctor? See, I didn't even know that. A good player, though, and I wanted to get him into sets with others. We've got a good club thing going with our squash courts, even though they're new." He eyed me. "You could do with some exercise. Anyway, Wendt always kept to himself. He was a nice guy, but he always kept to himself."

Frau Kleinschmidt didn't hold it against me that I wasn't Herr Wendt. "So you're a detective? Like Hercule Parrot?" She asked me in and put the kettle on. We sat in her kitchen, which had a corner bench, a cupboard, and a linoleum floor. The washing machine and the stove were brand-new. The drapes, the curtains in the glass doors of the cupboard, the oilcloth on the table, and the decals on the refrigerator all had Delft tile patterns.

"Are you in any way connected with Holland?" I asked.

"You saw the tulips in the garden and put two and two together!" She beamed at me with admiration. "My first husband was from there. Willem. He was a driver, a trucker, and when he had the Rotterdam route he always brought back the bulbs. Because he knew I liked flowers. He had connections, you see, and didn't have to pay for the bulbs. Otherwise we'd never have been able to afford all those flowers, what with the kids. Now that they're grown up, my second husband brings them from town—the bulbs, I mean."

"Your children have left home?"

"Yes." She sighed. The water whistled in the kettle and she poured it through the coffee filter.

"You must have been happy to get a nice young tenant."

"I was. We didn't ask for too much rent, because I said to my husband, 'Günther,' I said, 'the young doctor is in the psychiatric hospital. The only people who end up there are poor devils. The rich who pay their own doctors big money end up in other places.' But things didn't really go the way I hoped.

The young doctor was nice and polite, always said hello and asked how we were, but he never came in and sat down. He never came by for dinner, or to see us on a Sunday. Even after he spent the whole day studying. When I was out in my garden, you know, I could see him at his desk with his books."

"What about friends, or girlfriends?"

Frau Kleinschmidt shook her head. "We wouldn't have minded if he'd brought in a girl from time to time—we're not like that. And we've got nothing against friends either. But I guess he was a loner."

That was all she had to say. There were no unusual contacts, no unusual activities. A picture-perfect tenant. I had shown Frau Kleinschmidt Leo's picture before, but showed it to her again. I also showed her a picture of Helmut Lemke. She didn't recognize either of them.

"Have the police sealed Wendt's apartment?"

"Do you want to take another look?" She got up and took a key off a hook on the wall. "We can get in through the boiler room. The police said we can't go in through the front door until the investigation is over. We're not allowed to break the seal on the lock."

I followed her down the cellar steps, through the boiler room, and through the broom closet into Wendt's apartment. The police had done a thorough job in turning the place upside down. What they hadn't found I wouldn't find either.

The days passed. I did my job by the book, but wasn't really getting anywhere. I'd have liked to talk to Eberlein, but he was out of town. I'd also have liked to talk to Wendt's sister. She was living in Hamburg and, like her brother, didn't have a phone. Frau Büchler wasn't sure if the sister intended to come to the funeral. There had been some tension between her and her father, and also between her and her brother. I sent Dorle Mähler, née Wendt, a letter.

I also got a call from my old journalist friend Tietzke. "Thanks for having tipped me off the other day."

"For having tipped you off?"

But no sooner had I spoken the words than I knew what he was talking about. How could I have missed that! On the day of Wendt's murder, Tietzke had appeared on the scene at the same time as the patrol car and the ambulance. Only I could have tipped him off that fast. Or the murderer.

4

Peschkalek's nose

I saw everyone again at the funeral: Inspector Nägelsbach, Wendt's university friend, the card-playing pals, the woman from the Deutsche Bank, the instructor from the squash courts in Eppelheim, Frau Kleinschmidt, and Frau Büchler. Only Eberlein was missing. I came early, sat down in the back row, and watched the small chapel fill up slowly. Then some sixty people came in all at once. Their whispering gave away that old Herr Wendt had closed his offices and ordered his workforce to attend the funeral. He himself came late, a large, heavy man with a stony face. The woman on his arm was wearing a heavy black veil. As the organ began to play, Peschkalek darted into the empty seat next to me. During the first hymn he nimbly changed the film in his small camera. "Jerusalem! High tower thy glorious walls!" Despite this oblique allusion to real estate and Frau Büchler's stern glances, Wendt's employees did not join in wholeheartedly. The singing was sparse.

Peschkalek nudged me. "What are *you* doing here?"

"I could ask you the same thing."

"Then I guess we're both doing the same thing."

After the priest, a senior doctor from the psychiatric hospital spoke. He talked about his young colleague with respect and warmth, about his care for the patients, and about his dedication to research. Then the squash instructor from Eppelheim stepped forward and praised Rolf Wendt as having been the heart and soul of the squash courts. We were singing the final hymn when the door opened a crack and a young woman entered. She hesitated, looked around, and then marched determinedly up to the first row and stood next to Frau Wendt. Rolf's sister?

At the grave I stood a ways to the side. Nägelsbach, too, decided to keep his distance so he could observe everyone carefully. Peschkalek circled the mourners in a wide arc, taking pictures. When the last of Herr Wendt's employees had thrown their spadeful of earth into the grave, the mourners all made a quick getaway. I heard the motor start up on one of those small power shovels that today's gravediggers use to make their jobs easier for themselves.

Peschkalek came and stood next to me. "That's that, I guess."

"I was just thinking the same thing."

"You knew Wendt personally?"

"Yes." I saw no reason not to tell him. "His father has commissioned me to investigate."

"Then we really are on the same track. Not that I'm investigating for his father—I'm investigating for myself. But you and I are aiming to get to the bottom of this. Want to grab some lunch? You can leave your car here; I'll bring you back afterward."

We drove over to Ladenburg. In Zwiwwel they were

serving chervil soup followed by lamb with potatoes au gratin. Peschkalek had the waiter bring us a bottle of Forster Blauer Portugieser. For dessert we had fresh strawberries. Needless to say, I wanted to know why Peschkalek was investigating, what he was looking for, and what, if anything, he had managed to unearth. But I was in no hurry. Again our get-together was short and pleasant. He told me of his travels as a photojournalist all over Europe, America, Africa, and Asia, and quite nonchalantly touched on a colorful hodge-podge of wars, conferences, artwork, crime, famines, and celebrity weddings that he had covered. I was amazed. Wanderlust or no, I was happy enough to be the provincial that I am. Much as I like to head off to faraway places, my travels have been pretty much limited to a short trip to America, a few Aegean jaunts on a yacht with an old Greek girlfriend from my student days, and a few trips to Rimini, Carinthia, and Langeoog with Klara. I don't think I want to see a civil war, regardless of how photogenic it is, or Elizabeth Taylor marrying Boris Becker with the Taj Mahal as backdrop.

Over an espresso and a sambuca, his pipe and my cigarette lit, Peschkalek began of his own accord: "I bet you're wondering what I'm doing photographing all these things to do with Wendt. I'm not sure yet. But I have a nose for hot stories. And when there's a hot story somewhere, I take hot pictures. It's not the text that's the issue. If push comes to shove I even throw something together myself. Probing—that's what counts, and probing means photographing. If it isn't in the camera, it doesn't exist. Do you know what I mean?"

He had expounded his journalistic credo with passion, and I was happy to nod my assent.

"What did your nose get wind of?" I asked.

He reached into the inside pocket of his denim jacket and took out a piece of paper. "All you have to do is put two and two together. A week ago yesterday, Wendt was murdered. He had hidden a young terrorist, Leonore Salger, in the State Psychiatric Hospital. The police are looking for this terrorist because of an attack on an American military installation. The official search is initiated on the evening of the murder— Monday evening I saw it on TV, and Tuesday morning I read it in the papers. You're not going to tell me that's a coincidence, are you? Did Leonore Salger kill him? Or someone from the CIA, FBI, or DEA? Since the *Achille Lauro* incident, the Americans aren't too pleased about attacks on their installations or people of theirs being taken hostage or murdered. They retaliate. And from what I hear, there were some casualties during the attack on their installation."

I pointed at the piece of paper in his hand. "What's that?"

"Now we're getting to the mystery. I'm not sure how carefully you've been following things. So the police aren't saying anything about the circumstances of Wendt's death or about motives and suspects? Fine, I can understand that. I guess they don't know enough. But can you explain why not a word has been said about the exact time or place of the terrorist attack, or how the attack was perpetrated, and what came of it all? There's been nothing specific, not a single specific thing! Not on TV and not in the papers. I even went so far as to take a look at some of the old articles about Baader, Meinhof, and Schleyer. What they wrote back then was often wishy-washy, but still more precise than what we're reading and hearing now. Do you see what I'm saying?"

"I certainly do. And it's not just the media. The police, too, are pussyfooting more than they usually do."

"I said to myself, something's got to be wrong. You can't trumpet an attack like that to all the world on one hand, and keep your lips tightly sealed on the other. If such an attack had passed unnoticed . . . But I can't imagine that either. Perhaps people just didn't realize what was going on. But somebody must have noticed that something happened. And then that somebody wouldn't have kept it to himself. But I can't cover the whole area questioning everyone and his mother. However, I did look through all the newspapers, the local news. The *Mannheimer Morgen*, the *Rhein-Neckar-Zeitung*, the *Rheinpfalz*, and all their offshoots. I sifted through the local items, looking for something like, 'Last night Mr. L, a farmer, was shaken out of deep sleep by a blast that shattered the windows and rattled the plates in the cupboards. The incident remains a mystery . . .' Do you know what I mean?"

"Did you come up with anything?"

With a broad, proud smile he handed me the paper. Over the article he had written "*Viernheimer Tageblatt*" and a date in March.

"Go on, read it."

Explosions at the Munitions Depot?

"Have there been any explosions in the past few years at the American Forces Munitions Depot near Viernheim? Why has the guard detail for the last few months been issued special protective clothing?"

In the District Council yesterday, the Green Party put this question to the council chief, Dr. S. Kannenguth, in his function as the head of the Emergency Management Agency of the

Bergstrasse District. The speaker of the Green Party, J. Altmann, did not clarify the background of the question.

As was to be expected, the council chief could not provide an immediate reply, but promised an investigation and an official written response by the next session.

In fact, in January of this year, I happened to be driving through the woods one evening when I observed the glow of a fire above the munitions depot. The Viernheim police at the depot gates were not authorized to provide me with any information, and repeated queries to the press office of the American Forces have remained unanswered.

H. Walters

5

Gas needn't stink

I read the piece twice. And then a third time. Was I missing something? Was I slow on the uptake? The attack had taken place in January at a munitions depot near Viernheim, and had caught the attention of Walters. I could not gather more from the article than a confirmation of Leo's account. Peschkalek couldn't even do that. What did he find so exciting about it?

I kept to the matter at hand. "What were the district council chief's findings?"

"What do you think? Inquiries made to both German and American agencies indicated no explosions at the munitions depot. As for the guards at the depot, they're periodically issued protective clothing for training purposes. The safety of the people of Viernheim has at no time been compromised through activities at the munitions depot."

"Did you speak to Altmann? Or to Walters?"

"It was Altmann who provided me with the district chief's reply. Otherwise, he was a bit of a disappointment." Peschkalek grinned at me. "And I admit I'm a bit of a disappointment as a pipe smoker. I think I'd rather go for one of your cigarettes." He put away his pipe, which hadn't lit despite his desperate attempts, reached for my yellow pack of Sweet Aftons, and began smoking with relish. "Altmann doesn't have any insider information worth mentioning. Everything he knows comes from Walters. But what Walters happened to see that night was all Altmann needed to take a little swipe at the district council chief. I don't know if Walters knows more. I didn't manage to catch him yesterday." Peschkalek looked at his watch, out the window, and then at me. "What if we head over to Viernheim and have a chat with him? He should be in his office now."

It was three thirty already. I would rather have sent myself and the alcoholized lamb in my stomach for a nice long siesta.

As we drove through Heddesheim to Viernheim, I remembered an old case of mine, the Viernheim denominational wars. An altar painting of Saint Catherine had disappeared from the Catholic church, and the chaplain, suspecting the Protestants, fulminated from his pulpit against thieving heretics. The Evangelical church was sprayed with graffiti, then the Catholic church, then church windows were broken. That was all a long, long time ago. A presbyter with an ecumenical bent had hired me to get the painting back. I found it in the room of the chaplain's pubescent altar server, who happened to be a fan of the actress Michelle Pfeiffer. And Michelle Pfeiffer happened to be the spitting image of Saint Catherine.

Walters studied engineering in Darmstadt but had been born and raised in Viernheim and had deep roots there. He was a member of the male choir, the carnival association, the chess club, the shooting club, and the marching band. "That makes me the ideal local reporter, wouldn't you say? I'm not partial to any political group. I was happy to give Altmann the information about the munitions depot, but I'd just as readily tip off the CDU about the planned collectivization of the Rhein-Neckar Center, or the SPD about child labor at the Willi Jung company. That's how I work. So you read the little piece I wrote about the question Altmann put to the District Council—and I take it you want to know more, right? Well, I'd like to know more myself." His office was tiny. There was barely enough space for a desk, a swivel chair, and an extra chair for visitors. Walters had offered me the chair and Peschkalek a corner of his desk. The narrow window looked out on the Rathausstrasse. "Unfortunately I can't get it to open, so I'd be grateful if you didn't smoke."

Peschkalek put away his pipe and sighed as if he were forfeiting a true pleasure and not just another of his futile battles with tobacco, matches, and pipe paraphernalia. "Journalists never know enough," Peschkalek said. "We're all in the same boat, regardless of whether we're working for *Spiegel*, *Paris Match*, *The New York Times*, or the *Viernheimer Tageblatt*. I liked your article. It pinpoints the problem, it's written in a clean style, and you appeal to the reader by the fresh and direct way you introduce yourself into the article. One can see right away that the writer has solid background information and knowledge of the area. I'm impressed, Herr Walters."

At first I thought Peschkalek was laying it on too thick, but I was quick to see that Walters was lapping it all up. He leaned back in his swivel chair. "I like the way you put it. I see what I do as grassroots journalism, and myself as a grassroots journalist. I'd be happy to write an article for your paper about the situation here in Viernheim. You're with *Spiegel*, did you say? Or was it *Paris Match* or *The New York Times?* If I'm to do something in English or French for you, somebody will have to go over it and clean it up."

"I'll definitely keep you in mind. If Viernheim becomes a story, I could see to it that you get a column or a box in the coverage. But is Viernheim a story? A glow in the night is not necessarily a catastrophe. When did that actually happen?"

Peschkalek had roped him in. We found out that Walters had been driving from Hüttenfeld, where his girlfriend lived, to Viernheim at around midnight on January 6, when he saw three police cars in front of the gate to the munitions depot. He asked the officers what was going on but was brushed off. He drove on and saw the glow of a fire above the depot. "I didn't actually see the fire. But hey, my interest had been roused. So right away I headed onto the autobahn and took the turnoff to Lorsch. The depot is between Route 6 and the L 3111. But the glow was gone."

"That's all?" Peschkalek was disappointed and didn't hide it.

"I stopped, got out of the car, and sniffed the air. Later I sniffed it again, as I drove through the Lampertheim Forest. You see, I had to stay on the autobahn all the way to Lorsch, where I took a back road and returned to Viernheim by way of Hüttenfeld. I couldn't smell anything. But what I've found out is that poison gas doesn't necessarily stink."

"Poison gas?" Peschkalek and I burst out simultaneously.

"The rumor's been going around for years. Fischbach, Hanau, and Viernheim—after the war, the Americans are supposed to have set up depots there. Some people even say that the Germans stored and buried their poison gas there. Word has it that everything's been removed from Fischbach, and perhaps from Viernheim, too. Or that there was never anything there. Or that it's still there, and that all the commotion about its being removed from Fischbach was only a diversion from the poison gas stored in Viernheim. Be that as it may, I developed an interest in all of this after January sixth." He shook his head. "A real devil's brew. Phosgene, tabun, sarin, VE, VX—have you read up on what that stuff can do? Even when you read about that stuff, it's enough to turn your stomach."

"Were the police cars still at the gate?"

"No. But an American fire truck came out and drove away."

Peschkalek sat up. "Where did it go? And how come you didn't put that in your article?"

"I was going to disclose things bit by bit. But then my editor didn't think the fire truck was exciting enough to warrant a sequel. The truck had headed down the Nibelungenstrasse and the Entlastungsstrasse, I think over to the American barracks."

We thanked him. When we came out of Walters's cell, Peschkalek was ebullient. "What did I tell you? It's even better than I thought! The attack wasn't on any old American military installation, but specifically on an American poison-gas depot. You can bet your life that the Americans wouldn't turn a blind eye on such an attack. I wonder if Wendt orchestrated it all, and then had to pay for it with his life? Or did the Americans buy him off? Did he switch sides, and Leonore Salger assassinated him? Mark my word, Wendt wasn't murdered just like that."

6

A *summer idyll*

Nobody gets murdered just like that. The map in Wendt's briefcase showed the Viernheim triangle. When I stopped in front of the big map on the wall of the editorial office I recognized the Frankfurt-Mannheim autobahn and, leading straight down from it, the autobahn to Kaiserslautern.

Peschkalek stopped, too. "What's our next step, Herr Self? Shall we go take a look for ourselves?"

We drove along the Lorsch Road through the woods. A high fence ran alongside the road to our left, and just beyond it ran an asphalt path. Signs in German and English warned of explosives, of military and security patrols, of watchdogs, and that firearms were in use. The gate, which we passed half a kilometer down the road, was secured with iron bars and orange and blue warning lights and was plastered with signs that along with all the other warnings also cautioned against smoking. Then the fence veered to the left, and the road continued straight on. At the next left we made a big detour back to Viernheim, over and under the autobahn, but we no longer saw the fence.

"You ought to have a word with some of the local people, Herr Self." Peschkalek had not said much during our reconnaissance, but he became talkative once we reached Viernheim. "Poison gas. You heard it yourself. You'd think it would worry the people around here. But it doesn't. What surprises me is that our wild young reporter"—he pointed in the direction where he imagined the offices of the *Viernheimer Tageblatt* to be—"even managed to get his little article printed. Nobody here wants to read that kind of stuff." He headed along the road to Heddesheim, but soon took a right. "Just one more small detour, Herr Self."

We drove past long rows of fruit trees and rapeseed fields beneath a blue sky. In the distance mountains rose and quarries shone. A water tower and a small church with a roof turret appeared before us, surrounded by a few farms, cottages, and old meadows—the perfect summer idyll.

"Have you ever been to Strassenheim?" Peschkalek asked me. I nodded. He drove slowly. "You're wondering why I brought you here? Take a good look."

I was struck by the stately building next to the church. According to a sign, it housed the mounted detachment and the canine unit of the Mannheim police headquarters. "No, take a good look. There, that truck to the left, and those two to the right. Do you know what they are? They're tanker trucks, each carrying thousands of liters of water. Water for drinking and cooking, and also for the animals. Why do you think these trucks are here? Well?" He enjoyed the suspense. "It looks like the regular water isn't drinkable, wouldn't you say? I suppose that though Strassenheim belongs to Mannheim, it is not connected to Mannheim's water supply, nor to that of Viernheim or Heddesheim. Strassenheim must have its own wells. Can they have dried up? With all the rain we've had in the past few weeks? No, there's plenty of water around here, and the water looks perfectly clear. It might smell a little, but then again it might not. It might taste a little weird, but then again it might not. I'm not saying that you drop dead if you drink it. Perhaps you'll feel a bit queasy, or maybe even get sick as a dog; maybe you'll shit or retch your guts out."

Strassenheim lay behind us.

"How come you know all this?"

"I'm the kind of guy who puts two and two together. Know what I mean? The official agencies will never tell you anything, but here they're keeping such a low profile that that in itself is suspicious." He began driving faster again. "We're crossing the border of the Käfertal watershed area. The munitions depot lies in the outer perimeter. Viernheim junction, where the inner perimeter of the wells begins, is about two kilometers beyond Strassenheim. It's anybody's guess how the damn groundwater flows. Be that as it may, Strassenheim has had to bear the brunt of it." His right hand made a resigned wave, came clapping down onto his bald head, and then brushed back all the missing locks of hair. He chewed his mustache angrily, his teeth grinding.

I can't say that the sky looked any less blue or the rapeseed any less yellow. I've always had trouble believing in the existence of something I cannot see: God, Einstein's relativity, the harmfulness of smoking, the hole in the ozone. I was also skeptical because the munitions depot lay only a few kilometers away from the Benjamin-Franklin-Village in Käfertal, and I had a hard time imagining that the Americans would put their own people at risk. Not to mention that Viernheim lay closer to the depot than Strassenheim, and Viernheim's water supply didn't seem to have been affected. All things considered, had Peschkalek himself tasted the Strassenheim water, or had he sent it to be analyzed?

We were back in Edingen. As we drove down the Grenz-höfer Strasse, we saw Frau Büchler and Wendt's people coming out of the Grüner Baum Restaurant. The funeral meal had taken a long time. My old Opel was waiting in front of the cemetery.

"You and I have to talk this through at leisure," I said to Peschkalek.

He handed me his card. "Call me when you have a moment. You don't believe me, do you? You're thinking: These are the ravings of a reporter, this is journalistic gobbledygook. Well, let's pray that you're right."

7

Tragedy or farce?

Peschkalek's poisonous groundwater streams pursued me into my dreams, and I saw the small Strassenheim chapel grow into a cathedral, the gargoyles on its roof spitting green, yellow, and red water. By the time I realized that the cathedral was made of rubber, its walls bloating and distending, it was too late. It exploded, and revolting brown slime burst from it. I woke up as the slime was about to reach my feet, and I couldn't go back to sleep. During my conversation with Peschkalek I had not been frightened. Now I was.

My father's stories came back to me. Throughout the years I was at school, he hadn't said a word about his experiences in World War I. Some of my classmates bragged about their fathers' heroic deeds, and I would have liked to have done the same. I knew that mine had been wounded a number of times, that he had been decorated and promoted. I wanted to talk about that at school, to brag a little. But he didn't want me to. He only became talkative in the last few years of his life. Mother had died, his days had become lonely, and when I visited him he spoke about many things, and about the war.

Perhaps he also wanted to rid me of the idea that the Reich needed more lebensraum, even if it meant war.

He had been wounded three times. The first two times decently, as he put it, by a grenade splinter near Ypers and by a bayonet near Peronne. The third time, his company suffered a gas attack at Verdun. "Mustard gas. It's not a stinking, yellowish-green cloud, like chlorine gas, which you can see and so protect yourself against. Mustard gas is devious. You don't see it and you don't smell it. If you didn't see a comrade grab at his throat or didn't have a sixth sense and quickly slip on your gas mask, then that was it, in the blink of an eye." My father had had a sixth sense and survived, while most of the men in his company had died. But he had gotten a big enough dose of gas to suffer for months. "The fever went. But that dizziness, even when you weren't moving, and all the retching, retching, retching . . . and then, mustard gas burns out the eyes. That was the worst part, the fear that it had got you in such a way that you'd never be able to see again."

I heard the story of the gas attack more than once. Every time my father spoke about putting on the gas mask, he closed his eyes and covered his face with his hand, until he came to the part where he was released from the infirmary.

Had Leo known what her bonfire was capable of? Was that what she had wanted? Was that why she had accused and convicted herself so sternly? As for Lemke, I couldn't imagine that he didn't know what it was all about.

I was now fully awake. Terrorism in Germany. I had read somewhere that all major historical events happen twice, the first time as a tragedy, the second as a farce, and I had always seen the terrorism of the seventies and eighties, the commotion around it and the fight against it, as some kind of farce.

Now I had to ask myself if I had been wrong. Poison gas in the air, the water, and the ground was no farce. And there I was, driving with Leo through France and Switzerland as if the world were one long spring.

Now self-recrimination was added to my fear. Whichever way I lay in bed felt wrong. Whether my eyes were open or shut, my thoughts whirled in the same circle. They whirled crazily until the dawn broke, the birds sang, and I showered and was once again my conscious, rational, skeptical self.

8

It makes sense, doesn't it?

I had promised Brigitte and Manu that we would spend Saturday in Heidelberg. Shopping, some ice cream, the zoo, the castle—the works. We took a tram and got off at the Bismarckplatz.

I hadn't been there for a long time. Everything was purple: The tram stops, tram shelters, kiosks, benches, trash cans, lights. The purpleness was disturbed by a yellow mailbox and a pale bust of Bismarck.

"How do you like that! The women's movement has taken over the Bismarckplatz!"

Brigitte stopped. "You and your silly chauvinism. Füruzan is oppressing Philipp, I am oppressing you, and now women have occupied the Bismarckplatz and you, poor man that you are, no longer know—"

"Come on, Brigitte, I was only joking."

"Ha-ha-ha!" She walked off without beckoning me or Manu with a look or gesture to follow her, and I suddenly felt guilty, even though my conscience was clear. She marched into the Braun bookstore, and I waited outside. Should I have followed her to the Women's Studies section with suppliant eyes, drooping shoulders, and sensitive questions? Manu stayed outside with Nonni and me.

We watched the heavy traffic on the Sophienstrasse. "Where do they come out?" Manu asked, pointing at the cars disappearing down the entrance to the underground garage on the Sophienstrasse.

"Somewhere behind these trees, I think."

"Can they come out where we parked the other day?"

I didn't understand what he meant. "But that was . . . Do you mean the underground garage behind the Heilig-Geist Church?"

"Yes, that's how it is sometimes, isn't it?" Manu said. "I mean, you come up somewhere different from where you disappeared. It would be great if you could go under the earth from one underground garage to another whenever all the parking spaces are full or if there's a traffic jam. It makes sense, doesn't it?" He looked at me as if I were a little slow and launched into an intricate explanation.

I stopped listening. His vision of an underground flow of traffic took me back to Peschkalek's poisonous groundwater streams.

"You're not even listening!"

Brigitte came out of the bookstore. I bought her a skirt that flared out, and she bought me a pair of shorts in which I looked like a Brit on the River Kwai. Manu wanted a pair of jeans—not any old jeans, a specific brand—and we went all the way up the main street to the Heilig-Geist Church. I find the tide of strolling consumers in pedestrian areas no more agreeable, either aesthetically or morally, than comrades on parade or soldiers on the march. But I have grave doubts that

I will live to see Heidelberg's main street once again filled with cheerfully ringing trams, cars honking happily, and related, bustling people hurrying to places where they have something to do, and not simply to places where there's something to see, something to nibble at, or something to buy.

"Let's give the castle a miss," I said, and Brigitte and Manu stared at me, crestfallen. "Let's forget about the zoo, too."

"But you said we—"

"I have a much better idea. We'll go flying."

I didn't have to suggest it twice. We took a tram back to Mannheim and got out at the Neuostheim airfield. A small tower, a small office, a small runway, and small airplanes— Manu had seen bigger and better things on his flight from Rio de Janeiro to Frankfurt. But he was enraptured. I signed up for a half-hour flight. The pilot who was to take us up got his one-propeller four-seater ready for takeoff. We went rattling down the runway and rose into the air.

Mannheim lay beneath us like a toy town, neat and dapper. It would have been wonderful for the elector who had ordered the squares to be laid out centuries ago to see his city from this perspective. The Rhine and the Neckar glittered in the sun, the stacks of the Rhineland Chemical Works sent little white clouds puffing into the sky, and the fountains by the Water Tower danced in their basins. Manu was quick to spot the Luisenpark, the Kurpfalz Bridge, and the Collini Center where Brigitte has her massage practice. The friendly pilot flew an extra arc until Manu managed to spot his house in the Max-Joseph-Strasse.

"Could we swing over to Viernheim?"

"Is that where you live?" the pilot asked me.

"I used to."

Brigitte's interest was piqued. "When did you live in Viernheim?" she asked me. "I didn't know that."

"After the war. For a while, that is."

Beneath us were the blocks of the Benjamin-Franklin-Village. The golf course, the autobahn junction, the Rhein-Neckar Center, the narrow, crooked streets surrounding the town hall and churches. We had reached the last houses of Viernheim, and the pilot swung to the right.

I pointed left. "I'd rather fly back over the forest than over Heddesheim."

"In that case, we'll have to climb quite a bit higher."

"Why's that?"

He flew toward Weinheim and began to pick up altitude. "It's the Americans. They have a camp in the forest. There's no taking pictures either."

"What will happen if we don't climb higher? Will they shoot us down?"

"No idea. What is it you want to see?"

"To tell you the truth, it's the camp I want to see. Back in 1945, it was a prisoner-of-war camp—that's how I got to know the forest."

"Ah, old memories. Let's see what we can do." He swung to the left without rising any higher, but picked up speed.

I couldn't spot the fence, but I saw the grass-covered bunkers, some on the open field, others hidden among trees. I saw the connecting asphalt paths and the clearings in which trucks or trailers in camouflage paint were parked close to one another. An area farther on was practically without vegetation and had been flattened by truck or tank tracks.

Then, not far from the autobahn, I saw bulldozers, conveyer belts, and trucks at work. Dirt had been dug up over a surface the size of a tennis court. I could not tell how far down they had dug, or if something was being buried or dug up. It was surrounded by woods, but at one end of the tennis court the trees were black, charred skeletons. There had been a fire.

9

Old hat

"You weren't really in Viernheim at that camp, were you? You never mentioned it before," Brigitte said when Manu was already in bed and we were sitting like an old married couple on the couch in front of the TV.

"No, I wasn't. It has to do with the case I'm working on."

"If you want some inside information about Viernheim, I have a girlfriend who lives there. Actually, she's a colleague, and you know how we masseuses find out everything, just like hairdressers and priests."

"That sounds great. Can you set up a meeting?"

"What would you do without me?"

Brigitte stood up, gave Lisa a call, and arranged for us to meet for coffee on Sunday.

"She's a single mother, too, and her daughter Sonya is the same age as Manu. We've been wanting to set up a play date for the two of them, and Lisa's been saying she wants to see what kind of a man I—"

"Have managed to bag?"

"Your words, not mine." Brigitte sat back down next to me. In the movie we were watching, an old man was in love with a young woman who loved him, too, but they gave each other up because he was old and she was young. "What a stupid movie," Brigitte said. "But we had such a great day today, didn't we?" She looked at me.

At first I was worried that a straightforward yes would again conjure up the question of marriage and children, and I had every intention of answering with a noncommittal grunt. Never say yes or no when the other person will make do with an mm. But then I did say yes, and Brigitte snuggled up to me, quiet and content.

At ten o'clock the following morning I was at the Church of the Resurrection in Viernheim. I tried in vain to remember the name of the presbyter who'd commissioned me to find Saint Catherine all those years ago. After the sermon and the chorale, he sent a collection box down the rows, recognized me, and nodded to me. The sermon had focused on the dangers of addiction, and the chorale on the willfulness of the flesh, and the collection was to go to rehabilitate drug addicts. I was prepared to drop my pack of Sweet Aftons into the collection box and give up smoking forever. But what would I have smoked after church?

"To what do we owe this pleasure, Herr Self?" I had waited for him in front of the church, and he came over to me right away. Behind us the tram drove past.

"I have some questions to which you might know the answers. Let me invite you for a round or two."

We went over to the Golden Lamb.

"Hello there, Weller! You're early today!" the pub keeper called out to the presbyter, and took us over to his regular table.

"We can have a nice quiet chat," Weller said. "The others won't be turning up till later." We ordered two glasses of house wine.

"I'm working on a murder case. There was a map in the victim's briefcase that showed the woods to the north of Viernheim, the Viernheim Meadows, and the Lampertheim National Forest. I don't think he was killed on account of the map—but maybe on account of the forest? I keep hearing things about that forest, and I keep reading things about it. I'm sure you know the article that appeared in the *Viernheimer Tageblatt* back in March."

He nodded. "That wasn't the only article, you know. There was one in *Spiegel* about poison gas in the forest, and in *Stern*, too. Never anything specific, just rumors. And you're hoping I'll tell you what's going on, am I right? Ah, Herr Self." He shook his gray head.

I remembered that he was an upholsterer by trade, and that back then he'd had his own upholstery business and was complaining that everyone was going to IKEA to buy their couches and chairs at a discount. They'd sit on them till they fell apart and then throw them out.

"Do you still have your upholstery business?"

"Yes, and things have picked up again. I have quite a few clients from Heidelberg and Mannheim now who are into upholstering their old furniture. Things they have from Grandma and Grandpa, or just antiques. But what do you want me to tell you about the forest? To be honest, I don't give it much thought. No point. I'm sure they see to it that nothing happens. It's not my place to tell them how to run their business—just as it's not their place to tell me how to run mine. If something *were* to happen, I mean, because technically something *could* happen, what am I supposed to do? Move away? Kiss my house and business good-bye, just because some muckrakers are dredging up mud in the papers?"

A stubby little man with an important air approached us, tapped the table twice with his fist, greeted us with a playful "Enjoy," and sat down.

"This is Herr Hasenklee," Weller told me, "our headmaster." Drawn into the conversation by Weller, he lost no time in assuring me that he wouldn't be running a school here if his pupils were in any kind of danger.

"And if they were, what would you do?"

"What kind of question is that? I've been a teacher for twenty years and have always been totally committed to my pupils."

Other regulars joined us: a pharmacist, a doctor, the manager of the local savings bank, a baker, and a man who ran the local employment office. Poison gas in the Lampertheim National Forest? That's old hat. But the director of the employment office dropped a few hints, which the bank manager made specific: "I'll tell you something, it's not a coincidence that this rumor keeps surfacing. Viernheim is an industrial zone that's waging all-out competition on every side. First there's Mannheim, which needs every penny it can scrape together, then there's Weinheim, which is expanding its industrial zone around the autobahn junction, and the minute we here in Viernheim come up with an investor, the guys in Lampertheim snatch him away with a juicier offer. There are solid interests behind these rumors, I tell you, solid interests." The others nodded. "I'm glad they removed the stuff from Fischbach, though. That way, all the claptrap about poison gas has stopped making headlines."—"Then again, maybe it's our turn now. You know, Viernheim instead of Fischbach?"— "Nonsense. All the papers said that with Operation Lindwurm all the poison gas was cleared out of Germany."—"It's

205

incredible that the *Viernheimer Tageblatt* printed that story in March."—"Have you noticed the reporter who's been creeping around here for the past few days?"—"And then on top of everything, we have to be nice to those guys, otherwise they take it out on us."

"Don't forget the Communists," Headmaster Hasenklee, sitting next to me, mumbled. "For them something like this would be heaven-sent."

"In this day and age?"

"We used to have old Henlein around here—back in the sixties and seventies he kept handing out fliers about the forest and making a big stink. He was a Communist. It's true you don't hear anything about him anymore, or about Marx or Lenin. But if you ask me, our Karl-Marx-Strasse here is an outrage. Leningrad has been changed back to Petersburg, and in a few years you won't find a single street or square with Karl Marx's name on it anywhere in the East—except here in Viernheim!"

I asked if they knew about the tanker trucks in Strassenheim. They did. "You mean the orange trucks from the Federal Emergency Management Agency? They're always around, doing exercises and things."

I took my leave. The streets were empty. Everyone was already sitting at their Sunday roast, and I hurried to the green dumplings and the Thüringer leg of mutton that was roasting in Brigitte's oven. She has managed a seamless culinary unification of East and West German cuisines.

I didn't know whether Weller and his friends at the Golden Lamb had been putting on a charade for me or for themselves, or if they had told me what they really and truly believed. Weller's position was clear. Even if poison gas was being stockpiled in the forest, posing a threat to him and everyone else, you couldn't simply get up and leave, turning your back on everything you had worked for all your life. Were you supposed to start all over again at the age of sixty in Neustadt or Gross Gerau? One didn't do that at fifty, or even at forty. The only difference is that when one is younger one might still have a few illusions. I understood all that. And yet the presbyter and his friends at the pub struck me as weird, as I thought of them sitting there at that gloomy, smoky table, spinning out their conspiracy theories.

The afternoon was bright and breezy. We had our coffee in the garden. Manu followed in his Brazilian father's footsteps by flirting up a storm with Sonya, while Brigitte's friend Lisa turned out to be a very nice young woman. She knew all the stories about poison gas in the forest. She also remembered old Henlein, a hunchbacked little man who, for a long time, Saturday after Saturday, had stood on the Apostelplatz handing out flyers. She also knew about patients who periodically complained of rashes, suppurative sinusitis, cramps, vomiting, and diarrhea—this more often than in Rohrbach, where she had lived and worked before.

"Did you ever discuss this with any of the local doctors?"

"I did, and they knew exactly what I was talking about. But at the end of the day, none of us was really sure. You'd have to do a statistical analysis with control groups. And there is the Association of Insurance-Approved Physicians, which does all the accounts and has an overview. You'd think that the Association would notice if things in our district were different than elsewhere."

"Are you worried?"

She looked me straight in the eyes. "Of course I'm worried. Chernobyl, global warming, the destruction of the rain forests and biodiversity, cancer, AIDS—how can one not be worried in this world?"

"Do you think one should be particularly worried in Viernheim?"

She shrugged her shoulders. By the end of our discussion I realized that I hadn't dug up any more than I had that morning at the Golden Lamb. And that it was Sunday, and that Sunday is not a day for digging, was no consolation.

10

And both sound so harmonious together

I brought Turbo back home. He had broken Rudi the rat's neck, and Röschen had retaliated by giving him some tuna. He seemed to be losing his figure.

I dedicated the evening to my couch. I took a razor blade, one of those big old ones that are nice and sturdy, not the platinum-laminated, double-track blades embedded in a springy razor head. I tipped the couch on its side, cut open the seam at the bottom, plunged my arm into the stuffing, and groped around for the bullet from Lemke's gun. The other bullet, which had sent Dante's marble Beatrice plunging into the Inferno, I had thrown out with the fragments in my befuddled confusion. But that bullet hadn't been preserved as well as the one I had managed to fish out of the couch. The other one had finished off the marble, which in turn had flattened and scratched it. The first bullet had been gently buffered by the stuffing of the couch. I showed the smooth, shiny, shapely and malignant projectile to Turbo, but he didn't want to play with it.

Sewing the seams back together again proved harder than cutting them open. I see sewing and ironing as active meditation and often think with envy of the many, many women to whom this meditative bliss falls in such abundance. But in the case of my couch it was a tough battle with leather, needle, thimble, and a thread that kept breaking.

When the job was done I set the couch upright, put away the sewing kit, and went out onto the balcony. The air was mild. The first moths of summer beat against the window or found their way in through the door and danced about the ceiling light. I have no bone to pick with my age, but there are early summer evenings when, if you're not young and in love, you're simply out of place in this world. I sighed, closed the door, and drew the curtains.

The phone rang. I picked up, and at first heard only a loud crackling and a low, distant voice I couldn't understand. Then the voice sounded near and clear, although the crackling continued in the background and every spoken word was echoed. "Gerhard? Hello? Gerhard?" It was Leo.

"Where are you?"

"I'm to tell you . . . I want to tell you, that you needn't be frightened of Helmut."

"What I'm worried about is you. Where are you?"

"Hello, Gerhard? Hello? I can't hear you. Are you still there?"

"Where are you?"

The line had gone dead.

I thought of Tyberg's pleading for us to mind our own business. I could see Leo with Lemke in Palestine or Libya. When we were together, I was certain that she wasn't setting her sights on a career in terrorism. She had gotten mixed up in a foolish thing, wanted to leave it behind her and get out of it unscathed and lead a normal life again—if not the old life, then a new one. I was also certain that this would be the best solution. Children don't get better in prison. But they don't get better in guerrilla training camps in Palestine or Libya either.

These are not the kind of thoughts that are conducive to sound sleep. I was up early, and early at Nägelsbach's office in Heidelberg.

"All's forgiven and forgotten?" I asked.

He smiled. "You and I are working on the same case. I hear that your new client is old Herr Wendt. But all things considered, neither you nor I know where the other stands. Am I right?"

"But you and I both know that whatever the other is doing can't be all wrong."

"I should hope so."

I put the bullet on the desk in front of him. "Can you find out if this comes from the same gun that killed Wendt? And can we get together this evening? In your garden or on my balcony?"

"Come over to our place. My wife would be pleased." He picked up the bullet and balanced it in his hand. "I'll have the results by this evening."

At the editorial office of the *Rhein-Neckar-Zeitung* I found Tietzke at his computer. The way he was sitting there reminded me of one of those Jehovah's Witnesses who stand with their *Watchtower* on street corners. The same gray, joyless, hopeless conscientiousness. I didn't ask him what gray subject matter he was writing about.

"Do you have time for a coffee?" I asked.

He continued typing without looking up. "I'll meet you at the Café Schafheutle in exactly thirty minutes. A mocha, two eggs in a glass, a graham roll, butter, honey, and a couple of slices of Emmental or Appenzell cheese. We got a deal?"

"We got a deal."

He ate with gusto. "Lemke? Sure I know him. Or rather, knew him. Back in 1967, '68, he was quite a figure here in Heidelberg. You should have heard how he whipped up auditorium thirteen. When the right-wingers, who hated him with a vengeance, started chanting 'Sieg Heil Lemke, Sieg Heil Lemke!' and he would lead a competing chorus of 'Ho, Ho, Ho Chi Minh!' all hell would break loose. At first if the chanting wasn't at full blast, he could shout them down. Then they'd get louder, and he'd fall silent and stand motionlessly on the podium, wait for a moment, raise his arms, and then begin hammering the lectern with both fists to the beat of 'Ho, Ho, Ho Chi Minh.' At first you couldn't hear him above the shouting of the others, then some would begin chanting with him, and then more and more. Then he would stand there silently. After a while he'd stop banging his fists on the lectern and start waving his arms, just like a conductor. Often he'd turn this into a comic skit, and the auditorium would end up roaring with laughter. Even when the right-wingers were a majority, 'Ho, Ho, Ho Chi Minh' would win out over 'Sieg Heil Lemke.' He had a great feel for timing and would start at the moment when the others were still yelling for all they were worth but beginning to run out of breath."

"Did you know him personally?"

"I wasn't into politics back then. He was in that radical Students for a Democratic Society party, and sometimes I'd show up there the way I'd show up at the other political parties. I was just an observer. I didn't meet Lemke there, but in a movie theater. Do you remember those spaghetti Westerns back in the late sixties? Every week a new one would hit the theaters, a Leone movie, a Corbucci, a Colizzi, and whatever else their names were. For a while the Americans caught on that that was the new style of Western and made some good movies themselves. Back then the movies didn't premiere on Thursdays but on Fridays, and every Friday at two Lemke would be in the first row at the Lux or the Harmonie, sitting there with a couple of friends from the SDS—he'd never miss any of those openings. I, too, was eager to see the movie at the very first showing, and as the theater was empty except for us, sooner or later we got to talking. Not about politics, but about movies. You know *Casablanca*, right, the scene where the German officers sing the 'Wacht am Rhein' and the French sing the 'Marseillaise,' and both sound so harmonious together? He once told me that that was how he wanted it to be with 'Sieg Heil Lemke' and 'Ho, Ho, Ho Chi Minh.' That was the most political conversation we ever had. Back then, you know, I actually liked him."

"Later you didn't?"

"After the Students for a Democratic Society were outlawed, he joined the Communist League of West Germany, a cadre party with a Central Committee and general secretary, and all that crap. He started out as a candidate, then became a member of the Central Committee, lived in a high-rise in Frankfurt, edited party information bulletins, and drove around in a big black Saab—I don't know if it had a driver and a curtain or not. I don't think he finished university. Sometimes I'd bump into him at the Weinloch Bar, but he stopped going to the movies, and I was in no mood to talk about world revolution and the Russian, Chinese, and Albanian paths. At the beginning of the eighties the Communist League was disbanded. Some of them went over to the Green Party or to the German Communist Party, some ended up with the anarchists, and some simply were fed up with politics. I don't know what became of Lemke. There was a rumor that he'd made off with a hefty chunk of cash from party funds when the Communist League was disbanded and that he settled in America, where he speculated in stocks. There was also talk that Lemke was Carlos, the arch terrorist. But all of that is rumors and bullshit."

"Have you run into him recently?"

"No. Not too long ago I did bump into someone else from those first-row movie seats, a theologian who is now the head of the Evangelical Academy in Husum. We talked a bit about old times, and it turns out he's still reappraising the '68 radicals in his seminars at the academy. That's it. I've got to get back to the office. So—are you going to tell me what's in it for me, besides coffee and cake? What are you looking into right now?"

"I wish I knew."

11

Under the pear tree

Nägelsbach shook his head when I looked over at his work-shop. "I don't have anything to show today. In fact, I've dropped the idea of doing Rodin's *Kiss* in matchsticks—it was a crazy idea. I could see how embarrassed you were the other day when I was carrying on with all that nonsense about matchstick sculpture. Thank God I have Reni."

We were standing on the lawn. He had his arm around his wife, and she nestled against him. They'd always struck me as a loving couple before their recent crisis, but I'd never seen them so much in love.

"Don't look so surprised," she said to me, laughing, and smiled up at her husband. "Come on, let's tell him."

"Well . . ." Nägelsbach grinned. "When the model arrived—it's standing over there—Reni said we ought to sit like that, too, so I could get a better feel for the sculpture. And so we . . ."

"Made up again?"

A replica of Rodin's lovers kissing stood among the flower-ing rhododendrons; Nägelsbach looked somewhat gaunter in the flesh, and his wife plumper, but Rodin would surely have been delighted by this double echo.

We sat under the pear tree. Frau Nägelsbach had made some strawberry punch.

"The bullet you brought over is from the same weapon with which Wendt was shot. Are you also bringing me the murderer?"

"I don't know. I'll tell you how far I've gotten. On January sixth, four men and a woman launched a bomb attack on an American military installation in the Lampertheim National Forest—"

"In Käfertal," he interrupted.

"Don't interrupt him," Frau Nägelsbach intervened.

"The woman and two of the men managed to escape, but one of the others was killed and another arrested. The media mentioned two dead men: The other one must have been a soldier or a guard. I don't know if there had been an exchange of gunfire or if it was the explosion. That's not important."

"I heard it was the bomb," Nägelsbach said.

"For the police it was bad luck in disguise. They had caught some guy called Bertram and made him talk, but he didn't know all that much about his accomplices. He knew Leonore Salger and the man who had died—some Giselher or other—but he didn't know the two men who got away. Now I'm not saying that the terrorists put their team together willy-nilly, so that the members wouldn't know each other and couldn't give each other away. The way I see it, the attack was more a spur-of-the-moment kind of thing. Anyway, Bertram could give only a vague description of the two men, because he didn't know them. And, let's face it, in the night all terrorists are gray—not to mention that they'd blackened their faces. The pictures that are being used for the manhunt are composites, right?"

"I'm not working on this case," Nägelsbach replied, "but if the Agency doesn't have their names . . . Did the media say these were composites?"

"Maybe they did and I missed it. Anyway, on January sixth we have the attack, and it's not until May that the search is made public? There could have been a public appeal for information right after the attack. There could have been pictures in the media the moment the arrested man began talking, identified Leonore Salger, and described the two men. That would have been in February at the latest, because at that point the police were already looking for Leonore Salger. And yet when the public appeal for information finally came, we were given as good as no information about the time, place, and circumstances of the attack. You're not going to tell me that this is the way things are usually done, are you?"

"As I said before, I'm not working on this case. But if the Americans request that we treat the attack on their terrain confidentially, and that we tread carefully, then that's exactly what we do."

"Why would they make such a request?" I asked.

"How should I know? Maybe Holy Islamic Warriors had threatened them with an attack like this in retaliation for their support of Israel, or perhaps some Panamanians were trying to free Noriega. In that case the Americans would have to weigh how to handle this from a foreign-policy perspective. There could be thousands of reasons."

"Then how come they went public on the very day Wendt was killed?" I asked him.

"Was it the same day?"

Frau Nägelsbach nodded. "Yes, it was," she said. "When the name 'Salger' came up in the late-night news, I remembered it right away because of the spat the two of you had just had. And then by the time you came home late that night, because you were working on the Wendt case, my asparagus soufflé had collapsed."

"It all fits together, because in Wendt's briefcase there was a map showing the section of the Lampertheim National Forest where the Americans have their depot and where the attack took place. I know you're saying that the attack was in Käfertal, and that Viernheim is not in your jurisdiction, and that it is the Federal Criminal Investigation Agency that deals with terrorist attacks. But someone in your office had to have seen the connection and made it clear to the decision makers that it was high time for them to go public. Because they couldn't take the risk that the attack would trigger God knows what else after Wendt's murder. And that someone in your office was right."

Nägelsbach's face remained a blank. Was he the someone who had seen the connection? Had he known from the start that the attack had been in Viernheim and nowhere else? Was the matter so secret and delicate that he preferred to play the fool rather than give anything away? I shot a glance at his wife. I knew from experience that she was up-to-date on everything that preoccupied him. "There are no professional secrets in a childless couple," was one of his mottos. She eyed us nervously.

"The bullet that killed Wendt comes from a gun that belongs to one of the two men you're looking for," I said. "Helmut Lemke, mid-forties, not unknown in Heidelberg. I don't have a recent photograph of him, but the one I've got here is better than the composites you have, and I have no doubt that the photographers from the Agency will know how to make him look fifteen years older." I gave him a copy of one of the pictures I had from Leo's photo album.

"Why would Lemke have shot Wendt?" Frau Nägelsbach asked.

"I don't know," I replied. "All we know for sure is that Wendt was killed with Lemke's gun. I'm hoping your husband and I might put our heads together on this one."

"I don't know how much I can contribute," Nägelsbach said. "You seem to know more than I do. Of course we put out a search for the man and the VW Golf that Frau Kleinschmidt saw, questioned the neighbors, and looked for people who'd been out walking. But it was pouring that day, as you well know, and nobody saw anything. Or at least anything we could use. In the house the Golf was parked in front of, the children kept looking out the window, as they were waiting for their mother. The girl says the Golf was red, the boy says black—and they don't recall the license plate." He laughed. "Crazy as it may sound, every time I come across a red or a black Golf, I try to catch a glimpse of the driver. Does that sort of thing ever happen to you?"

"You bet it does." I waited, but Nägelsbach did not continue. "It almost sounds as if the Wendt case has ended up in the files," I said.

"To tell you the truth, we didn't know what else we could do," Nägelsbach said. "Now that you have brought us all these new leads, we can set things rolling again. But who is Lemke? Where did his and Wendt's paths cross? Might Wendt have been the fifth man in the attack after all?"

"No, he wasn't."

"You're handing me that on a silver platter, too. I guess you won't want to tell me how you come to know that either?"

"If you're hinting that I haven't told you where I have the bullet from, I'll be glad to make amends."

I told him about my encounter with Lemke.

"But now you have definitely found out a good deal more from me than I have from you," I said.

Frau Nägelsbach agreed with me. "I think you owe Herr Self something, too."

He disagreed. "I will keep him posted, I assure you. But he had a bullet, and I had one. Both he and I had to bring them together so we could compare them and ascertain that they came from the same weapon. Now we're both moving forward. My progress I have already mentioned. And he can call his client tomorrow morning and announce his first success."

12

Tearing along

That is exactly what I did. Frau Büchler was pleased. No, I could not speak to Herr and Frau Wendt yet. They were in Badenweiler with their daughter.

The morning was cool, and I wore a sweater with my corduroys and hiking boots. I drove over the Friedrich-Ebert Bridge, the Friedrich-Ebert Strasse, through Käfertal and Vogelstang, and over the Entlastungsstrasse to Viernheim, where the Nibelungenstrasse took me to yet another Friedrich-Ebert Strasse. Everything flows: We drive along the same Friedrich-Ebert Strasse and yet it is not the same Friedrich-Ebert Strasse, we are the same and yet not the same.

To my left the fence reached the Lorscher Weg Road, and I parked my old Opel and walked. I followed the fence westward through the woods. The ground was springy beneath my feet, the birds were singing, the trees were rustling in the wind, and an aroma of pine resin, decaying foliage, and fresh green hung in the air. I didn't see any watchdogs or security patrols on the asphalt path behind the fence, nor did the fence look as if it had been damaged or repaired in the last few months. After a quarter of an hour, the rustling grew louder—it wasn't the wind anymore, but the autobahn. The fence ran northward alongside it. The cars tore past me, and once an empty can barely missed my head. I was glad when the fence veered back into the woods again.

But then I changed my mind. I knew that the tire tracks left by the car Leo's group had used to get to the depot would no longer be there, but I wanted to see what route they might have taken. The embankment that I found posed no problem for a regular car. I also found a wide path through the woods that a car could easily have used, and which could be reached from the embankment. The path led out of the woods and into an open area with stunted shrubs, dried grass, blueberry bushes, and wildflowers. Leo had said that they followed a path leading across the meadows to the woods, and I followed the path to where I imagined the fence to be behind the trees. I made a mental note of the rampant brambles along the edge of the woods so I could come back in August for some berry picking. In the woods I soon came upon the fence again.

I saw right away that this part of the fence had been repaired. I listened for the bulldozers, the conveyer belts, and the trucks that I had seen from the airplane. I heard the birds, the wind, the distant rumbling of the cars—otherwise there was silence. My watch showed ten o'clock. Was the construction crew on a break? I sat down on a rock and waited.

Then I heard something that at first I couldn't place. Did conveyer belts rattle like that? Did bulldozers squeak like that? But the rumble of engines was missing. I couldn't believe the guards would be patrolling the fence on mountain bikes, but that is exactly what it sounded like. Then I heard voices, one light and one deep.

"Do be careful, Eva!"

"I am being careful, Grandpa, I am."

"If you keep tearing along like this I'll end up with a broken neck. And when you rattle me like this, I can't stop coughing—*cough cough cough.*"

"It's not the rattling that makes you cough, it's the smoking!"

"No, no, Eva. The cigarettes have hit me in the legs, not the lungs."

Eva, flushed and sweating, must have been about eighteen; Grandpa in his wheelchair was somewhere between eighty and a hundred and ten. He was a shriveled little man with sparse white hair and a thin beard like that of a Chinese sage. He was hunchbacked and sat crookedly in his wheelchair, his hands gripping the armrests, and the stump of his leg, which had been amputated below the knee, rested against the raised footrest. In their struggle, Eva and Grandpa only saw me when I got up from the rock I was sitting on. They looked at me as if I'd come from another planet.

"Good morning," I said. "Fine weather we're having." I couldn't think of anything better.

Eva returned my greeting. "Good morning."

"Shh!" Grandpa cut into Eva's and my budding conversation. "Can you hear them? I knew it!"

We listened, and now the bulldozers, conveyer belts, and trucks could clearly be heard.

"I suppose they're just back from their break," I said, and the two of them looked at me, even more surprised. "You meant the construction going on beyond the fence, didn't you? The new fence. Does the construction interest you?"

"Does it . . . ? You're not from these parts, are you? When I got my pension and still had both legs—*cough cough*

cough—I used to walk along this fence every day. Later I came as often as I could, at least once a week. Now she brings me here whenever she can. If you were from around here, I'd know you. And you'd know me, too—*cough cough*—No one else ever comes here."

"I've heard about you, Herr Henlein."

"What do you say to that, Eva? People have heard about me. Are you with the Green Party? Are you interested in the forest again? I heard about that—*cough cough*—you're all rearing to go, and then you fizzle out because you can't get quick results. All you guys want to make the world a better place, but you don't even take the time to hear what I've got to say."

"I didn't know you were still active. Where do you live? Could we meet somewhere?"

"You'll have to come over to Mannheim. I don't live in Viernheim anymore. I live near my children—*cough cough*—in E 6, in a retirement home. Come on, Eva, off we go."

I followed them with my eyes. She was dexterous and had a knack for steering the wheelchair clear of roots and stones, but didn't manage to dodge them all. She needed all her strength to push the wheelchair, with Henlein cursing loudly, over some of the obstacles.

I hurried after them. "Would you like me to help you?"

"I can manage, thank you very much—*cough cough*."

"*You* can manage, Grandpa, but I wouldn't mind a little help," Eva said.

It took us almost two hours to reach the road. Henlein cursed, coughed, and reminisced about his campaigns in the sixties and seventies, with which he wanted to get to the bottom of things. "The Americans' poison gas—that wasn't even the worst of it. You can bet they'd be pretty careful when they handle that stuff. But what about the old stuff . . ." In 1935, he'd been interned in a concentration camp, and in 1945 put to work moving and burying the Wehrmacht's stocks of poison gas. "Near Lossa, Sondershausen and Dingelstädt in East Germany—I wrote about that later on and even managed to go there and hand out flyers. But the East German authorities deported me back to the West. Ha, there's model Communists for you! Then I did the same thing here in Viernheim. There were rumors that there was poison gas from World War I still buried in Viernheim. Yellow-cross gas, blue-cross gas, mustard gas, and later on we dug in tabun and sarin." After Henlein had been freed from the concentration camp, he'd drifted around for a while, and in 1953 came to Mannheim. There he worked at Brown Boveri & Co., married in 1955, and built a house in Viernheim. He saw it as preordained (if for a Communist there is such a thing) that he ended up here. His calling in life was to fight to defuse the time bomb in the Lampertheim National Forest. "Maybe it stopped ticking ages ago. Maybe the Americans dug everything up after '45 and took it all away. But would you believe a thing like that?"

I invited Grandpa and Eva for lunch in the Kleiner Rosengarten, and then drove Henlein back to his retirement home. His room was filled with binders. He had been collecting material since 1955. I read how poison gas is manufactured, stored, and employed, how it works and how one can protect oneself, and where it was manufactured and stored in Germany—and that nobody really seems to know where it was buried after World War I and II. Henlein had cut out every local and regional report containing the slightest evidence of poison gas in the Lampertheim National Forest or on the

Viernheim Meadows. He had also saved all the reports about local and regional projects for which the ticking time bomb could be particularly dangerous. Both the realized and unrealized projects reflected the development of the Federal Republic of Germany: Hunting preserves, woodland communities, adventure parks, waste management plants, test tracks, nature preserves, golf courses—all kinds of grand plans had been made for the area, anticipating the time when the Americans would give back the Lampertheim National Forest and the Viernheim Meadows.

"Do you know if maps of the stockpiling areas were made in '45?"

"I think so. And I think they also had maps back then that showed where the leftover stuff from World War I had been buried. But I've never managed to track any of those maps down. Think about it: That stuff is still lying buried all over the place, and the Americans give us back the land—those maps would be worth a fortune!"

13

Life's illusions

Worth enough to lead someone to murder? A woodland community on the Viernheim Meadows and in the Lampertheim National Forest would interest a real-estate mogul like old Herr Wendt, both for itself and for its effect on the real-estate market. I admit I haven't shown much talent in my occasional speculations in the stock market, but even I could see that one could make hefty gains with such maps. All you needed was to publish such a map at the right moment: Planning in the area would grind to a halt, and land prices would rise or come crashing down.

I left Henlein's retirement home and crossed the Planken Boulevard to the Ring, where I had parked the Opel. I bought a whole carton of Sweet Aftons, a tie with little white clouds on a night blue background, and an ice-cream cone with five scoops. I sat down in the park behind the Water Tower, ate the ice cream while listening to the splashing of the fountains, and thought, not for the first time, how nice it would be to live in one of the round towers that crown the two corner houses at the Augusta-Anlage. Would old Herr Wendt pull a few strings for me? Herr Wendt, I imagined myself saying, my investigations have revealed that you used some old maps to pull a shady trick or two for some crooked deals. You used your son, and lo and behold he got murdered along the way. Now I'm not saying that you pulled the trigger, Herr Wendt, but you let it happen. So here's the deal: I want you to fix me up with one of those two tower apartments up there, and I'll be happy to look the other way.

People don't murder simply for money. In fact, they murder for one reason, and one reason only: to save their life's illusions. There's the one who murders out of jealousy: If my beloved is dead, she's mine and nobody can take her away from me, not a lover, not she herself. There's the one who kills as a professional: He knows no trade, is nothing, but wants to hold his own in a world in which professional success makes the man. Tyrants murder because they want to be greater than they are and are murdered in turn because somebody wants the world to be a better place than it is. There is collective murder for collective illusions—the history of the twentieth century is riddled with it. Then of course there is also murder sparked by greed. But its aim is not to gather and hoard money: It, too, aims to salvage dreams of greatness and eminence. It had been many years since old Herr Wendt had stopped dreaming of being the emperor of a real-estate empire in favor of being a father who has reconciled with his son. No, old Herr Wendt had nothing to do with his son's murder.

While we're on the subject: What about your own illusions, Gerhard Self? There was that matter of you and Korten. But Gerhard Self was in no mood for a dialogue with Gerhard Self.

In my office there was a message from Peschkalek on the answering machine saying that he had an idea, and a message from Philipp asking me to call him back. A few callers had hung up. Then I heard a distant whir of voices, humming, and the synthetic twitter of an international call. I knew it was Leo before she even spoke. "Gerhard? Gerhard, this is Leo." There was a long pause. "I just want you to know that Helmut didn't kill Rolf." There was another long pause before she went on. "I'm far away. I hope you're doing well." She hung up. As if Lemke would admit to her that he'd killed Wendt!

Philipp complained when I returned his call: "How come I can never reach you? Are you spending the merry month of May rolling in the hay? A bit of action to charge up those old batteries of yours?"

"Nonsense! I was over at Brigitte's one evening, but . . ."

"You don't have to excuse yourself to me, I'm a man of the world. In fact, I'm bristling with envy. My days are numbered—I count on you to keep the flag flying."

"What happened?" I asked him. What could put a stop on Philipp other than AIDS?

"The wedding's on Friday," he said. "Will you be my best man?"

I don't mean to say that Philipp, who's pushing sixty, is too old to get married. Nor do I mean that because he chases every skirt that comes his way he's too young to get married. But the simple truth is that I can't imagine him as a married man. "Are you pulling my leg?"

"Don't give me any of that bullshit. Be in front of the city hall at five to ten. The ceremony's at ten o'clock sharp. After that we'll be celebrating at Antalya Türk. And I'm warning you to bring lots of time and Brigitte." He was in a hurry. "I'd love to hit the town with you one last time before I get married, but there's so much to do. I'm sinking with all hands, even though my little Fur-ball has taken time off from work. We can hit the scene sometime after the wedding; I'm sure she won't mind."

My impression that in a Turkish marriage the man was king of the castle was somewhat dated. Or had his little Fur-ball Füruzan specifically not chosen a Turkish husband? Or was Philipp making a mistake? Should I train him as a fighter in the marriage war—me, of all people?

Peschkalek didn't just have an idea, he had a suggestion, about which he wanted to talk to me. We decided to meet at the sauna in the Herschelbad pool.

He, too, liked a sauna to be piping hot and without steam, and he, too, smoked between sessions. We also shared the same sequence: three Finnish sauna sessions one after the other, and then, after a lengthy break, two Turkish ones. In the big pool we launched a water battle worthy of Admiral Pushkin. With his large stomach, bald head, and bushy mustache glittering with water drops, Peschkalek looked like a friendly sea lion. We lay on the loungers, covered with white towels, napped for a while, and then stretched, feeling that we had had some good bonding.

"What was that little song and dance the other day at lunch all about, Peschkalek?" I asked him with a smile. "You were acting as if it had just struck you what a good idea it might be to drop by the *Viernheimer Tageblatt*. And then acting like it only struck you during our conversation with Walters that there might be poison gas in the munitions depot. You knew the story about the poison gas, also about the munitions depot, not to mention Strassenheim."

"You win, Self, you win. I admit I put on a little show to whet your appetite. I don't think I can handle this case on my own. I didn't want to run the risk of you not taking the story about the poison gas seriously and not wanting to look into it. I need your help." He hemmed and hawed. "Which brings me to my suggestion. Let's go to the Americans and tell them to lay their cards on the table."

"Great idea!"

"No, I'm serious! I'm not saying we should drive over with a 'Permit me to introduce myself, my name is Peschkalek, and this is Herr Self. Please be so kind as to explain the January attack.' No, we would go there officially."

"You mean as General Peschkalek and Sergeant Self of the Marines?"

"No, not the Marines, the German army, and I'll be happy enough with the rank of major. I'll be the military man, and you could be from the office of the president. The president wants to award some medals to the men of the fire brigade who fought the fire and the guards who were injured in the line of duty. We'll go speak to the American fire chief and discuss the number of medals to be awarded, the names to be engraved on them, and the wording of the citations."

"Unauthorized assumption of authority, falsification of documents, perhaps there is also something like abuse of uniforms and medals—this is playing for real! If we're lucky, we'll walk away knowing that the attack was in Viernheim and not in Käfertal or Vogelstang, and that they're storing new or old poison gas there. As for the Wendt case, this wouldn't bring me a single step closer to solving it."

"I'm not so sure. Your only lead up to now is that Wendt had something to do with this mysterious attack that is being covered up. If there's nothing mysterious or covered up, you can kiss your lead good-bye." He sat up straight, held his palm before his mouth, and blew the lead away.

"And you're not concerned about the long list of felonies?"

"Don't worry, I'm going to set up our little excursion to the Americans so that nothing can go wrong." He explained where he was going to get hold of the uniforms, how he would manufacture our laminated IDs, and who would instruct him about the relevant names and ranks.

He saw that I was still not satisfied. "What is it? Are you afraid the Americans will call our departments to check up on us? We're not supposed to have a regular central office, that's the whole gist of it. The foolish husband who wants to have some fun on the side will tell his wife that he has business trips, meetings, and appointments with colleagues—all of which he has, but not to the extent he pretends he does. This course of action inevitably runs aground. The clever husband, on the other hand, invents new friends and associates and new activities. Where nothing exists, nothing can run aground. The Americans won't call the president of Germany. As far as they know you're working for him, while I'm one of his representatives, and I will invent my department in a way that though it doesn't exist, it very well could. I still haven't convinced you? Let's leave it for now—I'll get everything ready, and give you a call in a couple of days."

14

Not a particularly good impression

He called me two mornings later. "I'll drop by at nine. The whole thing won't take more than two hours. I'll bring your ID along—wear a dark suit."

"What happened to all the careful preparations? You think that in a single day you can—"

He laughed. "I won't lie to you. I've been working on this for ages. The reason I asked you two days ago was because by then I was sure I could pull the whole thing off. And I only know if I can pull something off once the preparations are under way."

"How do you know I'll play along?"

"You will play along? Great! I've already called and announced our arrival."

"You did what?"

"I'm not pressuring you, am I? It's up to you. If you don't want to do it, that's fine with me. See you later."

I put on my dark blue suit and slipped my reading glasses into my pocket. When I let them slide halfway down my nose and peer over the top, I look like an elder statesman. I wasn't going along only because I wanted to find out what was happening at the American depot. I also felt that if I didn't go I'd be letting Peschkalek down.

We walked to the train station. His uniform was too tight, but he assured me that German army uniforms were notoriously bad fits. "As I said, we're from the president's office. You will make a few general statements, and I'll discuss the details. You don't have to say more than that the firemen and guards are to be awarded medals for their service on January sixth. Should your English fail you, I'll jump in."

From the station we headed to Vogelstang in a taxi, as if we had just come on the train from Bonn. Peschkalek took two laminated, credit card–sized ID tags out of his jacket pocket and clipped one on his lapel and one on mine. They looked good. I liked the color photo of me; Peschkalek had taken it at Wendt's funeral.

Despite his assurances, I was worried about having to chatter away in English. I called to mind the sixties, when jokes about old President Lübke's English bloopers were all the rage. More often than not I didn't understand them, a fact I would hide from others with a knowing chuckle, but I couldn't hide from myself that I didn't know any English worth mentioning. Could this be why I remember Lübke so warmly? No, I have a soft spot for all politicians once they're out of office: for our singing President Scheel, our hiking President Carstens, and I even have a soft spot for grim Gromyko.

"Sir!" The soldier at the gate stood to attention in his white cap and belt.

Peschkalek greeted him with military abruptness, and I raised my hand to an imaginary cap. Peschkalek explained that we had an appointment with the chief of the fire brigade.

The soldier put through a call, an open jeep pulled up, and we got in. I sat next to the driver and rested my foot outside, which is the thing to do when sitting in a jeep, if American war movies are anything to go by. We drove along a path bordered by lawns and trees. A squad of trotting women soldiers in bobbing T-shirts came toward us. In the distance, a white wooden building came into view, with fire trucks parked outside its large doors. The fire trucks were not red and gold, the way I had imagined them, but the same green as everything else.

The driver walked us up an outside staircase to the office floor above the garages. A dapper officer greeted us, and Peschkalek did the honors. My ears didn't fail me: Peschkalek introduced me as Under-Secretary Dr. Self! We sat down at a round table and were served watery coffee. The large window looked out onto some trees. Behind the desk was an American flag, and President Bush stared down at me from the wall.

"Dr. Self?" The officer looked at me questioningly.

I launched into an English sentence: *"Our president wants place an order on the brave men of the night of sixth Januar."*

The officer continued to look at me questioningly. Peschkalek jumped in. He spoke of Viernheim and the terrible threat of terrorism. The German president did not want to place an order, but to give the men a medal. Peschkalek also talked about documents, a speech, and a reception. I didn't understand why the men should have to go to a reception desk to get their medals, but then it dawned on me that he might be talking about a reception as in a soirée. I spoke up, suggesting that a *pathetic speech* should be given; after all, soldiers always like a bit of pathos, but that didn't seem to go down too well either. The word "sensitive" kept cropping up—were American soldiers worried about our rough German ways? *"Make you no sorrows,"* I quickly said, but before I could calm the officer's fears about German brusqueness, Peschkalek cut in and asked him for a list of names that would go on the medals. He also asked if what the individuals had done should be recognized uniformly, or whether the actions of different men warranted first- and second-grade medals.

The officer sat down at his desk, took a folder from a pile, opened it, and began leafing through it. I leaned over to Peschkalek: "Don't lay it on too thick." As far as I was concerned, since we'd talked about the attack of January 6 and the officer had not contradicted us our mission was accomplished. Peschkalek leaned over to me. He grabbed the leg of my chair and pulled it away, and the chair and I went crashing to the floor. I banged my head and elbow. My elbow ached, my head buzzed. I didn't manage to get up right away.

In an instant the officer was at my side, and helped me first of all to a sitting position, then onto my knees, and finally back onto the chair, which he had set upright again. Peschkalek emitted regretful and worried sounds. Lucky for him he didn't touch me, otherwise I'd have tackled him, wrung his neck, cut him into tiny pieces, and fed him to the birds.

But he wasn't afraid of me. He seized my left arm and marshaled the officer to my right, and both of them helped me to the door and down the stairs. Peschkalek talked and talked. Downstairs the jeep was waiting for us and all three of us got in the back, with me in the middle. As Peschkalek helped me out of the jeep at the main gate, I managed to ram my healthy elbow into his solar plexus. That winded him, but he quickly got his breath back and continued talking at the officer.

The taxi came. The officer was sorry, Peschkalek was sorry, I was sorry. "*But we must make us on the socks,*" I said, and the officer again looked at me oddly. The soldier with the white cap and belt held the door open for us, we got in, and the soldier slammed the door shut. I rolled down the window to say a few last words, but the officer and the soldier had turned away.

"*That's what happens when you have an army with nothing to do,*" I thought I heard the officer say to the soldier, and if I had heard right, our visit had not made a particularly good impression.

15

Black on white

"Are you out of your mind?"

"Please!" he hissed. "Wait till we're out of here!"

He had told the taxi driver to head for the train station. He asked him to hurry so we wouldn't miss the 12:11 train. He also asked him all kinds of questions: How was the local Lorenz Standard Electric Company doing, and Brown, Boveri & Co., since when did Mannheim have streetcars, what was playing at the National Theater, was there actually any water in the Water Tower, and he wove into the conversation that this was our first time in Mannheim and that we needed to get back to Bonn on time. I felt he was laying it on a bit thick, that all this was unnecessary and embarrassing. I leaned my buzzing head in my hands, looked out the window, and hoped to God that the driver wouldn't recognize me if he ever picked me up again.

Peschkalek and I went into the train station through the main entrance and out again through a side door on the left. "Take off your jacket. The Heinrich-von-Stephan Strasse is visible from the taxi stand."

Here, too, I played along. When we were safely out of view, Peschkalek flipped out. "I got my hands on it!" he shouted. "I got my hands on it!" He threw his jacket on the ground and triumphantly held up the binder. In the commotion after my fall he had snatched it from the fire chief's desk and hidden it in his jacket. He grabbed me by the arms and shook me. "Self! Cheer up! You were great—we were great! Here's the proof, and nobody can say there was no attack!"

I freed myself from his grip. "You don't even know what's in that binder!"

"Well, let's take a look. How about grabbing a bite somewhere nice and elegant. We have something to celebrate, and I owe you one. You know, I thought of telling you what I was thinking of doing, but then you'd have tensed up and really ended up hurting yourself. Plus, you'd never have been as convincing as you were!"

I was in no mood to have lunch with him. Nor was he too pleased that I wanted to make myself a photocopy of the file at the nearest copy center. He tried to forestall it, but in the end couldn't refuse. When my copy was ready we said a cool good-bye.

I went home and took two aspirin. Turbo was out roaming the rooftops. In the refrigerator there were eggs, Black Forest ham, tuna, cream, and butter, and in the freezer a package of spinach. I made a béarnaise sauce, warmed the spinach, poached two eggs, and let the ham sizzle for a bit. I placed the can of tuna in hot water. Turbo enjoys his tuna just as much when it's ice cold, but I can't believe it's good for him. I served lunch on the balcony.

Over a cup of coffee I began going through the American file with the help of a dictionary. When the fence had been cut, the alarm had gone off in the guardhouse. There had been fog, and it took the guards a while to locate the hole. The fog also made a systematic search of the terrain difficult. At one point they thought they had found the intruders. They had called out to them and then fired, both actions specified by regulation 937 LC 01/02. Then came the first explosion, and when they reached the area there was another, the result of which was that one intruder and one guard were killed, and a second intruder was injured and taken into custody. The second explosion had ignited stored chemicals. The fire brigade and the ambulance had been called in and appeared promptly. The fire was extinguished within minutes. No toxic substances were released. There was also a reference to two further reports: numbers 1223.91 CHEM 07 and 7236.90 MED 08. Along with report number 1223.91 CHEM 07, there was a further reference to suggestions for future storage of the chemicals. There had been no authorization at any time for the involvement of the German police, who had appeared at the entrance of the depot. A brief report furnished by the fire brigade was enclosed. The reports identified the fire brigade and guard patrol units, and named the two dead men and the arrested man: Ray Sachs, Giselher Berger, Bertram Mohnhoff. The respective superiors had signed the reports.

Now I had it in black and white. I could imagine Peschkalek cursing up a storm, trying to figure out how to get his hands on those other two reports, 1223.91 CHEM 07 and 7236.90 MED 08. Perhaps he'd return to the depot as a member of a cleaning detail? Or disguised as an American army chaplain? I, for one, had no intention of heading out with Peschkalek, dressed as Donald Duck and Daisy, to entertain the poor boys of the chemical and medical divisions.

16

Mönch, Eiger, Jungfrau

The afternoon was still young. I drove down the autobahn, realized when I got to the Waldorf junction that I'd gone too far, turned off at the next exit, and meandered back through villages I'd never been through before. When I reached the psychiatric hospital and drove up the winding road leading to the old building, I saw it shining in the distance. The scaffolding had been removed, and the building was covered in fresh yellow paint.

I found the temporary director ensconced in Eberlein's office. "What I have to say," he told me, "I shall say to the police and to the Public Prosecutor's Office." He let there be no doubt that I was not welcome.

"When will Professor Eberlein be back?"

"I don't know if he will return, or when. Do you have his address on Dilsberg Mountain? He lives on the Untere Strasse—my secretary will give you the number." He bade me good day. He hadn't even asked me to sit down, and I was standing before his desk like a corporal before an officer. I walked to the door, and through an intercom he ordered his secretary to give me one of Eberlein's remaining business cards. I had barely crossed the threshold when I found her standing at attention with a little envelope in her hand. Would the janitor salute as I walked past? No, he was reading a tabloid and only looked up for an instant.

I headed straight over to Dilsberg without calling Eberlein first, parked my Opel in front of the old town gate, and found his house on the Untere Strasse. There was a note taped to the door. "I'm at the Café Schöne Aussicht. E." I found him on the terrace of the café.

"You? The detective?"

"I realize you were expecting someone else—I figured the note wasn't meant for me. But do you mind if I sit down for a moment?"

"Please." He made a hint of a bow, seated as he was. "Look at that!" He pointed to the south.

The Dilsberg Mountain blended into the gentle hills of the Kleiner Odenwald. It was a spectacular view. The restaurant on whose terrace we were sitting definitely merited its name: Schöne Aussicht—beautiful view.

"No," he said, "look higher."

"Are those the . . . ?" I couldn't believe it.

"Yes, the Alps. Mönch, Eiger, Jungfrau, Mont Blanc. I don't know the names of the others. You can only see them a few days a year; one would have to ask a meteorologist why. But I've lived here for six years, and it's only the second time I've seen them."

On the horizon the sky was a deep blue. Where it became lighter, a delicate white brush had painted the chain of peaks. To the right and left they faded into the mist. Above them arched the clear sky of early summer, a normal Rhine-Neckar sky that did not betray anything of the wonder that it showed on the southern slope of the Dilsberg.

"You and I might well be the only ones who are witnessing this," I said. There was no one else on the terrace.

He laughed. "Does that make it twice as nice?"

In the magic of the moment I had forgotten that he was a psychiatrist. What would he have deduced from my remark? That I am incapable of sharing? That I was a single child? That I became a private investigator because I want the truth for myself instead of leaving it for others? That I'm infantilizing, and I shit and don't get off the pot—

"Herr Self, I imagine you want to talk to me about Rolf Wendt. The police have told me that you are working for his father. How far have you got?" He looked at me attentively. Tanned, relaxed, his shirt unbuttoned, his sweater over his shoulders, the cane with the silver knob leaning against the railing as if he no longer needed it—there was no sign that the last few weeks might have shaken him, or at least I couldn't see any sign.

I told him that the bullet that killed Wendt had come from a gun belonging to Lemke, whom he knew as Lehmann, and that I didn't know if Lemke had killed Wendt, or why he might have wanted to. I also told Eberlein that all murders were committed by people who wanted to save their life's illusions, and that I would have to know the illusions of all the parties involved, but that I didn't know them.

"What was Wendt's illusion?" I asked. "What kind of man was he?"

"I know what you mean by life's illusions, but I don't believe that they exist in your sense. There are life issues, and Wendt's issue was doing it right."

"It?"

"Everything. He was the only person I could really and truly rely on, whether it was attending patients and dealing with their families, collaborating on articles, or just administrative stuff. Rolf Wendt wouldn't rest until whatever he had undertaken to do was done as well as possible."

"Hence that look of strain on his face?"

He nodded. "To shield himself from excessive strain, a perfectionist must limit himself, must ration and budget himself. He cannot live life to the fullest. He can set up his work environment that way, but in his personal life he often ends up being miserable. In his attempt to do the right thing by his friends, the perfectionist doesn't get to enjoy his friendships, and in his attempt to do the right thing by women, he doesn't get around to loving them. Wendt wasn't happy, either. But I must say that in his unhappiness he actually managed to develop an empathy for the unhappiness of others."

"How does one become a perfectionist? How did Wendt—"

"What a question, Herr Self! We Swabians have perfectionism in our blood. Protestants become perfectionists so that they get to heaven, and children become perfectionists because their parents expect it of them. Does that answer your question? Wendt was a clever, sensitive, competent, and agreeable young man. There was no reason whatsoever to analyze his perfectionism. OK, he wasn't happy. But where does it say that we are here in order to be happy?" He picked up his cane and tapped the dot beneath the question mark.

I waited a few moments. "Did you know what the deal was with Leo Salger, and about Wendt's relationship to her?"

He laughed. "That's why I was fired, so I ought to know a thing or two about it. I did in fact know what Leonore Salger was mixed up in. I took it the way I take all entanglements, entanglements with drugs, with relationships, with work. It was obvious that she wanted to break free from it. It was also obvious that her childhood friend, or friend from her adolescent years—Lemke, Lehmann, this archangel Michael—was playing a disastrous role. You are aware that Wendt knew him? They had had quite a few dealings with each other in the early seventies, when Wendt participated in that radical Socialist Patient Collective, and Lemke was building up his cadre."

I know nothing about psychiatry and psychiatric hospitals. I know that the idea of the lunatic asylum, with screaming, raving lunatics and barred doors and windows, is out of date. I'm glad it is. The way things were back when Eberhard was in the hospital was not good. But I couldn't agree that Leo belonged in a psychiatric hospital. The therapy offered by Wendt did not seem particularly professional to me: He was a friend of hers, was even in love with her, not to mention that he knew Lemke, from whom Leo wanted to break free with the help of this therapy. The whole thing sounded more like a therapeutic cover for something quite different: Leo's hiding from the police. And all of that was going on right in front of Eberlein's eyes. I could understand the decision of the authorities to suspend him.

I told Eberlein my doubts.

"When Leonore Salger came to us, she was suffering from severe depression," he replied. "It didn't come out until later, and then only bit by bit, that she had known Wendt from before, and that Wendt knew Lemke, and that she knew Lemke. You are right that these aren't the best conditions for a cure. But then again it is always a delicate matter to break off therapy in the middle. I must say that once all the problems were laid out on the table, Wendt went ahead and did the right thing: He brought Leonore Salger's therapy to a quick conclusion and arranged for her release from the hospital."

I must have looked skeptical.

"I can't convince you? Your view is that I should have handed Wendt and Leonore Salger over to the police?" He waved his left hand in resignation.

The Alps had disappeared.

17

Too late

When I got into bed that night, I hoped I would dream about the Alps. I would take a running start on the Dilsberg, swing into the air, and with wings calmly beating fly over the Odenwald Range, Kraichgau, and the Black Forest, all the way to the Alps, where I would circle around the peaks and land on a glacier.

I had just fallen asleep when the phone rang. This time, too, there was a rustling and an echo on the line. But I could hear her voice clearly, and as far as I could tell she could hear mine, too.

"Gerhard?"

"Are you doing OK? I've been worrying about you."

"Gerhard, I'm frightened—and I don't want to stay with Helmut anymore."

"Then don't stay with him."

"I think I want to go to America. What do you think?"

"Why not? If you like the country and the people. After all, you liked it there when you were in high school."

"Gerhard?"

"Yes?"

"Must one pay for everything in life?"

"I don't know, Leo. Tell me, did you know about the poison gas in the American military depot?"

"I have to go. I'll call you again." She hung up.

I lay awake listening to the bells from the tower of the Heilig-Geist Church pealing off the time, quarter hour by quarter hour. At dawn I fell asleep. Again the phone woke me. This time it was Nägelsbach.

"A warrant for your arrest has just come up on our computer."

"What?" I looked at the clock. It was eight thirty.

"Aiding a terrorist organization, obstruction of justice—according to this, you warned little Miss Salger and got her across the border. For Christ's sake, Self—"

"Who said I did that?"

"Don't play cat and mouse with me. The Agency got an anonymous call and followed up on it. They say you were seen together in Amorbach, and then an innkeeper in Ernsttal saw you. Tell me it isn't true."

"Is a Mannheim patrol car going to come get me?"

I suddenly remembered that at ten I was supposed to be best man at Philipp's wedding. I hadn't even gotten him a present yet. "Will you do me a favor? I need you to put things on hold. Tell the computer system that you've already taken me into custody. I promise to come in this evening. Philipp is marrying Füruzan, that nurse—you know her from the New Year's party—and I'm to be their best man. 'For one brief sun my fate delay, to wed the nurse, and then away.'"

He was silent for a long while. "So it's true?"

I didn't reply.

248

"This evening at six. At my office."

I flicked the switch on my coffeemaker, rushed into the shower, and then threw on my blue suit. I was already on the stairs when I remembered my little suitcase. Corduroys, sweater, pajamas, toothpaste and toothbrush, shampoo, and my eau de cologne. Presumably the cell would reek of rat piss and the sweat of fear. I picked up a volume of Gottfried Keller, my traveling chess set, and Keres's *Best Games of Chess*. Turbo was roaming the roofs instead of waving farewell.

Frau Weiland promised to look after him. "Are you off on a little weekend getaway?"

"Something like that."

I put my suitcase in the car. All kinds of foolish thoughts flashed through my mind. Did prisons offer parking for inmates? Short-term and long-term parking like at the airport? Wouldn't it be a great idea if there were something like prison insurance that paid prisoners on remand a daily allowance, as well as paying the state the necessary supplement for a single cell? On the way to the city hall I bought a large umbrella for Philipp's balcony. He didn't have one, as he rarely sat outside. But that would change now. I could see them there, Füruzan crocheting, Philipp polishing his surgical instruments, from time to time a little chat with the neighbors, and geraniums in bloom along the railing.

Füruzan and her family were waiting outside the registrar's office beneath a balcony that was propped up by two stone men on either side of the entrance. Füruzan was wearing a pale apricot-colored dress, had a white rose in her dark hair, and looked most charming. Her mother had gained with girth the kind of distinction only found in emperors, kings, and chancellors. Füruzan's spindle-thin little sister giggled. Her brother looked as if he had just come galloping down a wild Kurdish mountain and then got all dressed up.

"My father passed away three years ago," Füruzan told me when she saw my eyes flit over the group. She pointed at her brother. "He is going to give me away to Philipp."

The city hall clock struck ten. I tried to make small talk. But her mother only spoke Turkish, her little sister answered all my questions with the same fit of giggles, and her brother seemed unable to unclench his teeth.

"He's studying landscaping at the Technische Hochschule in Karlsruhe," Füruzan said, building a bridge on which her brother and I could have met to chat about Semiramis's hanging gardens or the Luisenpark. But he remained silent, his jaws grinding.

Periodically the mother uttered a wordy Turkish sentence, sharp and fast like a blow. Füruzan did not react. She looked over the marketplace, her face cool and proud. The pale apricot-colored dress was turning dark under her arms.

I had broken into a sweat, too. The market was lively. A little old lady at a nearby stand was touting fine Mangold beets. On the Breite Strasse, a delivery truck honked and a streetcar jingled. Early strollers had settled at the tables outside the Café Journal and were enjoying the sun. A waiter was opening the umbrellas. Whenever there is a big catastrophe, when everything collapses, I always keep my cool. But small catastrophes, those treacherous crags in life's broad stream, finish me off.

Before I even caught sight of Philipp, I saw from Füruzan's hurt, startled eyes that he had turned up. He was holding himself upright and was impeccably dressed: a dark blue silk suit, a white and blue striped shirt with a white collar, a gold collar pin, and a paisley tie. He walked with long strides, bumping here and there into market stands and pushing people out of the way, because he wasn't in a state to walk around them. He saw us, raised his arm, waved, and smiled sheepishly.

"I'm late." He raised his shoulders apologetically. "Why don't we head over to the restaurant right away? I mean, it'll be nice for us to get to know each other, or see each other again. That in itself is reason enough for a celebration, even if we don't—"

"Philipp . . ."

He looked at the ground. "I'm sorry, my little Fur-ball. I can't go through with this. I downed a whole bottle of the stuff that Gerhard always drinks, but I still can't go through with it. I wish I could, but I . . ." He looked up. "Perhaps a little later. After all, now that I've drunk so much, it wouldn't even be valid."

The mother hissed, and Füruzan hissed back. The brother raised his hand and struck Füruzan across the face. She held her cheek, astonished, incredulous, said a few words to him that made the blood drain from his cheeks, and with a disparaging gesture slapped him across the mouth with the back of her hand.

I noticed his bleeding lip that had been cut by Füruzan's ring and didn't notice his hand, in which a knife flashed. "Easy, easy, young man!" Philipp said, stepping between brother and sister, and the knife plunged into his left side. The brother pulled it out, ready to take another stab, but I managed to knock the umbrella against him just in time. It surprised him more than it injured him, but the knife went clanging to the ground, and as he bent forward to pick it up, I quickly stepped on his fingers. Phillip collapsed, falling onto the knife, and the brother had to make do with spitting on the ground in front of his sister. He turned around and walked away.

"You have to bandage it up," Philipp said in a low but clear voice, pressing his left hand against the wound. "Real fast and real tight. The spleen bleeds like crazy. Tear your shirt."

I took off my jacket and shirt, tore at my shirt to no avail, and gave it to Füruzan, who bit at it, shredding it strip by strip.

She began bandaging him. "Harder," Philipp snapped.

People stopped, asked what had happened, offered help.

"Can your giggly little sister get a taxi from the Paradeplatz?" Philipp asked Füruzan. "She can? OK, Gerhard, call the hospital and tell them to get the operating theater ready. Shit, he got me in the lung, too." Philipp was talking with a bloody mouth.

Füruzan's little sister ran off. I saw from the phone box that she was back in a few minutes with a taxi. Füruzan had finished bandaging Philipp and led him to the taxi. The driver must have taken him for drunk and groggy, but obviously didn't see any blood, just that his dark blue silk suit might have gotten a little wet. Füruzan got in with him, while her mother shooed away the crowd. I don't know what Füruzan said to the driver, but he drove off with screeching tires.

18

A *little peace of* mind

"As far as we can tell, he should be fine. We took out the spleen and patched up his lung." The surgeon who had operated on Philipp took off his green cap, crumpled it up, and threw it in the trash. He noticed my cigarette. "Can I have one, too?"

I handed him the pack and a lighter. "Can I see him?"

"If you like. But you ought to put on a gown. It'll take a while, though, for him to come around. When his girlfriend comes back, she'll take over."

When I got to the room, Füruzan was no longer there. Perhaps she was in the process of shooting her brother. Or reconciling with him. Or was mad at Philipp and didn't want to see him again. I sat at his bedside listening to his labored breathing and to the low hissing of the pump from which a tube leading to his ribcage disappeared beneath his hospital gown. Another tube ran from a drip to the back of his hand. His hair, wet with sweat, was sticking to his head. It was the first time I noticed how thin and sparse it was. Was my vain friend a maestro with a hair dryer? Or had I just never noticed? The blood around his

mouth had not been cleaned away properly; it was brown and
dry, and flaking at the corners of his mouth. From time to time
his eyelids twitched. The sun and the blinds drew lines through
the room that slowly wandered across the linoleum floor, the
bedcover, and up the wall. When the nurse changed his drip, he
woke up.

"Maria with the pretty ears." Then he recognized me.
"Remember, Gerhard: Nice earlobes mean nice breasts."

"Really, Herr Doctor!" Maria said, playing along.

"I'd do better not to speak," Philipp whispered with some
effort.

The nurse left the room, quietly closing the door. After a
while Philipp beckoned me to come closer. "My spleen is out?
The pump is running? I used to dream sometimes that I was
dying. I'd be lying in the hospital, in a room and a bed just
like now, and I would bid all the women I ever knew
farewell."

"All of them?" I, too, was whispering. "You mean they'd
be lining up outside, along the corridor and down the stairs?"

"Each woman would say that after me she never met
another guy like me."

"I see."

"And I would tell each of them that I never again met anyone like her."

"What you'd need is a room with two doors, one in front
and one in back. The women you've already spoken to mustn't
come face-to-face with the women still waiting. Can you
imagine if word got down the line that you were telling every
woman that you never met another woman like her?"

Philipp sighed and was silent for a while. "You have no
idea about love, Gerhard. In my dream, all of them get

together anyway. They leave my deathbed and go to the Blaue Ente, where I've arranged a banquet for them, and they eat and drink and remember me."

I don't know why Philipp's dream made me sad. Because I have no idea about love? I took his hand. "Forget all that for the time being. You're not dying."

"No, I'm not." He found it increasingly hard to talk. "As it is, I couldn't even speak to all of them now. I'm much too weak." He fell asleep.

Füruzan came around five. I could see that her brother had beaten her, but she whispered to me that they had made up. "Do you think Philipp will forgive me, too?"

I didn't understand.

"Because the knife was meant for me."

I didn't feel that this was the time to give her a crash course in emancipation. "I'm sure he'll forgive you."

I didn't wait for Philipp to wake up again. At six I was in Nägelsbach's office, at seven in prison at the Fauler Pelz. Nägelsbach was taciturn, and so was I. He did, however, tell me that there'd be no more food by the time I got to the prison and took me shopping. Pretzels, some Camembert, a bottle of Barolo, and a few apples. I remembered the Mangold beets being sold at the market in Mannheim. I have a soft spot for this underrated local vegetable when it is cooked au gratin or served as a salad—but one has to put the beets in a marinade while they are still warm and let them sit for a few hours.

I hadn't been at the Fauler Pelz prison since the days when I was a public prosecutor. More than forty years had passed, and I no longer recognized the layout. But I did recognize the smell, the echoing sound of steps, the correctional officer's fumbling for the right key on the jangling bunch, and the unlocking and relocking of the cell door. The warden closed my door and locked it. He and Nägelsbach walked away, and I listened to the echo of their steps. I ate a few of the pretzels with some cheese and apples, drank the Barolo, and read Gottfried Keller. I had taken along his Zurich stories, and learned from the Bailiff of Greifensee to what extent one can be driven to gather together all one's old loves. I wondered if Philipp, too, was seeking a graceful and edifying end to a ridiculous story, as well as a little peace of mind.

I was doing quite well until I lay down on the bunk for the night. Numbing cold seeped through the thick walls, and yet a summer breeze blew waves of warmth through the openings in the window. It also brought the voices of reveling barhoppers, calls of greeting and good-bye, the droning laughter of men and the bubbling laughter of women. Once in a while there was utter silence, until I heard faraway steps and voices approaching, getting louder, and then fading again in the distance. Sometimes I caught shreds of conversation. Sometimes a couple would stop beneath my window.

Suddenly I was gripped by longing for the bright, warm, colorful life outside, as if I had been locked up and would be locked up in this cell for years. Locked up for years—was that what was in store for me? I thought of the pride that comes before a fall, and of the fall that follows pride. I thought of the successes I had striven for in my life and the failures I had had. I thought about Korten's death. Was I experiencing the victory of poetic injustice?

The next morning I attempted a few squats and push-ups. They are said to help you survive years of solitary confinement. My joints ached.

19

Pending proceedings

At nine thirty I was taken for questioning. I had expected Bleckmeier and Rawitz. Instead I sat opposite a young man with a clever face and manicured hands who introduced himself as Federal Public Prosecutor Dr. Franz from the Federal High Court. In a clear, pleasant voice he read me the charges, ranging from aiding a terrorist organization to obstruction of justice. He asked me if I wished to be represented by a lawyer of my choice. "I am aware that you have a legal background," he said, "but so do I, and when it comes to my own affairs I wouldn't touch something as simple as a purchase or rent dispute. Never act on your own behalf in legal matters—that's a solid old legal principle. In your case, the main issue will be the severity of the sentence, so overview and experience will be necessary, neither of which you have." He smiled affably.

"You mentioned Frau Salger—and what did you say was the crime for which I am supposed to have obstructed justice?"

"I haven't said anything yet. The crime is an attack on an American military installation perpetrated on January sixth in Käfertal."

"Käfertal?"

Dr. Franz nodded. "But I think we'd better talk about you. You picked up Frau Salger in Amorbach and helped her cross the border into France. You need not worry about any infringements against the Passport Law, Herr Self; we will be happy to sweep that under the rug. I would like you to tell me what happened after you got her to France." He continued to smile affably.

After I had closed the book of my journey with Leo and put it away on my return to Mannheim, I hadn't touched it again. Now it flipped open of its own accord. For an instant I forgot where I was, didn't see the Formica table, the dirty yellow walls, the barred windows. I let myself be carried away by a wave of memories of Leo's face, the moon above Lake Murten, and the air in the Alps. Then the wave set me back down, and once again I sat facing Dr. Franz. His smile had frozen into a grimace. No, the book of my journey with Leo would remain shut for him. And what about the obstruction of justice? Does not obstruction of justice require that a crime has actually been perpetrated and can be punished? Without an attack in Käfertal on January 6, there was also no obstruction of justice. Without an attack, there was also no terrorist organization that I could have supported. What if, instead of the attack in Käfertal, there had been one in the Lampertheim National Forest?

When I asked him that, he looked at me, puzzled. "Instead of that attack another one? I don't quite understand."

I got up. "I'd like to return to my cell."

"Are you declining to make a statement?"

"I'm not sure yet if I will decline or not. I'd like to give the matter some thought." He was about to reply, and I knew what he was going to say. "Yes, I am declining to make a statement."

He shrugged his shoulders, pressed the bell, and without saying a word waved me off with the warden who came in.

Back in my cell I sat down on the bunk, smoked, and was incapable of thinking in an orderly manner. I tried to remember the name of the professor with whom I had studied criminal law as a young man, as if his name were of the greatest importance. Then images of my years as a public prosecutor went through my mind: interrogations, trials, and executions at which I had been present. In the flood of images there wasn't a single one that might have instructed me about the specifics of obstruction of justice, or otherwise about the legal problems of my situation.

The warden returned and led me into the visiting room.

"Brigitte!"

She was crying and could not speak. The officer allowed us to embrace. He cleared his throat, and Brigitte and I sat down at the table, facing each other.

"How did you know I was here?"

"Nägelsbach called me yesterday evening, and this morning another friend of yours, a journalist, Peschkalek. He was the one who actually brought me here. He wants to talk to you, too." She looked at me. "Why didn't you call me? Were you trying to hide the fact that you are in jail?" Nägelsbach had told her my situation was serious, and she had immediately set out to get me a good lawyer. Because the sick like to be treated by a professor, she wanted me to be represented by a professor and had called the Heidelberg professors of law. "Some of them said it wasn't their field, which sounded like internists who don't want to operate; with others it seemed to be their field but they couldn't understand what I was talking about; and then there were also those who didn't want to get involved in pending proceedings. Is that how it is? Aren't defense lawyers allowed to get involved in pending proceedings? I thought that that's what they're there for."

"Did you find one?"

She shook her head.

"It doesn't matter, Brigitte. I might not even need one. If I do, I know one or two lawyers I can turn to. What does Manu say to my being in prison?"

"He thinks it's great. He's behind you—we're both behind you."

Peschkalek also assured me he was behind me. He twirled his mustache anxiously and asked if he could do anything. "You could bring me a meal from the Ritter Restaurant. It's only a few steps away." He had brought a carton of Sweet Aftons.

"How did you find out about my arrest? Was it in the papers?" If I was to get out quickly, I didn't want Frau Büchler to hear the news and hit the roof.

"I tried calling you at home, and when I couldn't reach you there I called your girlfriend's place, and she told me the news. No, there's nothing in the papers yet. I don't think it will hit the local or regional press till the middle of next week. But things won't really get going till you appear in court. A former public prosecutor being cross-examined: You'll be the star of the show! Then you'll turn the tables on them, and become the accuser instead of the accused. You'll question them on the exact location where the attack took place, what the damage was, what the aftereffects were, and then the bombshell: The attack was in the Lampertheim National Forest, the target was a poison-gas depot, and all this is being covered up because the fact that there is poison gas stored there is itself being covered up. What a tour de force! I admit I'm quite jealous." He beamed, delighted by the scenario he had created and my role in it. "And then we have the romantic touch—not that I think the judge will be interested, but the readers will love it. Ticking bombs, beating hearts, an old man and a young girl: That kind of stuff makes for a great story. The old man and the young girl," he savored his words, "that would make a good title, wouldn't it? If not for the whole story, then at least for an episode."

"You're skinning me, basting me, roasting me, carving me up, and serving me—I am still alive, Peschkalek, and old stag that I am, it is closed season right now, not shooting season."

He blushed, ruffled his mustache, clapped his hand on his bald head, and laughed. "Oh no! The vultures of the press, the hyenas! Am I confirming all those preconceptions about reporters? Sometimes I frighten myself when I can't see or hear anything without thinking whether it would make a good story. Reality is only real when I've captured it"—he tapped his hand against his hip, where his camera usually hung—"or, rather, when the story has been aired or is in print. We've talked about this before. Who cares about anything that isn't in the media? And when nobody cares, the thing itself has no effect, and if it has no effect it's not real. It's as simple as that."

I let Peschkalek have his media-driven idea of reality. I didn't hold it against him that he reduced my story to a feature article.

He asked me to forgive his *déformation professionelle*, asked anxiously how I was, and looked at me again the way a friendly sea lion might. No, I didn't hold any of it against him. But the favor I had wanted to ask of him I asked of Brigitte instead, and also asked her not to tell him anything about it.

20

As if

If the first night in prison was bad, the second was worse, not to mention the fear now plaguing me that things would escalate, each night proving worse than the one before.

I dreamed that I had to arrange the layout of the front page of a newspaper. Every time I thought I had artfully put together the pictures and articles I had been given, another picture or article would turn up. And every time, I was faced by the insolubility of the task: The page was full and there was no space for additional material. But I would start over every time, moving things around, thinking I had pulled it off, but then realizing yet again that I had missed a picture or an article. I was unsettled, but hard-nosed and persistent. Then it struck me that I hadn't really looked at the material properly. The articles all had the same foolish headline—"Self Himself"—and the pictures showed me always with the same wide eyes and awkward grin. But even this didn't wake me up. I continued moving the pictures and articles around, failing each time, until the sun woke me.

"We want to set up an interrogation on Sunday. We'd like to talk to you one more time before you are brought before the judge." Dr. Franz was again sporting his affable smile. Nägelsbach was sitting next to him unhappily, Bleckmeier looked glum, and Rawitz had grown even fatter, holding his paunch in place with folded hands. "Unfortunately we had a silly little slipup, and your arrest was entered on Saturday instead of Friday. As a result, we couldn't secure the judge yesterday and will have to do it today. We'd be grateful if you wouldn't mind considering yourself as having been arrested on Saturday."

Had Nägelsbach entered me under the wrong day? Was that why he was looking so unhappy? I didn't want to cause him any problems, and waiting an additional day for a hearing before a judge didn't make much difference to me. But what was I to make of the prosecuting attorney's "as if" philosophy?

"I will be brought before the judge *as if* I'd been arrested yesterday. I am being accused of obstruction of justice *as if* a sentence for Frau Salger is imminent for a crime she committed in Käfertal. An attack in Viernheim is going to be handled *as if* it had occurred in Käfertal. Wouldn't you say there are a few too many 'as ifs' here?"

Rawitz unclasped his hands and turned to Franz. "There's no point. Let him tell the judge whatever he wants to. If the judge decides to release him, we'll just bring him in again. And don't worry, we'll purge him of that Käfertal-Viernheim nonsense by the time of the hearing."

"You have arrested one of the men and are intending to put him on trial," I said. "Are you intending to convict him of a crime he didn't commit? Are you—"

"The crime, the crime," Franz interrupted me impatiently. "What a strange notion of crime you have. It is the charge that generates the crime. The charge scoops up a few specifics from the infinite and overwhelming flood of occurrences, activities, and actions, and puts them together into what we call the crime. One man shoots, another falls dead, at the same time birds are chirping, cars go by, bakers are baking, and you're lighting a cigarette. The charge knows what it is that counts. The charge turns the shot and the dead man into a murder, and neglects everything else."

"One man shoots, you say, and another falls dead—but the attack was not in Käfertal but in Viernheim. Käfertal is neither here nor there."

"Oh, yes?" Rawitz said sarcastically. "Käfertal is neither here nor there? So where is Käfertal, then?"

"A place is one thing, and what happens at a place is another," Bleckmeier jumped in. "What is punished is what happens, not the place." He looked at us uncertainly and, when there was no reaction, added, "so to speak."

"The place is neither here nor there and isn't punishable," Rawitz said. "How long do I have to listen to this bullshit? It's Sunday, and I want to go home."

"Bullshit?" Bleckmeier was prepared to take quite a lot, but not that.

"Gentlemen, gentlemen," Franz said soothingly, "let us forget the philosophical questions of space and time. You, too, Herr Self, have more important issues you should be thinking about. You are right, we have arrested someone. He has confessed to the attack in Käfertal and will also confess in court. Furthermore, we will have the statements of our German officials and our American friends. Let us leave the pointless preliminaries and come to you and Frau Salger."

"Could you have the envelope brought here that arrived for me this morning?" I asked. I had found out from the officer who had brought me to the questioning that the folder Brigitte had sent me had arrived, but that it was going to be given to me on Monday, after inspection by the court. "You, of course, are authorized to open and view it without a judge."

After some back and forth Franz had the folder brought in, opened it, and took out a copy of the American file.

"Go ahead, read it," I said.

He read it, and his mouth tightened. After he read each page he handed it to Rawitz, who then handed it on to Bleckmeier and Nägelsbach. For ten minutes there was complete silence in the room. Through the small window I could see a section of the Heidelberg Castle. From time to time a car drove along the Oberer Fauler Pelz. In the distance someone was practicing on the piano. Everybody was silent until Nägelsbach had read the last page.

"We have to get the original. We'll have his place searched."

"I doubt he'd have the original lying around at home."

"Perhaps he does—it's worth a try."

"Why don't we go have a word with the Americans?"

"I don't like this business either," Nägelsbach said, looking at me sadly. "But an attack in Viernheim in which poison gas was released—poison gas belonging to the Americans or from old German stockpiles—that's simply not acceptable."

"Was poison gas released?" I asked

"Our American friends . . ." Bleckmeier began, only to fall silent at a glance from Rawitz. I repeated my question.

"Even if poison gas was not released—if the trial centers on it and the press zeros in on the story, all hell will break loose. Even if mass panic can be avoided, Viernheim will be a branded town. People will want to avoid it the way they would avoid Chernobyl. The terrorists should not be allowed to boast of this potential damage and threat. And the inhabitants don't deserve to be plunged into such fear by the terrorists."

"Are you trying to justify—" I tried to ask.

"No," Franz interrupted, "you've got your logic all mixed up. The trial can't take this course, but that certainly doesn't justify letting the perpetrators get away. What it boils down to is that we have a double responsibility: on one hand to the people of the area, particularly in Viernheim, and on the other for the implementation of the government's charge. And our responsibility doesn't end even there. We must consider the Americans, and the relationship between Germany and America, and the fact that the abandoned hazardous sites of the world wars have to be approached with a systematic solution. If there is ice in Viernheim, then we are dealing with the tip of the iceberg and we can't do things by half. You know as well as I do . . ."

I stopped listening. I was tired of all the talk, and tired of the grand words of double, triple, quadruple, and quintuple responsibility, and all the bickering surrounding my head. Suddenly I was no longer interested in threatening to throw a wrench into the Käfertal trial, nor in them letting me go free in order to save the trial. I just wanted to go to my cell, lie down on my bunk, and not give a damn about anyone or anything.

Franz looked at me. He was waiting for a reply. What was it that he had asked? Nägelsbach helped. "Dr. Franz is referring to a mutual rapprochement—on one side your role in the legal proceedings, and on the other the question of guilt and punishment." They looked at me expectantly.

I didn't want to take on the role they were trying to foist on me. I told them that. They called the warden and had him take me back to my cell.

21

Stuttering a little

By late afternoon I was a free man. There had been no further questioning and no hearing before the judge. The trusty had brought me a tray with cauliflower soup, spareribs, a vegetable platter, potatoes, and a vanilla custard. Otherwise I had remained alone, and with the help of Keres's *Best Games of Chess* had cornered Alyekhin into checkmate, until the warden came, told me I could go, and walked me to the gate. Thank God prisons don't follow the example of hospitals, which never release a patient on a weekend, even if he is cured.

I stood outside the prison gate with my little suitcase, savoring the smell of freedom and the warmth of the sun. And when I reached the Neckar River I took pleasure in the smell of dead fish, motor oil, and old memories. In the lock by the Karlstor a barge was being lowered. A blanket was spread out over the top of its hold with a little playpen in which a child was playing.

"Can you take me along?"

The bargeman could see that I was calling out something to him, but couldn't make out what I was saying. I pointed at myself, at the barge, and waved my hand downriver. He laughed and shrugged his shoulders. I took this as a yes, hurried down the embankment, and jumped from the edge of the lock onto the barge, which quickly disappeared into the lock's depths. It was darker and colder than up above, and water, menacing and forceful, was seeping through the gap in the back gates. It was a relief when the front gates opened and we had the river in front of us, the old bridge, and the silhouette of the old town.

"What you did was dangerous," the bargeman's wife said. She was holding the child in her arms, eyeing me with a mixture of curiosity and rebuke.

I nodded. "I wish that I'd at least brought along some cake. But when I passed a pastry shop just now, I didn't know I was going to meet you. Is your husband going to throw me overboard?"

Needless to say he didn't, and his wife offered me a slice of the sponge cake she had baked. I sat down, let my legs dangle from the side, ate the cake, and watched the town wander by. We passed beneath a bridge, the Alte Brücke, the child's squeals of delight echoing as its mother kissed its tummy. Under the Neue Brücke, I recalled the wooden bridge that had crossed over the Neckar River after the war, and the sight of the island awoke my childhood longing for both adventure and the snugness of home. Then we pulled into the canal and the autobahn bridge came into sight. From the dam I could have seen the spot where I had found Wendt.

I had cleared up a case that had mystified me, but which I had not actually been working on: A group of youngsters organize an attack, the police want to cover up the attack but still punish the youngsters, and so the police come up with the clever idea of moving the attack to another site. Relocating it, so to speak, as Bleckmeier would rightly say. But the police had to proceed with caution and a light touch. They couldn't afford to trumpet to the world that they were looking for these youngsters. It wouldn't do to mount a big search in connection with an attack in Käfertal and then, as they were being arrested, have them blabbing to cameras and reporters with pens poised about their attack in Viernheim. So the police initiated their search in secret, until Wendt's death, which was somehow linked to the attack and raised God knows what fears and no longer allowed further delay. The police had to go public with their search. All the same, they had struck a deal with one of the perpetrators that he could secure a milder sentence by confessing to the attack in Käfertal. He might even become the chief witness. The only thing the police would be risking was that the others might slip up or refuse to play along. But slipups can be fixed, and why shouldn't they want to play along?

In fact, I myself had not been aware that Wendt's death had somehow been connected with the attack. Wendt had a map of Viernheim on him when he was found. He had been killed by a bullet from Lemke's gun. He had known Lemke from before, had been introduced to Leo by Lemke, and had helped Leo after the attack. Had he been the fifth man Lemke had brought along on the attack, and whom Leo had not recognized, and who then made it back to the psychiatric hospital before she did?

I got off the barge at the Schwabenheim lock. I sauntered along the riverbank to the Schwabenheimer Hof and sat down at a table in the garden of the Zum Anker pub. Many families had come on foot or by bicycle from Ladenburg,

Neckarhausen, or Heidelberg. It was past the hour of coffee and cake and the fathers had switched to beer, while the children were beginning to whine because they, too, wanted something but didn't know what. A Madonna in a light blue dress and dark blue cloak stood in a niche in the wall. Two tables farther down sat a middle-aged woman cheerfully reading a newspaper and drinking wine. I liked her. To go to a pub alone, and sit comfortably with a newspaper and a glass of wine, is something that men do, not women, and never mind about emancipation. But she was an exception. Occasionally she looked up and our eyes would meet.

The taxi that I had the waiter call for arrived. I paid the check, walked over to her table, sat down, told her how very attractive she was, got up, and was gone almost before she could thank me for the compliment with a bemused smile. I think I stuttered a little.

During the ride to Heidelberg I was initially proud of myself. In fact, I'm somewhat shy. Then I got angry at myself. Why had I run away? Why hadn't I stayed at her table? Had there been an invitation in her glance, a promise in her smile?

I was about to have the driver turn back, but I didn't. One should never want too much at once. And as for the promise—perhaps she'd only made it because she could tell that she wouldn't have to keep it.

22

Write an article!

I found Peschkalek at Brigitte's place. "We were coming over to visit you when Chief Inspector Nägelsbach called. Congratulations! Have you been released till the trial?"

"I don't know. I might not even be called. I somehow think the last thing they want at the trial is a stubborn old man who keeps insisting that the attack was in Viernheim and not in Käfertal."

Peschkalek frowned. "You told them the attack was in Viernheim?"

I nodded. "I think they released me because—"

"Are you out of your mind?" he cut in, bewildered. "I thought we had agreed how we'd handle this. Your statement at the trial was supposed to explode like a bombshell! Now the only thing that has exploded is a little firecracker that nobody saw or heard! What's going to become of the trial now?" He grew increasingly irate. "What were you thinking? All that work for nothing! Am I supposed to start from the beginning? Are you no longer interested in the fact that the police are covering up a terrorist attack? You don't care that the trial will turn into a farce?" Now he was shouting.

I didn't understand. "What are you going on about? Bombshells are your job, not mine. Go ahead and write an article!"

"An article!" He waved his hands dismissively, no longer furious, just tired. "It's crazy. Here we had our goal within reach: We have the American report, you're about to go on trial—and then, nothing."

Brigitte looked at him and then at me. "You mean the report that I—"

I didn't want her to continue. As long as it wasn't clear why Peschkalek was making such a fuss, I didn't want him to know that I had shown the report to the police. So I shouted: "What do you mean 'nothing'? And furthermore, what do you mean by the goal being 'within reach' and me about to go on trial? What goal are you talking about?"

But he waved his hands again and got up. He smiled painfully. "I'm sorry I raised my voice. Don't take it personally, it's a legacy from my father. My mother can only bear to live with him because she has a hearing aid that she can turn off whenever he gets too loud."

Brigitte talked him into staying for dinner. After dinner, he helped Manu with his essay. "A visit to the planetarium" turned into a sharp, fast-paced report, and Manu was filled with admiration. Brigitte was charmed, too. As he helped her wash up in the kitchen, he suggested that they speak informally. As we sipped our wine, Brigitte suggested that he and I should call each other by our first names as well, and I could hardly refuse. "Gerhard"—"Ingo"—we clinked glasses. But I felt wary.

23

R. I. P.

The next day I drove to Husum. It's a journey to the end of the world. Beyond Giessen the mountains and forests become monotonous, beyond Kassel the towns become poor, and by Salzgitter the terrain turns flat and bleak. If we were to banish dissidents in Germany, we would banish them to the Steinhuder Lake.

I had called the main office of the Evangelical Academy and been told that the director, whom Tietzke had identified as a former comrade of Lemke's, was currently conducting a workshop: *Abused—Aggrieved—Affected: Coping with Threat in the Whirlwind of Time.* I was told that I could sit in on a session and talk to him during one of the breaks. I found the room and tiptoed to the only free chair. The speaker announced that he was coming to the end of his paper, and finally did so after a few lengthy detours. I learned that aggrievement was a passive state while affectedness was an active one, and that we could not hide behind the whirlwind of time but had to stand our ground. I was also initiated into the law of entropy, according to which the world doesn't have much of a prospect to end well. A bearded man of about fifty thanked the speaker. His paper, he said, had extended a hand to us that we would all want to clasp heartily, and we would have ample opportunity to do so during the two-thirty session; now it was time for lunch. Was this the director who had sat with Lemke in the front row at those spaghetti Westerns in '68 and '69? He was immediately besieged by the workshop participants, but when they dribbled away, taking the speaker with them, he remained behind, jotting down notes.

I greeted him and introduced myself. "I have a question that has nothing to do with your workshop. I'm a private investigator and am investigating a murder. I believe that you know, or knew, the main suspect. Were you a student in Heidelberg around '68, '69?"

He was a careful man. He made me show him my ID and had his office call Wendt Real Estate in Heidelberg to ask Frau Büchler to confirm that I had indeed been commissioned by old Herr Wendt to investigate young Wendt's murder. He was pale when he hung up. "This is terrible news. Someone I knew well becoming a victim of a crime. I suppose this is a daily occurrence in your profession, but in my world I experience it as severe aggrievement."

He seemed shaken, so I refrained from offering him my hand and advising affectedness instead of aggrievement.

"When were you involved with Rolf Wendt?"

"Let me see, when was the Socialist Patient Collective in Heidelberg? When all that ended, Wendt was looking for a new path, a new direction. He met us and for a while was something like a little brother to us. He must have been about seventeen or eighteen back then."

"You said 'us'—do you mean Helmut Lemke and yourself?"

"I mean Helmut, Richard, and myself—the three of us spent a lot of time together." He reminisced. "You know, as much as the news of Wendt's death has shaken me, when I think back, I realize that for me Rolf, dead as he now is, is not more dead than the other two, who I imagine are still alive but from whom I haven't heard in years. Though I must say that back then we lived like there was no tomorrow; all our thoughts and feelings were for the present. Despite world revolution—or because of it? As one grows older, a part of one's heart clings to the past while one's head worries about the future, and one no longer believes that friendships are forever."

I don't know what a man can still believe in when year after year he parcels out questions of fate into topics for workshops. He stood up. "Let's go and sit outside. Nowadays I hardly get out."

He leaned far back on the bench in front of the building and held his face up to the sun. I asked him if back then Lemke and Wendt had had a particularly good or particularly bad relationship to each other, and found out that everyone had a special relationship with Lemke. "You either admired him or locked horns with him, or both. But you couldn't deal with him as an equal. And when I said we were Rolf's big brothers, that's not quite right. It was Helmut Lemke who Rolf particularly looked up to."

"Admiration, locking of horns, not dealing with him as an equal—and yet you remember it as a golden time?"

He sat up and looked at me. His forehead was smooth for a man of fifty, but his eyes were tired with age—the eyes of a man who is duty-bound by his profession to love people, although by now they only get on his nerves. As a priest, therapist, or whatever he basically was, he had offered more advice, given more comfort, and granted more forgiveness than he had within him. "I didn't say it was a golden time, nor would I say such a thing. There is a photograph from those days hanging on the wall of my office in which I can see everything: what was golden—if it was golden—compulsions and conflicts, the living in the present. I can show it to you, if you'd like."

"How long did your gang-of-four last?"

"Until Helmut's career at the Communist League of West Germany took off. Then he no longer had time for tabletop soccer and spaghetti Westerns, and in politics only what had to do with the Communist League. What is strange is that none of us went over to the Communist League with him, even though he had been so dominant in our group that without him we scattered to the winds. Maybe he didn't want us there with him. Anyway, he didn't proselytize us. I'd say, one day he was simply gone."

"Did he also drop Rolf from one day to the next?"

"Yes, I think they had a fight or something. Richard was the only one who kept in touch with Helmut and whom Helmut seemed to want to keep in touch with. I don't know how long that lasted. The last time I saw Richard was when I passed my exams and was heading to Pforzheim for my internship as vicar, and was waiting in the Heidelberg station for my train. Richard was no longer working as a laboratory assistant, which is what he'd trained for, but was now working for a lawyer. A divorce lawyer, he said, though I wondered if it was really a divorce lawyer or a terrorist lawyer—you know, I mean one of those who are in cahoots with terrorists. Richard had always been frustrated that we could only watch those spaghetti Westerns and not actually live them: On one side large-scale landowners, corrupt generals, greedy priests, and on the other poor Mexican farmers in white pajamas and revolutionaries with ammunition belts crossed over their chests, and then lots of ripe mangoes, wine, and mariachis. He'd have loved to import all that over here."

Lunch was over. The participants of the various workshops had walked their legs off in the park. When one group caught sight of us and started heading over, he got up. "They think you are the next speaker, or they want to corner me. The workshop's starting up again in a few minutes. Come along, I'll show you the photograph."

It was hanging in his office. I had expected a photo the size of a postcard, but it had been enlarged to poster size and placed behind glass in a black frame. It showed a picnic in black and white: a lawn, a white cloth spread with fruit, bread, and wine, and Wendt and Lemke lounging across from each other. Behind them, the current director of the academy, already sporting a beard, was bending over picking flowers, and a few steps away was a Borgward with its sunroof pulled back. Instead of a number on its license plate it had the letters "R. I. P." Lemke was talking at Wendt, gesticulating wildly, and Wendt had been listening to him with his head resting on his hand and his hand resting on his knee, but now he looked up, and the flower-picking future director of the academy had also raised his head and was looking up, bent forward as he was. They had planted a presumably red flag on a thin, glittering stick: At this instant a magpie was flying off with the stick and the flag.

"Is that . . . no, it's not a snapshot, is it?"

"You mean because of the Manet motif? No, we didn't arrange ourselves like that on purpose. We didn't arrange for the magpie either, though it had already stolen a silver fork from us, and Richard had planted the flag lightly enough so the bird could snatch it away. Richard had been hovering around us all afternoon with his camera, shooting us from a distance, in closeup, with a telephoto lens and without one. He took hundreds of pictures. This was the last one. Do you like it?"

It was an attractive picture. But at the same time it made me sad. Lemke in his dark jacket, white shirt, and dark, narrow tie looked boyish in an old-fashioned way, energetic and self-confident. Wendt's face was already showing the over-taxed quality I had seen. A fearful, childlike face eager to be excited about the bird flying off but not quite daring to.

"Why should that beautiful Borgward automobile rest in peace?" I asked.

He didn't understand.

"R. I. P., *requiescat in pace*. Wasn't that meant for the car? Was it meant for capitalism, or . . ."

He laughed. "That wasn't on the car. Richard retouched the picture later. He always smuggled his initials into photos that he thought were particularly successful. R. I. P.—that's short for Richard Ingo Peschkalek."

24

After Fall Comes Winter

Shouldn't I have realized it? This was of course a futile question. But it preoccupied me all the way to Göttingen. I remembered the conversation in prison, when Peschkalek had spoken of Leo and me: the old man and the young girl. I hadn't ever told him anything about her. Had he got that from Lemke? It also struck me now that he had turned up at Brigitte's place, even though I'd never mentioned her. Had he been spying on me? Had our first meeting on the autobahn not been a coincidence, but set up by him? Had he been spying on me at that very moment?

Everything became even more confused. That Peschkalek might have heard about me and Leo from Lemke, but had come to me wanting to dig up the facts about the attack Lemke had launched, didn't pan out. Had he heard about Leo and me and the case I was investigating from the police, and not from Lemke? Let's say he'd read the article in the *Viernheimer Tageblatt*, his curiosity was aroused, he started investigating, found out from a police source that I, too, was investigating, and fastened onto me . . . And then, as coincidence would have it, his old comrade Lemke turned out to be behind everything? There was a little too much coincidence in all of this for my liking.

When in the evening, after a long drive, I reached Mannheim, I had a backache but no answers. All I knew was where I wanted to search for those answers. The phone book listed Peschkalek's apartment and studio in the Böckstrasse. I called Brigitte, told her I was still on the road and would be at her place by eight, and asked her to invite Peschkalek for dinner at eight, too. Then I parked my car in good time outside his place in the Böckstrasse. Shortly before eight he came out, got into his VW Golf, and drove off. He didn't look right or left. I read the names on the buzzers and went inside.

The hallway was narrow and gloomy. After a few steps it widened out on the left into a stairwell. Straight ahead it led to a backyard. Peschkalek's buzzer was on a board with six others. When I got used to the dark, I could make out a sign with his name on it and an arrow pointing to the back.

In the yard were an old elm tree and a two-story wooden shack leaning on the firewall of the building next door. Next to the outside staircase that led to the second floor was another sign, ATELIER PESCHKALEK. I climbed the stairs following the arrow. The landing was wide enough for Peschkalek to put a table and two recliners on it and use it as a balcony. The door had only a peephole, and the window that looked out onto the landing was secured with a grille. I reached into my bag, snapped open the large key ring that had a good hundred different keys on it, and tried them one by one. It was quiet in the yard. The wind rustled in the elm tree.

It took a long time for me to find the key that released the pin tumblers and turned the lock. The door opened into a large room. The back wall showed the unplastered firewall of the neighboring building. To the right were three doors, leading into a tiny bedroom, a kitchen that was no larger than a closet, and a bathroom that also served as a darkroom, in which the necessities of personal hygiene had surrendered to the developing of film. On the left I could look out into the neighbor's yard through two large windows. A gap in the buildings of the Hafenstrasse even offered a narrow vista of the warehouses and cranes of the harbor and the red strip that the setting sun had left behind on the pale sky.

Dusk was setting in, and I had to hurry. His place was filled with lamps that could have made the interior bright as day, and there were also black blinds on the windows—but one of the blinds was stuck. So I had to look things over as best as I could and take as close a look as possible at anything interesting in the windowless bathroom.

Despite the tangle of lamps, curtains, and folding screens, the Venetian chair, piano stool, grandfather clock, Styrofoam column, and fake jukebox, I soon realized that Peschkalek had an eye for order. In one desk drawer he kept stationery with a letterhead, in another stationery without, in the second drawer envelopes arranged by size, and in the last drawer supplies ranging from punchers to scissors. His unanswered mail and unpaid bills lay in a little basket on his desk. Everything that didn't have to be dealt with right away must have been in the binders lining the right-hand wall between the doors. They didn't have labels, but were numbered from 1.1 to 1.7, and under fourteen heading numbers there were between two and eleven further numbers. The heading numbers stood for topics such as portraits, nudes, fashion, politics, and commercials, and the further numbers stood for single big projects and also the small projects of a given year. It was quite straightforward. Under the heading number 15, Peschkalek had filed away his big features, the first about Italian contrabass makers, the second about closed steelworks in Lorraine, and the next three about football, alpine-horn blowing, and child prostitution in Germany. Binder number 15.6 was dedicated to the Viernheim attack.

Before I sat down on the toilet in his bathroom with the binder, I called Brigitte and told her about traffic jams and construction. "Is Ingo there yet? I won't make it before ten—don't wait for me with dinner."

They had finished the soup already and were about to start on the monkfish. "We'll keep a plate warm for you."

As in the other binders, in this one, too, were pictures first and then the text. It took a while till I realized what the photos showed. They were dark, and I was at the point of judging them failures. But they were night shots. A car, disguised figures in a forest, dug-up mounds of earth that the disguised figures were doing something with, uniformed figures, and an explosion with two bodies flying through the air, a fire, people running. The Viernheim attack in pictures.

The texts began with a letter to the local and regional press, in which the group After Fall Comes Winter took credit for the attack on the poison-gas depot in the Lampertheim National Forest and made threats against capitalism, colonialism, and imperialism. In a later letter, Peschkalek wrote about a terrorist who wanted out, had confided in him, and had handed him a confession and a video recording showing the Viernheim attack. Peschkalek praised the material and enclosed stills as proof of the video's quality, and excerpts from the confession. He wanted a million marks for it. The letter was to the ZDF television network. The next page in the binder listed who else he had contacted: the various broadcasting corporations, a Hamburg magazine and weekly, the serious press, the tabloids, and finally the gutter press. Then came the responses. At best they were surprised: The material looked interesting, but nothing was known about an attack on a poison-gas depot in the Viernheim Meadows. Some of the replies were curt, saying that the police knew nothing of such an attack—someone had spent time looking into it and was angry. More often than not, the replies were form letters thanking him, but unceremoniously turning him down. Finally I found in the binder the confession of the terrorist, an eighty-page manuscript, obviously printed on the same printer as Peschkalek's letters, and, in a plastic cover, the American file. I did not look at the video marked 15.6—the stills were enough.

I needed a breather before I could head over to Brigitte's place. I put a few photos in my bag, turned out the light in the bathroom, put the binder back, sat down in the Venetian chair, and looked out the window. On a balcony across the way three men had settled down to a game of Skat. I heard the bidding and calling of suits and sometimes a fist banging on the table along with a card. A red light blinked over the harbor, warning airplanes of a crane.

Had Lemke and Peschkalek mounted a spectacle for the media? I ought to have figured out much earlier that Lemke no longer believed in political battles or waged such battles anymore. A fanatic, a terrorist—that didn't pan out with him. He was able to slip into the role and play it convincingly. But that was all. Lemke was a player, a strategist, a gambler. He had staged a terrorist attack with a few foolish youngsters, staged it in a way that ought to have pitched the media into a feeding frenzy. There were even casualties, presumably unplanned, but heightening the worth of the spectacle and the price of the material. But nobody played along: not the Americans, not the police, not the media. None of the million marks they had intended to rake in had materialized.

25

That's strange

I didn't call Nägelsbach. I drove over to Brigitte's place, where I found her, Peschkalek, and Manu having chocolate, espresso, and sambuca over a game of Risk. I had a hard time responding to their cheerfulness. But I'd had a long drive and could plead tiredness. I ate the leftovers and watched them play.

It was a heated game. After years of living in Rio, Manu conquered and defended South America tooth and nail. His strategy was to occupy North America and Africa in order to secure South America—he didn't care about the rest of the world. Brigitte had only joined in the game because she didn't want to be a wet blanket. She had captured Australia, was fantasizing about harmonious coexistence with aborigines, and was not interested in further conquests. So Peschkalek managed to capture Europe and Asia without effort. But his mission was to free Australia and South America, and unlike Brigitte or Manu he took his mission seriously, got entangled in a hopeless war on two fronts, and didn't rest until he was utterly defeated. Manu and Brigitte were overjoyed, and he laughed along with them. But he was rankled. He wasn't a good loser.

"Time to go to bed!" Brigitte clapped her hands.

"No, no, no!" Manu was in high spirits and ran from the living room to the kitchen and back to the living room, and turned on the TV. Yugoslavia was falling apart. Rostock was bankrupt. A baby had been abducted from a hospital in Lüdenscheid and found in a phone booth in Leverkusen. The Frenchman Marcel Croust won over Viktor Krempel in the Manila chess tournament, establishing himself as the challenger to the world champion. The Federal Public Prosecutor's Office announced the arrest of the suspected terrorists Helmut Lemke and Leonore Salger in a village in Spain, from where they were to be extradited to Germany. The TV showed them being led in handcuffs to a helicopter by policemen in black-lacquered hats.

"Isn't that . . ."

"Yes."

Brigitte knew Leo from the picture leaning against the small stone lion on my desk. Brigitte shook her head. Leo, with her unwashed, stringy hair, bleary-eyed face, and grubby checked shirt, did not meet her approval.

"Are you going to see her again?" she asked me casually. Even when I had told her about my trip with Leo to Locarno, she had not made much of a fuss. Even then I hadn't fallen for it.

"I don't know."

Peschkalek stared at the television screen without a word. I couldn't see his face. When the news was over he cleared his throat and said, "It's amazing what the teamwork of the European police can pull off nowadays." He turned to me and launched into a minilecture about Interpol and the Schengen Treaty, the investigative role of the computer, Europol, and the new European forensic database.

"You'll try to get to see those two . . ." I began.

"I guess I ought to, don't you think?"

". . . and you'll try to talk them into playing the role I didn't want to play?"

He weighed which answer would trigger what question, wasn't sure, and dodged. "I'll think about it."

"What can you offer them?"

"What do you mean?" He seemed uncomfortable.

"Well, the Federal Public Prosecutor's Office can drop charges, apply for a lower penalty, or even grant pardons in order to salvage its story of the Käfertal attack. What can you offer? Money?"

"Me, money?"

"For a good feature article there's always good money, wouldn't you say?"

"Things aren't that good." He got up. "I've got to get going."

"Things aren't that good? There should be hundreds of thousands of marks in something like this, and with the real photos and documents even more. What would you say to a million?"

He looked at me, vexed. He was trying to figure out whether I'd just hit on that number or if I was hinting at something. His flight-instinct won. "Well, so long, then."

Brigitte had listened to us annoyed. When Peschkalek had gone, after kisses on both cheeks, she asked what was going on. "Are you fighting?" I dodged her question. As we lay in bed, she rested her head on my arm and looked at me.

"Gerhard."

"Yes?"

"Is that why they let you out of prison? I mean, did you tell them where to find the two of them?"

"For God's sake . . ."

"What would be wrong with that? I don't know the girl, but she's on the run with him, and he did assault you, after all. That was him, wasn't it? The one I met at the door when I found you in terrible shape and covered in blood."

"Yes, but I had no idea they were in Spain. Leo called me once or twice, and it sounded far away—that was all."

"That's strange." She turned around, nestled her back against me, and fell asleep.

I knew what she found strange. How would a policeman in a godforsaken village in the Spanish provinces come upon German terrorists? Not without a tip-off. I conjured up the image of a German tourist abroad going to the police to make a statement that he recognized the inhabitants of a neighboring bungalow as the terrorists for whom there was an alarm out. Then I remembered the tip-off that had led Rawitz and Bleckmeier to me, not to mention the tip-off that had landed me in prison. These had not come from a tourist. Nor had the tip-off that had brought Tietzke to Wendt's corpse. I might have been pointed out by someone who happened to see me, someone from Mannheim who had been drawn to the Odenwald and Amorbach by the warm summery day. But the tip-off about Wendt's corpse had come from Wendt's murderer.

26

A pointed chin and broad hips

Philipp wasn't in his hospital room.

"He's out in the garden." The nurse followed me to the window. Philipp, in his dressing gown, was walking around a pond, every step as cautious as if he were treading on thin ice. This is how old men walk, and even if Philipp were able to walk normally again, there would come a day when this would be the only way he could walk. A day would come when this would be the only way I could walk, too.

"This is my third round already. Thanks, but I don't need your arm. I'm not using the cane they've been trying to foist on me either."

I walked beside him, resisting the urge to tread as cautiously as he did.

"How long are they going to keep you here?"

"A few days, perhaps a week—just try pinning one of those doctors down. When I tell them they really don't have to treat me with kid gloves, they just laugh. They tell me I should have operated on myself, then I'd be fully up-to-date on my condition."

I wondered if that was possible.

"I've got to get out of here!" He waved his arms. The pretty young nurses were unsettling him. "It's crazy! I've always liked them, the sweet ones as much as the mean ones, the firm ones, the soft ones. I'm not one of those guys who need big breasts or blond hair. It used to be, if they were young and had that look in their eyes, that blank look where you can't tell if it sees through everything or is utterly clueless, when they have that scent that only young women have—that was it. And now"— he shook his head—"now a girl can be sweet and flutter her eyelashes at me all she wants, but I no longer see the young girl she is, just the old woman she will one day turn into."

I didn't understand. "You mean, a sort of X-ray vision?"

"Call it whatever you want. In the mornings there's Nurse Senta, for instance—the cutest face, soft skin, a pointed chin, small breasts, and broad hips. She acts stern, but loves to gig- gle. In the past, the air would have been charged. Now I look at her and see that one day her stern act will crease her mouth with scowling lines, blood vessels will spot her cheeks, and love handles will bulge over her midriff. Have you ever noticed how all women with pointed chins have broad hips?"

I tried to conjure up the chins and hips of the women I knew.

"Then there's Verena, the night nurse. A hot-blooded woman—but what looks wild now will look ravaged soon enough. In the past I wouldn't have given a damn. Now I see it, and it's like a bucket of cold water."

"What do you have against ravaged women? I thought you saw Helen of Troy in every woman?"

"I did. That's the way I liked it, and that's the way I'd like it to be again." He looked at me sadly. "But it doesn't work anymore. Now I only see a shrew in every woman."

"Perhaps it's just because you're still under the weather. You've never been sick before, have you?"

He had already weighed this explanation, too, but brushed it aside. "I used to fantasize about being a patient in a hospital and being spoiled by the nurses."

I wasn't able to cheer him up. On the way back to his room, he steadied himself on my arm. Nurse Eva helped him into bed. She wasn't just called Eva, she also looked the part, but he didn't grace her with a single glance. As I was about to leave, he grabbed my arm. "Am I paying now for having loved women?"

I left. But I left too late. His morose brooding had gotten to me. Here was a man who had made women the center of his life. His passion had not been for anything fleeting like fame or glory, nor for something external like money or possessions, nor for deceptive erudition, nor vain power. But it didn't help. The brooding and the life crisis still came, as they did for everybody else. I couldn't even think of a crime with which Philipp could salvage his life's illusion.

I called Frau Büchler. "I know who the murderer is. But I don't know his motive, nor do I have proof. Perhaps Herr Wendt knows more than he realizes. I really must speak to him at this point."

"Can you please call back in a few hours? I'll see what I can do."

I went to the Luisenpark and fed the ducks. At three o'clock I spoke again with Frau Büchler. "Could you please wait at your office tomorrow morning," she said. "Herr Wendt doesn't know yet when he will come by, but he will." She hesitated for a moment. "He is a man used to having his own way and can be somewhat imperious and gruff. But he is also sensitive. Whatever painful things you have to say to him about his son or his son's death, please say them carefully. And please don't hand him the invoice—send it to me."

"Frau Büchler, I—"

She had hung up.

27

If we had put our money where our mouth is

At nine o'clock I was at my office. I watered the potted palm, emptied the ashtrays, dusted the desk and filing cabinet, and neatly laid out fountain pens and pencils next to one another.

The phone rang. Herr Wendt's chauffeur informed me over his car phone that Herr Wendt would be at my office in half an hour.

A Mercedes pulled up. The chauffeur opened the car door. Before Herr Wendt got out, he eyed the building and my office, the smoked glass and the display window of the former tobacconist's, and the golden letters GERHARD SELF, PRIVATE INVESTIGATIONS. He got out of the car with difficulty and hesitated, carefully steadying himself, as if with his heavy body he had to find his balance: an elephant swaying his rump, head, and trunk, and one is uncertain whether he has forgotten how to use his power, or if he will stampede and flatten everything in his path. He approached my door with heavy steps. I opened it.

"Herr Self?" His voice boomed.

I greeted him. Despite the summer temperature, he seemed chilled and kept his coat on.

We sat down at my desk facing each other, and he immediately came to the point. "Who killed him?"

"You wouldn't know him. He and your son used to be friends, then for years their ways parted, but their paths crossed again and the two of them clashed. I am not yet sure whether he put pressure on your son, or whether your son put pressure on him; in other words, if he wanted something from your son or if your son wanted something from him. Were you in touch with your son in the days or weeks before he died?"

"I resent that question, we are father and son! He is a man of letters. He has his master's and a doctorate, and I'll be the first to admit that what he does and says is sometimes beyond me. And more often than not he simply doesn't understand how things are done in my world. But he has always respected me! Always!" Old Herr Wendt was blustering, but his face remained set. The bones of his temples were strong and his cheeks and chin square despite the considerable fat, and his eyes peered from beneath a wide forehead and profuse eyebrows, his pupils not vacillating, his eyelids not twitching. Only his mouth moved, letting the words drone out.

"Do you know the area between Viernheim and Lampertheim, Herr Wendt? The forest where the Americans have a depot."

"Why do you ask?"

"Your son was involved in the attack that was perpetrated there. To be precise, he was involved with the people who perpetrated the attack. There was a map of the region in his briefcase. Didn't the police tell you about that?"

He shook his head. "What map?"

"Nothing special. It was a map of the autobahn triangle near Viernheim and a few kilometers around it, with boundary or section numbers. It was a letter-size black-and-white photo-copy."

"Rolf . . ." He didn't continue.

"Yes?"

"I would have liked to have done more for my son. You know where he lived and how. Ah, Herr Self, the apartments he could have had! Why did I work my fingers to the bone all my life?"

I couldn't tell him why, so I waited.

"I would have given him everything, everything! But that map . . ."

"What do you mean?"

He stared down at the desk between us, reached for a pencil, and turned and twisted it in his gnarled hands. "I didn't want all of that to start again. Not that I know how deeply involved he was back then. Be that as it may, he didn't break free from it easily, let me tell you. When he started working, all that nonsense caught up with him, and now, when he was on the brink of making something of himself, with his own practice or his own hospital, he couldn't get mixed up in all that again!"

"What's the connection between the political things your son was involved in during the early seventies and the map you mentioned?"

The pencil snapped, and Herr Wendt slammed the two halves onto the desk. "I didn't hire you to cross-examine me!"

I remained silent.

He didn't say anything either and looked at me as if I were a bitter pill. To swallow or not to swallow, that was the question. I made to say something, but he waved his hand dismissively and began to talk. "A few days before his death, Rolf had asked for the map I have that indicates where poison gas had been buried at the end of the war in the Viernheim Meadows and the Lampertheim National Forest. He had wanted the map once before. He was still at school then and had just had an accident while driving a stolen car without a license. I moved heaven and earth to patch all that up, and I had just pulled it off when one night I caught him rifling through my desk and my safe, looking for the map. I gave him the hiding of his life. Perhaps . . ." There was a sudden uncertainty in his eyes. "That was the end of all the trouble. He finished school and passed his exams and his doctorate. So the hiding did him some good, don't you think? I learned to live with the fact that he didn't go on to become a surgeon; a man has to make his own choices. Also that he didn't talk to me much anymore—I don't know what people will have told you, but I was convinced that things would turn out well. At a certain age boys don't get along with their fathers. That's just a phase." He looked at me hard again.

"Why did your son want that map?"

"The first time around, I admit I didn't even give him a chance to explain himself, and the second time he wouldn't say. Did my son's murderer want that map? Are you saying that my son would still be alive if I'd given him that map?" He stood up. "It was him I was thinking of, do you understand, only him. I wanted him to be done once and for all with all that crazy political nonsense. As far as I was concerned he could have had the map; I don't need it anymore."

I couldn't tell him what he wanted to hear. I didn't know what had preceded Rolf's death that rainy afternoon beneath the autobahn bridge. But even if the map was worth murdering for, I couldn't imagine that somebody would murder Rolf if he were trying to extort the map from him. I told Wendt as much. "Is the map worth killing for?"

"Today? In the old days, perhaps. Take the metropolitan area of Ludwigshafen-Mannheim-Heidelberg: If one intended to establish a city, a real city, instead of letting it sprawl haphazardly, then only the area between Lampertheim, Bürstadt, Lorsch, and Viernheim would have come into question. There is access to the autobahn and the train, twenty minutes on the high-speed train to Frankfurt and twenty minutes by car to Heidelberg, there's nature all around, the Odenwald Range and the Palatinate Forest right at your fingertips—sounds good, doesn't it? In the sixties and seventies it sounded very good indeed. But today we don't think and plan that way anymore. Today we like everything to be small and cozy, with little towers and bay windows. Only the expansion of the high-speed train network is in the works. If you ask me, we wouldn't be in the mess we're in if we had put our money where our mouth is."

"Were the Americans planning to leave back then?"

"They were, by all accounts. And so we started buying. Prices rose in Neuschloss, and one Realtor tried to be particularly clever and put down half a million for the old forester's lodge on the road to Hemsbach." He laughed, slapping his thighs. "Half a million!"

"And with that map, you knew what was worth buying and what to avoid?"

"No. You couldn't get at the actual terrain. The Americans were there, and they still are. But *if* they had left, and *if* they had not cleaned up the place while they were still there, and *if* the city were to be built, then the map would have been a gold mine. If, if, if—that map was never a jackpot."

"Where did you get it?"

"I bought it."

I looked at him, puzzled.

"Needless to say, not at my local bookstore. A young man found it in his father's papers and was clever enough to realize its value for the real-estate market. I had to fork out a good chunk of cash for it."

I showed him young Lemke in a photograph from Leo's album. He looked at it: "Yes, he was the one who sold it to me."

I didn't for a moment believe that Lemke had found the map among his father's papers. Leo had told me about Lemke's internship at her father's office in the Ministry of Defense. Lemke had to have come across the map there and stolen it. Then he had sold it to old Herr Wendt and tried to get it back from young Rolf Wendt—presumably to cut the same deal with the next Realtor, for the funds of the Communist League, or for his own pocket.

"Herr Wendt, did you tell your son how you got the map?"

"I suppose so."

"That is what helped your son, not the beating you gave him. Lemke, who sold you the map, was trying to get your son to take it away from you again. He wouldn't have told him that he had sold you the map. He wouldn't even have spoken of money, but of high political aims. He was your son's political idol, and your son believed in him, until he realized that Lemke had duped him and used him."

"Did he . . ."

"No, he didn't kill your son."

He took the two halves of the broken pencil and tried to put them back together again.

"Can I have the map?" I asked.

"Will it help with your investigation?"

"I think it will."

He eyed me silently. Our conversation had exhausted him. Without asking me, he picked up my phone, called his chauffeur, and told him to pull up outside. He got up, steadied himself on the desk, found his balance, walked to the window, and waited for the car. "You'll hear from me," he said over his shoulder as he walked out the door.

28

Marked red

I didn't have to wait long for Wendt's reply. I got off the phone with Brigitte and immediately received a call from Frau Büchler. She had just sent a messenger to my office, and Herr Wendt hoped I would know to use what was in the package prudently—he didn't want it back. After the close of the investigation he expected a detailed written report. "You are to send the report to me, and the invoice, too," Frau Büchler said. "I wish you much success, Herr Self."

I waited for the messenger and looked out the window. There are seldom pedestrians out and about on the Augusta-Anlage. There are a couple of schools in the area, but the children use the side streets. There are also several offices, big and small, but the people who work there use their cars. I watched the traffic cop writing out tickets. Then my vista remained empty for a while, until two dark men in light suits came into view, stopped, talked vehemently at each other, and continued on their way, one of them angrily in front, the other anxiously following. A young woman pushed a stroller through the picture. A small boy ran by carrying a schoolbag. I lit a cigarette.

The messenger arrived on a motorbike. He didn't switch the engine off while he handed me a large yellow envelope on the steps leading up to my door, and he had me sign a receipt. Before he thundered off, he tapped his index finger on his helmet.

I had to clear my desk in order to lay out the map. It looked utterly insignificant. Little green numbers, ones and twos, denoted evergreen and deciduous woodland. To the west of the small pond called Baumholzgraben were a few brown altitude lines, and the whole area was cut into rectangles by cleared areas in gray, numbered between ten and forty. At eleven points, matchstick-thin areas about two centimeters long were marked red next to the cleared areas. Some were marked with a particularly wide hatching, and some with an additional question mark. Was that where poison gas from World War I was buried, or thought to be buried? The map bore no caption, and no heading either, just a multidigit number, an indication of the scale, a stamp with eagle and swastika, and an initial that was illegible.

I folded the map up again. I don't have a safe, but nobody has ever broken into my file cabinet. I laid the map on the middle shelf, under my blank-cartridge pistol. I wondered if there were any copies. I supposed that Lemke must have made a copy before he sold it to Herr Wendt, which he then could have used in preparation for the attack. Maybe the map had even given him the idea. Otherwise copies were not of much use, not then and not now. No Realtor would have paid for a copy, and no newspaper would have been interested.

I gazed at the shadow play that the sun and the gold lettering on my glass door conjured up on the floor: long, airy letters stretching upward and away from one another. I didn't have anything to do till evening. But I wasn't particularly interested in doing anything. I wanted to finish this case and put the whole thing behind me.

At the Kleiner Rosengarten I had a veal schnitzel in lemon sauce. I saw a matinee of a movie in which at first she loved him but he didn't love her, and then he loved her but she didn't love him, and then nobody loved anybody, until finally, after a chance meeting years later, he loved her and she loved him. I sweated, swam, and napped at the Herschelbad. I woke up to Peschkalek and Brigitte bringing me a birthday cake, whose candles I was supposed to blow out but couldn't. The two of them stood next to me, talked at me, and kept slapping my shoulders, their hands meeting. I felt they were holding onto each other and tried to turn around, but couldn't. They were holding me in a vise.

I disentangled myself from the sheet and looked at the clock. It was high time.

29

Another matter altogether

I remembered which key it was. The lock clicked open right away.

I looked around. An hour and a half had to be enough. I had asked Brigitte to invite Peschkalek again, which she readily did, but I wouldn't be able to put her off any longer than that.

I called her. "I'm sorry, but—"

"You'll be late?"

"Yes."

"Don't worry. Manu isn't home yet. When do you think you can make it?"

The grandfather clock struck. "It's eight now. Nine thirty—that shouldn't be a problem. *Bon appétit*—and don't forget to leave something for me."

"Will do."

It stayed light a little longer than last time. I could still see well. This time I looked not only at the desk, but also searched every compartment and drawer for the gun. I also looked behind every binder. I searched through the bedroom, groping my way through the closet from sweaters to shirts and under-wear to socks, and I patted down every jacket and pair of pants. I couldn't find his shoes. There was no shoe closet, no shoe shelf, nor were they lying around anywhere on the floor. A man without shoes—that couldn't be. When I tackled the bed and lifted the mattress, I found a drawer built in under the bed and packed with shoes, organized by color and polished to a spotless sheen. Pulling the drawer out all the way to look behind it proved difficult in the narrow room. But I managed that, too, crawling under the bed on my stomach and groping about in the area between the back of the drawer and the wall. Nothing.

It was very tight beneath the bed and I wanted to get out. But that proved more difficult than getting in. I pushed against the wall and kicked my legs but didn't get very far. I had used my legs to push my way under the bed, but I couldn't use them to pull myself out. More proof, I thought, that getting oneself into something is easy enough, but getting out again is another matter altogether. Just like monasteries or marriage, the foreign legion, or bad company, I reflected. I remembered a pool I had jumped into as a small boy. I had just learned to swim. After two laps I realized that there was no climbing up the smooth concrete walls. I was trapped.

Finally I stemmed and kicked, pushed and pulled myself centimeter by centimeter out from under the bed. Things got easier once my bottom was no longer stuck between the bed and the floor. First my shoulders got free, then my head. I breathed a sigh of relief, closed my eyes for a moment, and rolled onto my back—I simply couldn't get up right away.

When I opened my eyes, Peschkalek was standing over me. He was looking down at me, one hand in his pocket, the other twirling his mustache.

"How long have you been standing there?" This wasn't a good opening. I should have left him the first word and gotten up quietly.

"I should have pulled you out. Perhaps with a little apology, because it's so tight down there? And with an invitation, perhaps: As in, what would you like to see next? Where would you like to snoop around now, Mr. Private Investigator?" He took an ironic bow.

"What are you doing here?" I asked. That wasn't a particularly good beginning either. I was confused. Just the same, I got up.

He grinned. "I heard my clock chime when you called Brigitte." His grin grew malicious. "And three guesses how I managed to listen in when you called. Now why would your Brigitte and I be sitting cheek to cheek? Well?"

He took his hand out of his pocket and clenched his fist. I don't know whether he hoped or feared that I would fling myself on him. The thought didn't even cross my mind. I took my time.

"Well?" He hopped from one foot to another.

"Where is your gun?"

He stopped in his tracks. "My gun? What are you talking about?"

"Come on, Ingo. No one's here except you and me. There's no police inspector in the closet and no microphone in my tie pin. You know what I'm talking about, and I know that you know. Why play games?"

"I really don't know what you're talking about. How—"

"You're right. My question was a game, too. Why should you tell me where you've hidden the gun? Or did you throw it away?"

"Cut the bullshit, Gerhard. I told Brigitte I'd come get my

307

camera, and that's exactly what I'm going to do. Then I'll take the pictures of Manu she wants, and eat the potato soufflé that's in the oven. Feel free to turn on the light and continue your search for pistols, and don't forget to lock up when you leave."

He turned around and went into the other room. He was good. He was much better than I'd given him credit for. And the matter-of-factness with which he spoke of Brigitte, Manu, and the soufflé hit me harder than the sucker punch of him and Brigitte sitting cheek to cheek when I called. I watched him pack two cameras and a flash into his leather bag, and said, "I'd also take binder 15.6 and the video."

He pulled the strap very slowly through the buckle, pushed the prong into the hole in the strap, and pulled it tight. He shot a quick glance at the shelf.

"It's all still there," I said.

He had finished packing, but seemed unsure what to do next. He stood looking out the window, his hands on the leather bag.

"Not to mention that I have the map you wanted from Rolf."

Now he was even less certain what to do. Was I throwing him some bait? Was I making him an offer? With his left hand he tapped a disjointed rhythm on the leather bag.

"Isn't Lemke a risk, after all? You assumed he'd play along and keep his mouth shut. Then he'd have made his grand entrance at the trial, and you'd have had your feature in the media. When he gets out of prison, he'll have half the proceeds, with interest and compound interest. He'll get—what, eight years, ten? A high price, but as he got caught anyway and will be punished, what would he stand to gain if he didn't play along and keep his mouth shut?"

Peschkalek's hand tapped slowly and evenly.

"And yet he would stand to gain something," I said. "He'd be paying you back for squealing on him."

He turned and faced me. "Squealing on him? I don't understand."

"I don't know if one can actually prove that you squealed. Voice recordings, voice matches—nowadays there are all kinds of possibilities, but I doubt the police would go to all that trouble." I shook my head. "But Lemke doesn't need concrete proof. If I point him in the right direction, then he'll realize, just as I've realized, that it could only have been you who made that call to the Spanish police, not some German tourist, or whatever you passed yourself off as."

Peschkalek looked at me as if he were bracing himself for the next blow.

I took aim. "What's bad for you is that Lemke is not out just to get even. If he's going to start talking, it wouldn't surprise me if he chose to save his own skin. If he ends up as the chief witness, he might only get four to five years. So why not? He'll start talking and lay all the facts on the table. And he'll lay them out in such a way that you'll be the one who was behind it all: You came up with the idea, you masterminded it, and you saw it all through. You fired the gun— both in Viernheim and in Wieblingen. It was you!"

30

All's not lost

He gave up. Bait, offer, threat—whatever game I was playing, he no longer dared not play along. But playing along in my game meant giving his game up.

"You don't seriously believe that it was I who shot Rolf Wendt?" He looked at me, appalled.

"You put him under pressure. You had Lemke's gun. You contacted the newspapers. You—"

"But how—"

"How?" I shouted. "You want to know how it can be proved? One thing you can be sure of is that when the police have a lead they find the proof, too, and whatever they won't find, Lemke will provide them with."

"No, what I meant was, how could I have been the one who killed him if what I was after was to blackmail him?"

"Believe me, I won't lose any sleep over that one."

"It was an accident. Rolf—"

"The gunshot was an accident? Come on, Ingo—"

"If I'm going to talk, at least listen to what I have to say." He looked at me half desperate, half furious. I was silent.

"You don't have to tell me it sounds crazy! Rolf and I had gotten into a fight because I wanted the map and he wouldn't give it to me. I threatened that I would tell the police that he had hidden Leo in his psychiatric hospital. He grabbed hold of me and I slapped his hands out of the way and pushed him, and he fell backward."

"And?"

"He just lay there. At first I thought he was playing games, then I thought he had fainted. Then I suddenly got this really weird feeling and felt for his pulse. Nothing. He was dead." Peschkalek sat down in the Venetian chair, put his arms on the armrests, raised his hands, and let them fall again. I waited. He smiled crookedly and shot a quick glance at me. "I had taken the gun along to frighten him a little, and, well, as he was dead anyway . . . I fired it."

"All that just to sell your story? You thought—"

"I didn't just think. I'd have pulled it off if you hadn't gotten in the way. Then the reporter would have been on the scene before the police, would have found the little map, and would have started giving the matter some thought. Then it would have been easy enough for me to point the reporter in the right direction. But things have gotten moving anyway and become public."

"Did Lemke give you the gun?"

"Helmut give *me* something?" He laughed. "Helmut is a taker. And for years I was a giver. I was proud to be part of things, to let him order me about. The girls had to make coffee and cook spaghetti, and I had to see to electrical cables, equipment, and cars. That's why Helmut wanted me around when he was in Spain and got all that new-age stuff going with groups and seminars and nude bathing and hot springs.

When that didn't pan out and he came back here, things still went on the way they always had. I was to be part of things—in other words, see to all the technical stuff—but I had learned my lesson."

The lesson Peschkalek had learned was that nothing is free, that as you make your bed, so shall you lie in it—and nobody will come tuck you in. The whole thing had been Lemke's idea.

"You have to have something to offer people, was his motto. Soccer games, celebrity weddings, accidents, and crime are what excite people, and postmodern terrorism is just as much a media event and has to be organized and marketed like everything else." Lemke needed Peschkalek in order to fill the gap in the market. This time not only because it was more convenient not to have to worry about the technical side of things, but because Lemke wasn't capable of pulling off the whole thing on his own. He needed a cameraman. "But though he needed me, he didn't want to go fifty-fifty. I was to get only a third. I talked to him about it, but he wouldn't budge. He is . . . somehow, you can't talk with him. So I thought to myself: Just you wait, my time will come."

And Peschkalek's time did come. Initially, the horror was great. "The morning after the attack—you can't imagine. There we were, huddled around the radio. There was the news at the top of each hour, and every time we'd think: That's it, here comes the report! But each time, nothing. Even though we had two casualties to offer, and that's not to be sniffed at." On the following days there wasn't anything in the news either, and added to that disappointment came the uncertainty of what might have happened to Bertram and Leo, what Bertram might have said after his arrest, and if Leo had been arrested, too, or where she had gone into hiding. But Bertram wasn't actually in a position to reveal anything important because he didn't know anything of importance about Helmut and Ingo, and Helmut was certain that Leo would not want to reveal anything. So they set to work, writing to TV stations and newspapers. When that didn't pan out, Helmut wanted to drop the whole thing. "He still hired you to search for Leo and said he was doing it so we could put more pressure on the media without needing to worry that she might mess things up for us one day. He used my money for that. But I think he only did it because he wanted her back—because the way I see it, his mind was already on other projects."

Then Peschkalek had jumped in, shadowing me, had almost managed to trace her, and had set Rawitz and Bleck-meier on me. When shooting at Rolf didn't bring the whole thing out in the media the way he wanted, Peschkalek had first reported me to the police, then Helmut and Leo. "Hel-mut had stayed in constant contact with me. It never even occurred to him that he might pull the short straw one day."

Peschkalek had picked up momentum as he talked and looked at me hopefully. "All's not lost, Gerhard. When the trial comes, Helmut will put the record straight on Käfertal and Viernheim—that will be a real bombshell, and all the TV stations and papers that turned their backs on my story will have a feeding frenzy. With the map that you have, the story will get even better and more lucrative. There's at least half a million in it for each of us." He rummaged through his pants pocket. "Do you have a cigarette?"

I lit one for myself, threw him the yellow pack and the lighter, and leaned on the bookshelf. "Forget it. It isn't going to work. But you could give me the material."

"What would you do with it?"

"Don't worry, I won't turn it into cash. Perhaps I can use it to get Leo out."

"What, are you nuts? I've been working on Viernheim for over half a year! You want me to just chuck everything out the window?"

"Look, Ingo, it's over. The police know that Wendt was shot with Lemke's gun. When they confront Lemke with that, he'll know that you took it and shot Wendt with it. He won't want to pay for a murder he didn't commit. What other options does he have but to hand you over to the police? He has no choice. Give it up, Ingo."

I took binder number 15.6 and its video off the shelf, and he jumped up and tried to snatch them out of my hands. I held on to them tightly, but didn't have a chance. He was young, strong, and furious. There was a short scuffle, and the binder and video were in his hands.

He looked at me, malicious and ready to pounce.

"You won't get far with those," I said.

He grinned and threw a mock punch at me with his right hand. I stepped back. He put down the binder and video and came closer. I had no idea what he was doing. He launched into a shadowboxing dance, throwing punches first with one fist, then the other, and I kept stepping back. Had he lost his marbles? Then one of his punches hit me, and I staggered backward through the open bathroom door, taking glass beakers, bottles, and trays with me as I fell, and lay in the rubble of his darkroom.

I struggled back to my feet. I could smell chemicals. There was the gentle puffing sound with which a gas range lights up, and the cigarette I had dropped as I fell lit the puddle beneath the bathtub. I tore past the startled Peschkalek into his living room. Behind me there was another puffing sound, then another. I felt the warmth of the fire, turned around, and saw the flames leap out of the bathroom and seize the carpet and the shelf. Peschkalek tore off his jacket and started beating at the flames. It was completely futile.

"Get out!" I yelled. The fire began to roar. In the bedroom, the bed and closet were in flames. "Get out!"

The jacket with which he was beating at the fire was burning. I grabbed hold of him, but he tore himself loose. I grabbed hold of him again and dragged him toward the door. I tore it open. A gust of wind blew in, and the whole room was in flames. The heat drove us onto the landing. Peschkalek stood there, staring hypnotized into the burning room. "Let's get out of here!" I shouted, but he wasn't listening. He began walking back toward the door like a sleepwalker, and I pushed him down the stairs, hurrying after him. He tripped, caught himself, tripped again, and went tumbling head over heels.

He lay at the foot of the stairs without moving.

31

Rawitz laughed

The lights went on in the apartments all around and windows opened. People were leaning out and calling to one another what they could all plainly see: Fire! The ambulance arrived even before the fire brigade and took the unconscious Peschkalek away. The fire trucks arrived. Men in blue uniforms and funny helmets, with little axes on their belts, pulled the hoses through the hallway with surprising speed and turned the water on. There wasn't much left to extinguish.

Then I poked around in the hot, wet, black gunk. Even before the fire chief ordered me off the premises I could see that there was nothing left to be found. There wasn't anything even remotely resembling a binder or a video cassette.

The police began taking statements from witnesses, and I stole out of the courtyard. I would rather have headed over to the Kleiner Rosengarten or home than to Brigitte's. But I couldn't just leave her waiting. I gave her a sanitized version of my encounter with Peschkalek. She didn't probe further, just as I didn't probe into why she and Peschkalek had been sitting cheek to cheek. Later that night we called the hospital, where he was recovering from a concussion. He had also broken an arm and a leg, but had no other injuries.

Then I lay in bed mulling over the ruins of my case. I thought of the death of Rolf Wendt, who could have lived in a stylish apartment and had his own hospital; of Ingo Peschkalek, the miserable murderer; and of Leo's life on the edge, between flight and prison. I was worried that I wouldn't sleep a wink, but I ended up sleeping the sleep of the righteous. I dreamed I was running down some stairs and along corridors, pursued by flames. The running soon turned into floating and gliding, and I flitted cross-legged, with billowing nightshirt, over stairs and through more corridors, until I finally left the flames far behind me, braked, and landed on a green meadow among bright flowers.

The shortest way from Brigitte's place to mine is over the footbridge that crosses the Neckar to the Collini Center and then past the National Theater and across Werderplatz Square. At six in the morning the streets are empty, and only on the Goethestrasse or the Augusta-Anlage will you find some light traffic. It had not cooled off in the night, and the warm morning augured a hot day. A black cat crossed my path on the Rathenaustrasse. I could use some good luck.

I wrote my report for old Herr Wendt to the extent that I could. Then I faced the last chapter.

I put a call through to the Ministry of Defense and was passed from one department to another until I finally got hold of the official in charge of overseeing the poison-gas depots of the two world wars. He didn't want to say anything and couldn't say anything, but his department, naturally, was interested in anything that would help avert any potential danger and damage. Viernheim? A map from the archives of the

Wehrmacht and later the Ministry of Defense? A reward for handing over the map? He would be glad to look into the matter. I wouldn't give him my number, but he gave me his—his private line, his departmental number, and his number at home.

Nägelsbach, too, didn't want to say anything, or couldn't say anything. "You'd like to know how Frau Salger is doing? The preliminary proceedings are under way, and we have been issued strict instructions not to pass on any information to third parties. My inclination to make an exception in your case is minimal, to say the least." His tone was as sharp as his words. But Nägelsbach was prepared to arrange a meeting with Dr. Franz from the Federal High Court.

So I sat facing them once again in the Heidelberg District Attorney's Office: elegant Dr. Franz, the unavoidable Rawitz, and Bleckmeier with his gloomy glumness—so to speak. Nägelsbach had joined us but did not pull his chair up to the table, as if he were planning a quick getaway, or planning to stop one of us from doing so.

"You wanted to talk to me?" Dr. Franz asked.

"I have a few facts to put on the table, and an offer to make."

"Oh God!" Rawitz snapped. "Now he wants us to strike a deal with him!"

"I'll begin with the facts, if you don't mind."

Franz nodded, and I told them of Lemke's postmodern terrorism, of Wendt's and Peschkalek's first meeting years ago, and of their final meeting beneath the autobahn bridge near Wieblingen. I told them of my visit to Peschkalek's place, of Peschkalek's material, and about the map. All in all, I stuck to the truth. Except that I gave them to understand that I had saved the binder and the cassette from the flames.

"Are you saying that Wendt's murderer is lying in the hospital, waiting, so to speak, to be arrested?"

"So to speak. But I didn't say that he murdered Wendt. I find his version of the story entirely credible."

"Ha!" Rawitz barked.

"And what is the offer that you mentioned?" Franz asked. He was sporting his affable smile again.

I smiled back, letting the tension mount as I let them stew a little. "I shall hold on to Peschkalek's material. I'll keep it under lock and key and will guarantee that it will reach neither the media nor the defense lawyers. You can tell Peschkalek and Lemke that it was lost in the fire."

"I wonder what Dr. Self might want in return," Rawitz said with a smirk.

"There's something else. I'm prepared to give you the map."

"Like we're interested in geography!" Rawitz scoffed.

"Not so fast, Herr Rawitz. If it's worth something, it's worth something," Franz said.

I gave Franz the phone numbers of my contact at the Ministry of Defense, and he sent Bleckmeier to make the calls.

"And what would you like in return?"

"I would like you to release Leonore Salger and drop all charges against her."

"There we go!" Rawitz said, laughing.

"So that's what you want," Franz said, nodding. "And what does your client say to this?"

"One of the last things that Herr Wendt's son did was to take care of Leonore Salger. He hid her in the State Psychiatric Hospital and then found her a position in Amorbach. My client feels deeply for what his son was, and for what his son did."

Rawitz had started laughing again. Franz looked at him, irritated. "Will you furnish us with copies of Peschkalek's material?"

"No."

"Why not?"

"I don't want you to familiarize yourself with the material and orchestrate something that will defuse it."

"But surely we can at least take a look at it."

"That would entail the same risk."

"Are you expecting us to buy a pig in a poke?"

"You can get access to the material that Peschkalek sent out to the media. It's out there for the asking. And I did bring a few samples." I laid on the table the copies of the photographs I had pocketed during my first visit to Peschkalek's place.

"Can we trust him?" Franz asked, turning to Nägelsbach. "Can we be certain that he will hold on to this material, come what may?"

"That he'll hold on to it?" Rawitz mumbled, but he gurgled as if he were suppressing a chuckle. "Who can even guarantee that he has the stuff? For all we know, it went up in flames and he's only bluffing. Peschkalek and Lemke might even have other copies."

Nägelsbach looked at me, and then at Franz. "I would trust him. As for there being other copies, we'll see whether that's the case from Peschkalek's and Lemke's reactions when they're told about the fire."

Franz sent Nägelsbach off to arrange for Peschkalek's arrest. Bleckmeier returned, and Franz asked me to wait outside. When Nägelsbach came back, he and I stood awkwardly facing each other in the corridor.

"Thank you," I said.

"There's no need to thank me." He went back into the office.

I could hear them talking. Rawitz laughed from time to time. After about twenty minutes, Franz came out of the room. "We'll be in touch. And thank you for your cooperation." He dismissed me with a handshake.

I drove over to my office, finished my report, and wrote out an invoice. I leaned Leo's picture against the stone lion, sat, gazed, and smoked. At home I found Turbo sulking. I sat down on the balcony in the heat and he came over, turned away from me, and groomed himself.

Shortly before eight, the phone rang. Nägelsbach informed me that I could pick Leo up from the Fauler Pelz prison the following morning and told me to bring the map. He spoke in an official tone, and I imagined he would say good-bye right away and hang up. But he hesitated, I waited, and an uncomfortable silence ensued. He cleared his throat. "Expect difficulties with Frau Salger—I just wanted to let you know. Good-bye."

32

Too late

I had been too proud to ask Nägelsbach to explain what he meant. But I'd seen Leo on TV, and could imagine her being utterly exhausted, confused, perhaps even bitter and aggressive.

The following morning I tidied up my apartment, put a California champagne on ice that I had won a few years earlier as third prize in a seniors' surfing competition, and took a hot and cold shower. Then I spent a good twenty minutes in front of my closet until I finally decided on a brass-colored suit, a light blue shirt, and the tie with the small clouds. "Aren't you acting a little like a love-struck schoolboy?" an inner voice jeered as I drove to Heidelberg. I announced myself at the prison gate and handed the map over to a taciturn Bleckmeier. I had a good many reasons to feel queasy, and I did.

Leo was wearing the checked shirt she had been wearing on television after her arrest. But she had washed it and had slept away her bleary-eyed tiredness, and her brown curls again fell fully and softly over her shoulders. She saw me, waved, laughed, and stretched out her arms. It was a great weight off my mind. Where were the difficulties?

"Is that all you have with you?" I asked her. She was carrying a plastic bag.

"Yes, my things got lost along the way—the last ones when they arrested me. Your friend the chief inspector brought me a few things, even some eau de cologne, look!" She went over to the table and spread out her belongings. She started pushing the few items back and forth, as if she were trying to establish a certain order not yet discovered. The eau de cologne had to go in the middle and the other toiletries in an orbit around it, but there was no place for the handkerchief, the notepad, or the pen.

The correctional officer sitting behind a glass panel operating the gate buttons looked over at us. "What's going on?" he asked.

"Just a minute." She tried one last time. "No, it just won't work." She opened up the plastic bag and swept everything back into it. "Gerhard, I'd love to go for a drive somewhere and walk a bit, can we? The Heiligenberg Hill has been peeking into my cell the whole time."

We drove to the Mönchhofplatz, climbed up the Mönchberg, and followed the wide coils of the path to Michaels Basilica. It was almost like when we had climbed up to the ruins of Castle Wegelnburg: Leo often ran ahead of me, her hair flying. We barely spoke. She was skipping and jumping around. I watched her, and at times the memory of the trip we had taken together was as painful as if it had been a memory of distant years and long-lost youth. We sat at a table in the garden of the Waldschenke beneath tall old trees. It was only ten thirty in the morning, and we were the only customers.

"So tell me all about it."

"What do you mean?" she asked.

"How you've been doing since you left me."

"I didn't leave you. Did I leave you? I can't give you back the four hundred francs yet. I don't have any money. Helmut did have some, and I wanted him to send the four hundred francs to you, but he said you'd already made enough money off us. Did you? Helmut wanted to make money off me, and his friend did, too. I found out about that. But you . . ." She frowned and ran her finger along the squares on the tablecloth.

"If I hadn't been given the case, I wouldn't have gotten to know you. But by the time we were traveling together I no longer had the case and wasn't making any money. How did you get from Locarno to where Helmut was?"

"I called him and he came and picked me up. We traveled down the whole boot of Italy to Sicily, and then back up to the Riviera, and then over to Spain. Helmut was trying to drum up cash everywhere we went, but he couldn't." She spoke as if she were talking about two strangers and countered my questions with terse answers. I pieced together that they had gone on a spending spree, squandering all the money he had brought with him, and then slept in the car, pulled off con tricks, filled up their gas tank without paying, and shoplifted at supermarkets. "Then Helmut wanted me to . . . Well, there were tourists, and others, too, who had the hots for me, and Helmut said I should be nice to them. But I wouldn't play along with that."

"Why didn't you call me collect? You ran out of money— that's why you didn't call me anymore, right?"

She laughed. "That was fun, wasn't it, us talking on the phone at night? Sometimes you weren't there, but I suppose

I wasn't either." She laughed again. "I told Helmut to have his friend say hi to you from me, but I kind of knew he wouldn't."

We ate lunch. In the old days they served up nice plain home cooking at the Waldschenke. Today microwaves give the most modest establishment the ability to serve up a bad boeuf bourgignon in minutes.

"You and I have eaten better," she said, winking at me. "Remember the Hotel above Lake Murten?"

I nodded. "Let's go out and have a real dinner this evening," I said. "What are your plans, by the way? Are you going to stay in Heidelberg? Are you going to go on with your studies? Visit your mother? I'm sure she's been told about developments—have you heard from her?"

She thought awhile. "I'd like to go to a hair salon. My hair's all stringy." She took hold of a lock and tugged it straight. "And it stinks like hell." She sniffed at it and wrinkled her nose. "Go on, smell it yourself."

I was sitting opposite her and declined. "Don't worry, we'll go to a hair salon."

"No, I want you to smell it." She got up, walked around the table, bent toward me, and held her head in front of mine.

I smelled the sun in her hair, and a touch of eau de cologne. "Your hair doesn't stink, Leo, it has an aroma of—"

"It stinks! You have to take a better sniff!" She held her head even closer. I took her face in both hands. She gave me a short kiss. "And now be a good boy and smell it properly."

"OK, Leo, you win. We'll head over to a hair salon afterward."

Going back down the mountain was slower than the climb had been. The day had become oppressively hot; it was also strangely quiet. No breeze, no birds twittering in the heat, no cars or hikers, and the haze that covered the Rhine plain dampened the sounds rising from the city. Our steps were loud, heavy, and cumbersome. I felt tongue-tied.

Quite suddenly and spontaneously Leo began telling me about interpreting. She hadn't yet completed her studies, but for years had helped out with sister-town meetings between small German, French, and English communities. She spoke about mayors, priests, association chairmen, and other dignitaries, of the lives of the families that had put her up during these meetings. She mimicked the pastor of Korntal's Swabian attempts at English, and the pharmacist from Mirande who had learned German on a farm in Saxony as a prisoner of war. I laughed so hard that my sides hurt.

"It all sounds nice and fine, doesn't it?" she said, looking at me distressed. "But have you ever thought what interpreting really means? *Inter* is Latin for cutting between two things, plunging into, slashing through. And *pretium* means punishment, retribution, just deserts. That's what I've been trained for: slashing and punishing."

"Nonsense, Leo. I don't know what the exact etymology is, but I'm sure it's not that. If it had such a dark origin, why would it have become the term for the harmless activity of translating the spoken word?"

"You think translation is harmless?"

I didn't know what to say.

Leo arranging and rearranging her things on the table in the prison, speaking of herself as a stranger, holding her hair under my nose, saying wild things about interpreting—what was I to think? She didn't wait for my answer, but went on talking. By the time we got back to the car, she had given me a full lecture on her theory of translation that I didn't under-stand, and when I'd asked whether this theory came from Professor Leider, she filled me in on his strengths, weaknesses, and habits, and also on his wife, secretary, and colleagues.

"Do you have a particular hairdresser in mind?" I asked.

"You choose one for me, Gerhard."

Ever since I've lived in Mannheim, I've gone to a barber in the Schwetzinger Strasse and been satisfied. He has grown old along with me, and his fingers tremble, but the few hairs on my head don't challenge his capacity. He'd never do for Leo, though. I remembered that on my way to the Herschelbad I always passed a salon shining with chrome. That's where we'd go.

The young hairstylist greeted Leo as if he'd met her at a party the day before. Me he treated with the elegant respect befitting whatever I might be: her grandfather, father, or elderly gentleman friend. "You can wait here if you like," he said to me, "but perhaps you might prefer to return in about an hour?"

I sauntered over to the Paradeplatz, bought a *Süddeutsche Zeitung*, and read it at the Café Journal over an ice cream and an espresso. In the science section, I learned that cockroaches lead warm and caring family lives—we wrong them by abhorring them. Then I saw the bottle of sambuca on the shelf behind the bar. I drank one glass to Leo's health, another to her freedom, and a third to her new hairstyle. It's amazing how a shot or two of sambuca can make the world click into place. An hour later I was back at the salon.

"One more minute!" the Figaro called out from behind the partition, where he could see me, but I couldn't see him. I sat down. "One more minute and we'll be ready!"

I know that women leave salons looking quite different from the way they go in. After all, that's why they go there. I also know that afterward they are usually miserable. They need time—they need our admiration and enthusiasm. Any snide or critical remark, let alone a sarcastic one, must be avoided at all costs. As a daring Indian brave must never show pain, a daring participant at the premiere of a hairstyle must never show shock.

For a second I didn't recognize Leo. For a second I thought that the young woman with the buzz cut was someone else, and so dropped my attentive, enthusiastic expression. By the time I recognized her and quickly reinstated it, it was too late.

"You don't like it?" she said to me in English.

"Oh, no, I do! There is something strict and piquant about you now. Yes, you remind me of the women in those French existentialist movies of the fifties, and at the same time you look younger and more tender, more delicate. I—"

"No, you don't like it!"

She said it so emphatically that I lost courage. What I had told her wasn't entirely false, either. I liked those women in French existentialist movies, and Leo's new look had something of their vulnerable determination. I also liked her head—its beautiful shape was now revealed by the brushlike hair that had been truncated to a finger's breadth. I had loved her curls, but if they were gone they were gone. Curls invite you to plunge your hand into them, while a buzz cut invites you to sweep your hand over it—more appropriate in the circumstances. If only Leo didn't look so shorn, though. She had the air of an inmate of a prison or a psychiatric ward, and that frightened me.

"Okay, let's go."

I paid, we went to the car, and we drove home.

"Would you like to lie down and rest awhile?"

"*Why not.*"

She lay down on the couch. Its leather is cool, and even in the heat of summer allows for the cozy comfort of a light blanket. I covered her up and opened the balcony door wide. Turbo came in, crossed the room, jumped up onto the couch, and curled up beside her. Leo had closed her eyes.

I tiptoed into the kitchen. I sat down at the table, opened the newspaper, and pretended to read. The tap was dripping. A fat fly was buzzing at the window.

Then I heard Leo crying quietly. Was she crying herself to sleep? I listened and waited. Her crying grew louder, smooth, throaty, moaning, and wailing. I went back into the living room, sat down next to her, talked to her, held and caressed her. She stopped sobbing, but the tears continued to flow. After a while her wailing started up again, surged, and ebbed. This went on and on. Her tears never dried.

For a long time I didn't want to face that I wasn't equal to the situation. But then her wailing became so intense that she had trouble breathing. I called Philipp. He suggested that I talk to Eberlein. Eberlein told me to take her immediately to the State Psychiatric Hospital. On the way there she continued crying. She stopped as I walked her from the car to the old building.

On the way home I cried.

329

33

Imprisoned

It was to be a long, hot summer. For two weeks I took Brigitte and Manu to a beach resort, collected shells and starfish, and built a sand castle. Otherwise, I sat on my balcony a lot. I met Eberhard in the Luisenpark to play chess, and went out fishing with Philipp on his yacht. I occasionally practiced playing the flute or baking Christmas cookies. On a courageous day I went to the dentist. Tooth three-seven could be saved, and I was spared a removable prosthesis. Cases in the summer months had always come somewhat reluctantly. Now that I am older, they come very reluctantly indeed. I don't have to retire—I can just let my practice peter out.

In September the trial of Helmut Lemke, Richard Ingo Peschkalek, and Bertram Mohnhoff—the so-called Käfertal terrorist trial—began at the Karlsruhe Higher Regional Court. The newspapers were pleased with everything: the quick police investigation, the speedy court proceedings, and the terrorists who were eager to confess. Lemke was dignified and remorseful, Mohnhoff childishly eager. Only Peschkalek dug in his heels: He had had nothing to do with Wendt's death, he had not met up with him in Wieblingen, and the gun had not been in his possession. But then the news broke that the gun in question had been found during repair work in the Böckstrasse behind a brick in his apartment's firewall. When he presented the court with his version of the accident it didn't go over too well, even though the forensics couldn't exclude the possibility that Wendt had been killed not by the bullet but by a fall. Peschkalek was given twelve years, Lemke ten, and Mohnhoff eight. The newspapers were pleased with that, too. The lead writer of the *Frankfurter Allgemeine Zeitung* praised the idea the constitutional state had established by building bridges to repentant terrorists, bridges that were both golden and thorny.

I didn't go to the trial. Trials—like surgical procedures, holy masses, and sexual encounters—are events that I either participate in or stay away from. Not that I have anything against public trials, but I would feel like a voyeur.

After the trial was over I got a phone call from Nägelsbach. "These are the last evenings of summer where one can sit outside. Would you like to come over?"

We sat beneath the pear tree and made small talk. The Nägelsbachs were as little interested as I was about how and where we had spent our vacations—they in the mountains, I on a beach.

"How is Leonore Salger doing?" Frau Nägelsbach asked suddenly.

"I'm still not allowed to see her. But I called Eberlein the other day—he's been reinstated as director of the hospital now that the trial's over. He doesn't know when she'll be released, but he's certain that she will get well again and be able to complete her studies and lead a normal life." I hesitated.

"Why don't you put your cards on the table, Herr Self?" Frau Nägelsbach said. "If you and my husband don't clear this matter up now, you never will."

"But Reni, I think—" Nägelsbach began.

"That goes for you, too."

He and I looked at each other uncomfortably. Needless to say, Frau Nägelsbach was right. Frau Nägelsbach was always right. But we both wondered whether it was already too late.

I gave myself a push. "So you knew about the condition Leo was in?"

"She was acting very strangely. During the interrogations there were moments when she seemed completely elsewhere, as if she didn't see or hear us. At times she'd talk up a storm, and then again you'd have to wring every single word out of her. Rawitz said right away that she was insane and that her lawyer would have to be an all-out idiot for her to get convicted. That's why he couldn't stop laughing when you were so set on freeing her. I and the others, however, weren't so sure she'd get off." He hesitated. Now he, too, gave himself a push. "What's the deal with Peschkalek's material? Do you have it, or was it lost in the fire?"

"Self, the deceiver? I guess that would fit nicely. Lemke and Peschkalek deceived Leo and her friends, the police and the Federal and the Public Prosecutor's Office deceived the courts, perhaps the courts played along and did their bit of deceiving, and the deceived public heralds its deceivers. Is there even any poison gas in Viernheim?"

Nägelsbach looked at me angrily. Then he looked angrily at his wife. "You see, he has no intention of revealing anything— all he wants to do is to hurt me!" Then he looked angrily at me again. "I don't like it either when underhanded little tricks are being played, and I've been unhappy about the Käfertal terrorist case from the start, just as the others were. But we tried to deal with everything as best we could. You, on the other hand . . . first you wheedle your head out of the noose, and then that of Leonore Salger. Perhaps they couldn't have found her guilty. But even so, now that she has checked herself into the psychiatric hospital of her own volition, and will be free to leave of her own volition, she's in a better position than if a judge had had her committed, not to mention that she's been spared a trial. My compliments, Herr Self. And how does that make you feel? Would you say that the rules that apply to all of us don't apply to you? If so, your deception of yourself is far worse than your deception of others." He read his wife's glance as a summons to pull in his horns. "No Reni, it's high time that all this was put on the table. He's just sitting here, a successful deceiver, and considers himself above the deception of the police. Are you claiming that the wrong people were convicted? And can you deny that you and Leonore Salger should have ended up in the dock, too, with you, at least, being slapped with a conviction?"

What could I say? That I had, after all, helped the police bring in Lemke and Peschkalek? That I knew that the rules that apply to everyone apply to me, but that I also have my own rules, too? That not all rules are the same, not all deception the same? That he was a policeman and I wasn't?

"I don't raise myself above you, Herr Nägelsbach. And I don't have Peschkalek's material. It was lost in the fire. All I have are the pictures I showed you copies of."

He nodded, and for a long time gazed at the gnats that danced about the lamp. He refilled our glasses. "Poison gas? Well, I don't know if there's any poison gas in Viernheim. I wasn't informed, nor will I be. I hear, though, that they're out in full force at that depot. So if there is poison gas there, at least they seem to be dealing with it."

The wind rustled in the leaves. It grew cooler. Voices echoed from the neighbor's garden, and smoke came wafting over from their barbecue. "How about a nice hot goulash soup, and a blanket over your knees?" Frau Nägelsbach said.

"Even if I belong in prison, I must say I'm much happier here with you under your pear tree."

"You won't be able to dodge prison altogether, you know. My husband can't let you get away entirely unscathed. Come along."

Frau Nägelsbach got up and led the way to her husband's workshop. I had no idea what was awaiting me, but I couldn't imagine that it would be anything bad. Nägelsbach and I walked in silence. The workshop was pitch black, and I grew a little uneasy. Then the fluorescent light above his workbench flickered on.

Nägelsbach had returned to architecture. On the workbench stood a nineteenth-century prison made of thousands upon thousands of matchsticks. There were a main building and cellblocks in the form of a star with five points, and around the compound ran a wall with a gate and watchtowers. There were gossamer wires along the top of the wall, and minute bars on the windows of the cells. Nägelsbach never populates his models with figures. But in this case he or his wife had made an exception: a tiny cardboard man.

"Is that me?"

"Yes, it is."

I was standing alone in the prison yard in striped prison garb and cap. I was waving to myself.

ALSO BY BERNHARD SCHLINK

SELF'S PUNISHMENT
by Bernhard Schlink and Walter Popp

As a young man, Gerhard Self served as a Nazi prosecutor. After the war he was barred from the judicial system and so he became a private investigator. But he has never forgotten his complicity in evil. Hired by a childhood friend, the aging Self searches for a prankish hacker who's invaded the computer system of a Rhineland chemical plant. But his investigation leads to murder, and from there to the charnel house of Germany's past, where the secrets of powerful corporations lie among the bones of numberless dead.

Crime Fiction/978-0-375-70907-4

THE READER

Hailed for its coiled eroticism and the moral claims it makes upon the reader, this novel is a story of love and secrets, horror and compassion, unfolding against the haunted landscape of postwar Germany. When he falls ill on his way home from school, fifteen-year-old Michael Berg is rescued by Hanna, a woman twice his age. In time she becomes his lover—then inexplicably disappears. When Michael next sees her, she is on trial for a hideous crime. Hanna refuses to defend her innocence, and Michael realizes that she may be guarding a secret more shameful than murder.

Fiction/Literature/978-0-375-70797-1

FLIGHTS OF LOVE

A boy's fascination with an erotic painting leads him into the labyrinth of his family's secrets. The friendship between an idealistic young man from West Berlin and an upwardly mobile couple from the East is challenged by revelations about the collapse of Communism. A philanderer, juggling one wife and two mistresses, begins to crack under the weight of his abundance. By turns brooding and comic, *Flights of Love* is nothing less than masterful.

Fiction/Literature/Short Stories/978-0-375-72555-5